PRAISE FOR THE NOVELS OF
Penny McCall

The Bliss Factor

"An entertaining romantic frolic . . . Fast-paced and filled with humor." —*Genre Go Round Reviews*

"The author strikes just the right note . . . A terrific group of secondary characters round out the cast and contribute to some of the best lines and scenes in the book, many of which had me rolling with laughter. I thoroughly enjoyed *The Bliss Factor* and look forward to reading more books from Ms. McCall." —*The Romance Dish*

"The intrigue in McCall's latest is hilarious . . . This romp gets two thumbs-up for adventure." —*Romantic Times*

"A fast-paced, action-packed book, incorporating humor and sensual romance with edge-of-your-seat suspense. I could not put this book down!" —*Night Owl Reviews*

"Readers should buckle up and hold on as Rae and Connor race to beat the bad guys. I do have to say that *The Bliss Factor* did leave me blissfully happy." —*Manic Readers*

Packing Heat

"A great story, nonstop action, snappy dialogue, witty humor, and chemistry between the hero and heroine that is white-hot. I'm very happy to give *Packing Heat* the highest possible recommendation." —*Romance Junkies*

continued . . .

All Jacked Up

"Here is one pint-sized librarian with plenty of moxie! Aubrey Sullivan and Jack Mitchell are like highly combustible oil and water, and their head-butting is sexy and amusing. After a debut like this, there's little doubt that McCall has a bright future ahead."　　*—Romantic Times*

"A fast-paced bumpy ride with some surprising twists and turns that keep you on the edge of your seat. The chemistry between [Jack and Aubrey] was HOT."
—Romance Junkies

"A fast-paced story full of suspense and excitement. Sure to get your pulse racing and keep your interest all the way through."　　*—Romance Reviews Today*

MORE PRAISE FOR PENNY McCALL

"Smart, sexy, and fun, McCall knows how to deliver!"
—Suzanne Enoch, *New York Times* bestselling author

"A terrific new voice in romantic suspense: snappy dialogue, nonstop action, and sexy writing."
—Lori Foster, *New York Times* bestselling author

"Penny's writing is pure fun!"
—Ruth Ryan Langan, *New York Times* bestselling author

"Lots of witty dialogue and some laugh-out-loud funny scenes."　　*—Booklist*

WORTH THE TRIP

Penny McCall

BERKLEY SENSATION, NEW YORK

THE BERKLEY PUBLISHING GROUP
Published by the Penguin Group
Penguin Group (USA) Inc.
375 Hudson Street, New York, New York 10014, USA
Penguin Group (Canada), 90 Eglinton Avenue East, Suite 700, Toronto, Ontario M4P 2Y3, Canada
(a division of Pearson Penguin Canada Inc.)
Penguin Books Ltd., 80 Strand, London WC2R 0RL, England
Penguin Group Ireland, 25 St. Stephen's Green, Dublin 2, Ireland (a division of Penguin Books Ltd.)
Penguin Group (Australia), 250 Camberwell Road, Camberwell, Victoria 3124, Australia
(a division of Pearson Australia Group Pty. Ltd.)
Penguin Books India Pvt. Ltd., 11 Community Centre, Panchsheel Park, New Delhi—110 017, India
Penguin Group (NZ), 67 Apollo Drive, Rosedale, North Shore 0632, New Zealand
(a division of Pearson New Zealand Ltd.)
Penguin Books (South Africa) (Pty.) Ltd., 24 Sturdee Avenue, Rosebank, Johannesburg 2196,
South Africa

Penguin Books Ltd., Registered Offices: 80 Strand, London WC2R 0RL, England

This is a work of fiction. Names, characters, places, and incidents either are the product of the author's imagination or are used fictitiously, and any resemblance to actual persons, living or dead, business establishments, events, or locales is entirely coincidental. The publisher does not have any control over and does not assume any responsibility for author or third-party websites or their content.

WORTH THE TRIP

A Berkley Sensation Book / published by arrangement with the author

PRINTING HISTORY
Berkley Sensation mass-market edition / November 2010

Copyright © 2010 by Penny McCusker.
Cover art by Pando Hall/Photographer's Choice/Getty Images.
Cover design by Rita Frangie.
Interior text design by Laura K. Corless.

ISBN: 978-0-425-23847-9

BERKLEY® SENSATION
Berkley Sensation Books are published by The Berkley Publishing Group,
a division of Penguin Group (USA) Inc.,
375 Hudson Street, New York, New York 10014.
BERKLEY® SENSATION and the "B" design are trademarks of Penguin Group (USA) Inc.

PRINTED IN THE UNITED STATES OF AMERICA

10 9 8 7 6 5 4 3 2 1

To Cameron,
my new light
and
to Ian, Erin and Mike
still shining bright

chapter
1

"NO, HOLLIE, I'M NOT DATING ANYONE," NORAH
MacArthur told the perky blond host of *Chicago in the
Morning* for at least the fifth time, with enough sarcasm to make the live audience snicker and Hollie
frown at her. At least Norah thought it was a frown.

Hollie's eyes narrowed slightly, but the rest of her
face stayed Botox smooth. "But you wrote this book
on relationships . . ." she said, not even holding it up
for publicity's sake—*publicity* being a very loose term
since *Chicago in the Morning* was in the ratings basement and only a handful of episodes from gasping
its last televised breath. "*The Gender Bridge, or How
to Create Your Mate*," she read off the cover, sounding
perky with an edge of snark.

Norah appreciated the snark, but she could do without perky. She got her fill of perky from the coeds who
crowded into her classroom on a daily basis, thinking

she knew the secret to finding a husband. She might have told them that bouncy breasts, buns of steel, and pretty faces were enough to accomplish that task all on their own, but they knew that better than she did. Men were slaves to visual stimuli, after all.

But Hollie required verbal interaction, which she proved by clearing her throat daintily and prompting, "You were saying?"

"*The Gender Bridge*," Norah began with what she considered admirable patience, "is intended to demystify the workings of a relationship and give the reader some tools for bridging the communication gap between the sexes. Both males and females are preprogrammed to think and behave in certain ways. So many couples break up or get divorced, when all they really need is to read behind the words and behaviors of their partners."

Hollie smiled, just her mouth moving. It was train-wreck freaky, but Norah tore her eyes off the expanse of frozen, pink forehead, trying to stay in the conversation this time so she didn't get nervous. When she got nervous she tended to blurt out whatever was on her mind. Since her mind stored every useless fact she ran across, there was no telling what might come out of her mouth, but it almost always made her look like an idiot. She hated looking like an idiot . . . and she'd completely lost whatever conversational volleyball Hollie had just lobbed her way.

Myra Newcastle, student advisor at the college where Norah taught, turned agent extraordinaire and the perpetrator of Norah's current predicament, stood in the wings, both hands fisted in her spiky red hair and a panicked look on her face.

Hollie wasn't happy about the dead air, either. Hollie was probably taking Norah's inattention as an insult. "Your book is subtitled, *How to Create Your Mate*.

Can you tell us a little bit about your claim that any woman can turn the man of her choice into the ideal mate?"

She shot Myra a look, since the subtitle had been her idea. "Actually, *Hollie*, I haven't guaranteed anyone anything. We're all bombarded by perfection. Television, movies, the Internet, and especially magazine covers. Men subconsciously use those images of airbrushed models as a comparator, and consciously as status symbols, so women feel pressured to reach that impossible level of perfection, and if they can't achieve it naturally, there's always plastic surgery, liposuction, Botox . . ." Norah tried not to, but her glance twitched up, just for a split second, to that smooth, dead forehead.

Hollie attempted displeasure. She almost managed to pull it off. "And reading your book does what?"

"Twenty-first century relationships are under enormous pressure even without the evolutionary difference between male and female," Norah said evenly. Either Hollie had something against her, or she was trying to bump her ratings. Norah had no idea why Hollie would dislike her at first sight, but whatever was behind the woman's antagonism, Norah wasn't about to be played, not by a piker like Hollie Roget. Norah had spent half her life being manipulated by a master, and she'd learned how to fight back. "The basis for attraction is biological reproduction. There are physical characteristics that stimulate sexual arousal—youth, beauty, scent. Symmetry of features is a big one. But once you've gotten past the attraction phase, there are ways of securing affection."

Holly's artificially plumped lips thinned as much as they were able, but Norah bulled on, making sure her explanation was peppered with words like *hypothalamus* and *neotenic*. By the time she was done, the sparsely populated studio audience was near catatonia and her agent was all but hysterical. Hollie was sharpening her claws.

"Well, Norah," she sniped, "it would seem to me that someone who speaks with such authority on relationships ought to have some firsthand knowledge."

"Psychologists counsel people every day, schizophrenics, kleptomaniacs, even murderers, without any practical experience—"

"So you're admitting that you don't have any experience in relationships. Why should anyone trust what's little more than theory?"

The audience woke right up. They weren't sure what was going on, but they scented tension, like the burn of ozone on the air just before a lightning strike. The only question was, who was about to become a scorch mark on live television?

"My book is based in science. Sound science. It was written for the general reading audience, but I never expected this kind of—"

"Success? It's on the *New York Times* bestseller list. Millions of women are buying your book expecting to learn how to handle the men in their lives."

"It was never intended as a how-to manual for women who can't . . ."

"Women who can't what? Women who can't get a man?"

"No—"

"Now *there* is something you know about." Hollie plowed right over her, brandishing a sheet of paper. "I happen to have your dating history here."

"*Oh-h-h-h-h,*" the audience chorused while Norah's face heated and her mind went blank, except for a very vivid picture of her throttling Hollie before God and the city of Chicago. "You researched my personal life?"

"It's what any responsible journalist would do before an important interview."

"I doubt Barbara Walters does a sexual history on her guests."

"She interviews world leaders, famous actors, really important people. I'm just interviewing you."

Right, Norah thought, with a slight puff of laughter, and even though she knew it was just Hollie being passive-aggressive again, putting down another woman to assuage her own lack of self-esteem and establish control and power, Norah still couldn't help but buy in, just for a moment.

After all, she described herself as *medium*, so why shouldn't everyone else? Medium height, medium size, medium reddish brown hair that was medium length and somewhere between curly and straight. Her eyes were blue, but it was a medium blue, not crystal and bright, not dark and mysterious, more like the color of well-worn jeans. A comfortable color. Heck, even her life was medium.

She liked her life, though, and she was satisfied with the way it had been progressing. She taught psychology at the Midwest School of Psychology, founded over fifty years before and quickly becoming one of the preeminent universities dedicated to its chosen course of study. Norah had spent the last three years half in, half out of a relationship with the dean of the college, but she'd ended it not too long ago, and they'd remained friends.

She wasn't insanely happy but she wasn't desperate or depressed, either. The most ambitious moment of her life had been when she agreed to write a book on psychology for the general public. Through some freak of luck, and with the help of an amazing agent, she'd actually found a publisher. Myra had predicted her book would live a short but useful life among the self-help ranks before fading quietly into oblivion.

By some cruel joke of fate, it had become a phenomenon. Norah didn't want to be a phenomenon. She'd rather skip the whole *Chicago in the Morning* experience, being interviewed by a vapid quasi-journalist who considered her cereal box heavy reading. Norah didn't like fame, and she hated the public persona she seemed to have acquired, thousands of lonely women wanting her to give them the secret to turning some emotionally stunted man into the ideal life partner. Of course, she hadn't been raised by Father Knows Best. She hadn't been raised by her father at all, which might explain why she was so fascinated with relationships. She'd always wanted to understand why her mother had stayed married to a man who constantly disappointed her. And she wanted to give other women the tools to avoid that kind of lifelong heartache, which was why she'd written the book. She hadn't expected it to become a manifesto for finding *any* husband.

She opened her mouth to tell Hollie as much, and caught her agent out of the corner of her eye, breathing into a paper bag, her eyes pleading. The producer behind the camera was having apoplexy over the dead air space. Hollie just looked smug, something she had no trouble getting across since *smug* didn't rely on any Botoxed facial features. She lifted that damning sheet of paper and opened her mouth.

Norah snatched it out of her hand, gave it a cursory glance, then handed it back. "Let me save you some time," she said to Hollie, whose smirk only widened because, she must be thinking, she'd not only blindsided her guest, she'd made her angry enough to speak without thinking first. Poor, clueless woman. "I've dated, like all women, and every one of those relationships has ended, some of them badly. Success is a wonderful thing, but it's often our failures that define us. As I said before, I didn't set out to write a dating manual, but who better than someone who's been in the trenches?"

"You're single, aren't you? It says so right here on this paper. Why should we take advice from a woman who can't attract a man, let alone keep one?"

The audience drew its collective breath, and Hollie realized she'd crossed a line in her zeal to be a hard-hitting journalist. Her eyes flicked to the producer, the audience, back to Norah. She consulted the paper in her hands, remembered what it was, and laid it carefully on the table beside her chair, like it had grown eight legs and venom-filled fangs. "Um . . ." she sputtered. "Ah . . ."

"A simple 'I'm sorry' will do," a male voice said. A very deep male voice. The kind that commanded attention.

Like everyone else in the studio, Norah instantly gave him that attention, twisting around in her chair, her mouth dropping open when she laid eyes on him because, *wow*, did he live up to the voice. The phrase *tall, dark, and handsome* must have been invented for him, she thought, only they forgot to add the muscles, and the thousand-watt smile, and the way he carried himself, like the planet had been created so he'd have a place to walk around and show off those muscles and that smile. It wasn't arrogance, though, more like he was 100 percent comfortable in his own skin. The ultimate urban legend for a psychologist, someone with no phobias or eccentricities or downright craziness. Except for the way he was looking at her.

He was looking at her like he loved her—no, like she was the love of his life.

His eyes were locked on her face, his smile widened, and his pace quickened. Long legs carried him across the stage, and boy did he know how to walk, loose-hipped, arms swinging, easy, confident, strides. And he was walking straight to her.

Norah pushed back into her chair, the impact of him was so overwhelming, and even though she knew he was pretending, and every suspicious bone in her body was jangling like wind chimes, and she was pretty sure she should run like hell, she just sat there, palpitating and perspiring. Definite sexual arousal, the very symptoms she'd described to Hollie, some calm, clinical part of herself observed—the same part that was urging her to get herself out of his damage path. Apparently, however, physical action was beyond her. The only movement she managed was to curl her hands around the arms of her chair so she didn't launch herself at him.

Not that she would have had to, since he bent down and planted one on her, a kiss that was soft at first, questioning, and when she melted against him because she couldn't do anything else, he took it deeper, took her to a place where there wasn't an audience, just him, the heat of his mouth, the tangle of his tongue, the taste of him, shooting right to her spinning head, with an edge of danger that must have come from kissing a complete stranger. And liking it. Too mild a word, she thought as he pulled back, just enough to look into her eyes before he dropped another quick kiss on her lips and straightened. *Like* was definitely the wrong descriptor, but there weren't enough words in the English language to describe what that kiss had done to her.

He shook Hollie's hand—she was speechless, too, along with the entire audience—then he turned back to Norah, winking as he perched on the side of her chair and draped an arm casually over her shoulders as if they'd known each other forever.

"You know, Hollie," he said with a wide smile that completely camouflaged the sucker punch he was about to deliver, "you really aren't equipped to play mind games with a psychologist."

OKAY, IT WAS A CHEAP SHOT, PROMPTED BY SOME unexpectedly strong protective instincts, but Trip thought Hollie Whatsis, the plastic blond talk show host, was being a jerk. Sure, Norah had given as good as she got, but Norah was the guest, and there was such a thing as hospitality, even in television. He gave Norah a sidelong glance and flashed back to that kiss, and *hospitality* took on a whole different meaning. As in, they'd be spending a lot of time together, he and Norah, and he wondered just how hospitable she might be. It was the last thing he should be thinking.

Convenient, Trip decided, that there was some life-and-death stuff and some crime-of-the-century action, with a long-lost stolen treasure caveat, to take his mind off the three-dimensional reality of a woman who was only supposed to be a means to an end. And not that end, he reminded himself when his upper lip began to sweat and his pulse pounded hard—everywhere—and he began to wonder if that kiss had been such a brilliant idea. Sure it had accomplished his goal, which was to insert himself into Norah's life in such a way that she couldn't easily denounce him, not after she'd kissed him back in such a public forum. He hadn't actually anticipated the kissing back part. That had been unexpected, and while it sealed her fate, the side effects for him were irritating. And inconvenient.

He focused on the big picture, adding the kiss and his reaction to the list of things about Norah MacArthur he intended to ignore. The list did not include sticking around on the stage. The stage was little more than a shooting gallery, and he wasn't talking about Holly's paltry verbal barbs. He doubted anyone would take pot-shots at Norah in front of so many witnesses, but why risk it?

"I think we're done here," he said to Norah, taking her by the hand and pulling her out of her chair while she was still doing the deer-in-the-headlights thing and was too muddled to resist.

"But . . .What . . .Who are you?" Hollie sputtered. She grabbed a couple sheets of paper and brandished them. "It says here Norah isn't currently dating any-one."

"Cheap researchers," Trip said with a smile. "Budget problems?"

A red flush crept up Hollie's neck. But he had to give her credit—she recovered quickly, and she backed off the subject of *Chicago in the Morning's* money trou-bles, introducing the next guest instead as he and Norah exited stage left.

Norah was no slouch, either. He'd thought she was too dazed and confused to give him any trouble; as soon as they were out of camera range she tore her hand from his, and he knew differently. The look in her eyes, nar-rowed and sharp as they met his, confirmed it. She'd assessed the situation and chosen not to make a public scene. A woman with that kind of quick mind and reso-lute self-control would be no picnic for him to con. As if he had a choice.

But first he had to get her by the Amazon in the wings, a string bean of a woman with an inch of spiky red hair—barn red hair—and a look of avid determination in her eyes. Short of a Taser, or maybe a .45, they weren't getting around her.

Norah didn't even try, planting herself in front of the woman and huffing out a breath. "Can you believe that? She did a sexual history on me."

The woman shrugged. "Don't sweat it," she said around a wad of gum. "Probably nothing she didn't get from your biography. And it was worth it if she smoked him"—she pointed a bony figure at Trip—"out of the woodwork."

"I'm not a cockroach."

"You are an unwelcome pest," Norah observed. "I just haven't established the species yet."

"I'd settle for a name."

"My agent, Myra Newcastle, meet—"

"You can call me Trip."

"Fitting," Norah muttered, "since we've crossed into the Twilight Zone."

"Is there a last name?"

"Jones," Trip said.

Myra took the hand he offered, and sighed. "It's nice to look a man in the eyes once in a while."

In the eyes? Hell, she had at least an inch on him, and he was over six feet tall.

"So, Trip," Myra said, voice direct, studying his face, "I've known Norah at least three years, well enough that I would have sworn she'd tell me about someone like you. How long have you two—"

"Years," Trip supplied. "We were young and foolish."

"I was never foolish," Norah put in. "At least I never used to be."

"You were the one who broke up with me, remember?"

"That wins the crazy contest in my book," Myra said.

Norah folded her arms. "This would be the book you're judging by its cover, right?"

"Touché," Myra said, turning back to Trip with an expectant look on her face, waiting for the rest of the story.

Trip was only too happy to oblige. The deeper he pulled Norah into the pretense, the harder it would be for her to dig herself out. "I just got back to the States, and I couldn't wait to see Norah again." She frowned at him, so he tweaked her playfully on the nose.

Norah didn't take it for the affectionate gesture he'd intended. "You were quite a surprise," she said, smiling sweetly as she swatted him not so playfully.

Trip slung an arm around her waist and pulled her hard against him. He took an elbow in the ribs, but the sound of her breath whooshing out was worth it.

Myra opened her mouth, looking concerned about the physicality of their "relationship."

Trip cut her off. "Norah and I need to talk. She'll catch up with you later."

"Well then," Myra said as she handed Norah's purse over, "I'll leave you to your reunion. Try not to cause any permanent damage."

Trip didn't need any more urging, hustling Norah past the Amazon, who yelled out, "Call me," to Norah, but didn't come after them.

Not that Norah needed the protection. As soon as they were out of Myra's eyesight she shoved Trip's arm off and rounded on him. "Who the hell are you, and what do you think you're doing?"

"Those things didn't seem to be such a pressing issue a few minutes ago."

"I had to play along onstage."

"And what about your agent? Why didn't you tell her the truth?"

Norah whipped around and headed off, pulling out her cell phone as she went. "You're right, I should be honest with her. Maybe she'll know how to deal with you."

Trip plucked the phone out of her hand and shut it off. "I don't need to be dealt with."

She took her phone back. "Would there be any point in getting a restraining order?"

"What for?" Trip took her phone again, without being obnoxious about it this time, and dropped it into her purse. "You didn't exactly push me away in there. Nobody will believe you need protection from me."

"I should file a police report, at the very least."

"Go ahead, you'll get laughed out of the station house."

"Hollie's show is syndicated, but it's a late-morning program."

"Maybe only the stay-at-home moms of Chicago saw your interview this morning, but by this time tonight the rest of America, not to mention parts of Canada and Mexico, will have seen the clip of you and me kissing. Then there's the verbal catfight between you and Hollie. And before you tell me nobody cares, you should remember why your agent booked you on this show. You're a pretty big deal right now."

"The kind of 'big deal' an unscrupulous man like you would try to capitalize on. So why don't you tell me what you're after?"

"Do you really think I'm a threat?"

"I don't know, but it's wrong to perpetrate this kind of . . . fraud . . ."

Trip stopped walking when she did, both of them staring through the glass doors that led to the parking lot, except they couldn't see the parking lot because of the reporters and cameramen crowded around the exit,

not in Paris Hilton numbers, but enough to be daunt-
ing.

"Well," Trip said as they were spotted and the handful of reporters crowded closer to the door, "if you want
to set the record straight, here's your chance."

chapter
2

NORAH TUGGED ON THE BOTTOM OF HER
jacket, squared her shoulders, and stepped forward,
prepared to call his bluff. Damn her and her straightforward ilk.

He caught her by the arm, tugged her back. "Just
hear me out," Trip said, "then you can send me away if
you want to."

"Fine," she said, but she took off, out the door,
through the crowd on the other side, going as fast as
she could in an attempt to ditch Chicago's anemic form
of paparazzi, which turned out to be junior reporters
from the *Sun Times* and the *Tribune* with a couple of
freelancers thrown in for variety.

And she couldn't ditch them because she was wearing heels. Not great for speed-walking, but they did
amazing things for her legs. Too bad she wore such
unflattering clothes. Trip could tell there was a decent

package inside the ugly wrapping—not one of those Hollywood stick figures—he liked curves, and she moved with the kind of grace that told him she knew how to operate the equipment. Her face was good, too, pretty rather than beautiful, and full of character.

But it was the mind that worried him. Norah MacArthur was neither stupid nor naïve. She was a woman who held her emotions in a firm grip and controlled her expression enough that he found it a challenge to read her. She didn't make spot decisions either. She thought things through, worked out the pros and cons before she chose a course. In the current situation it worked to his advantage. In the long run it was going to be trouble. There would be times when he needed her to follow blindly without asking questions. Norah wasn't a woman who would be led. That meant he'd have to gain her trust. With her history that wouldn't be easy.

Trip stepped between her and the peanut gallery. A couple of steely looks were enough to convince them to drop the pursuit, that and the fact that Norah MacArthur wasn't exactly cover story material, and definitely not famous enough to get a black eye over.

Norah glanced over her shoulder and saw their audience dispersing. She slowed her pace a bit but kept walking in the opposite direction from Lake Michigan, which, it being the tail end of October, was a good thing. It might be Indian summer, but the temperature hadn't climbed much over sixty, and the wind coming off the water would be at least fifteen degrees colder than that. Trip wasn't exactly a cold weather kind of guy. He liked it hot . . . His eyes slid sideways. He jerked them forward again. Norah MacArthur might be hot under the right circumstances, but the rest of her screamed Happily Ever After. Trip didn't do Happily Ever After. Hell, he didn't do all that well with the morning after.

"Either talk or go away and leave me alone."

"She's curious," he said, grinning.

"She's also impatient."

"I could always go back inside"—he turned to do just that—"Hollie did press me for an interview—"

"Wait."

"Worried about your credibility?"

"It's worse than that. I'm worried about what people—women—will think of me for turning down a man like you."

"A man like me?"

She rolled her eyes. "Don't be self-deprecating. You know what I mean. If I send you off after the way you kissed me, every woman in the country will question my sanity, not to mention my sexual orientation. Not that my sexual orientation is the point . . ."

They came to the side street between the television station and the parking structure where she'd left her car. Four lanes of sporadic traffic zoomed through the intersection, slowing when the light turned yellow. Norah looked both ways, more by habit than anything else, since the little red hand on the crosswalk sign was holding her hostage at the curb. Then she frowned, her eyes drawn to a car that wasn't slowing for the yellow light. Then the light turned red and the car kept coming, changing lanes as horns blared and brakes squealed, veering around stopped cars until it was in the right lane, the engine roaring as it sped up. Heading straight for them.

Norah froze, eyes and mouth wide, mind completely empty as the car got bigger and bigger until she couldn't see anything else, and it began to seep into her brain that she was about to be killed by a complete stranger on a crowded downtown street, for a reason she couldn't begin to fathom—

Rough hands grabbed her, dragged her back as the car zoomed by, so fast it was a blur, a roar of sound and wind that whipped her skirt up and stole her breath. Or maybe that was because she was up against a stone wall with Trip plastered over her, cradling her head against his shoulder. Unless he'd forgotten to tell her he was born on Krypton, he wasn't going to be any protection from two tons of metal driven by a homicidal maniac. But he tried anyway, and darn it, why did he have to go and be a hero?

"Oh, my God, are you okay?"

"We're fine," Trip said, brushing by the concerned woman and the rest of the bystanders who'd rushed over after the black Lexus bumped back down the curb and took off.

Norah needed a minute; Trip gathered her close, overloading her already strained nerves to the point where she let him wrap his arm around her and hurry her off. They hadn't gone a block before she shoved him away. "What the hell was that?"

"Attempted murder."

"It wasn't a very good attempt."

"It seemed pretty good from where I was standing. Which was in front of you."

"Um, thank you?"

"And?"

"And I think it's time you started talking. You can start with your name—your real name."

"James Aloysius Jones, III," he said. "Trip for short."

She looked at the hand he held out. She didn't take it. "A little late for that, considering. Besides, knowing your name and knowing you are two different things."

"Then get to know me."

She blinked, took a second to process that, and still couldn't make sense of it. "Why?"

"Because I'm a nice guy?"

"Nice guys don't kiss complete strangers in front of an audience unless they have an ulterior motive. What's yours?"

"Well . . . I'm writing a book, and I was thinking you could help me get published."

Norah stopped walking, let her head fall forward. Trip Jones was handsome and charming and sexy, but she'd grown up with a man like that—at least the handsome and charming part—and having a father who was also a con man meant she could smell a snow job a mile away.

"Really," Trip said, "all I want is a little help, and I'm gone."

She started walking again, taking a right at the entrance to the parking structure. "Why don't you give Myra a call? I'm sure she'd like to hear from you."

"So you're too important to help me get my work out there?"

"Your work? Let me tell you about your work." She took in his jeans and long-sleeve Henley, meeting his eyes before she could get drawn into admiring the long, muscular lines of the body beneath the clothes. "You look all laid-back and relaxed, but your bearing is military."

He tried to slouch. He didn't quite pull it off.

"And when you talk to me, you stare me straight in the eyes."

"Which means I'm telling the truth."

"That's what everyone believes, but people who are telling the truth generally hesitate, and their gaze shifts to the right as they search their memory. Liars rehearse, so they look you in the eyes. And there, the muscle in your jaw flexed once, and your eyes narrowed just a little. You're annoyed, but you suppressed it without even trying."

"So you have me all figured out."

"How could I? You're too practiced at controlling your expression, letting the world see only what you want it to see. That means you're either a grifter or a cop."

"You don't sound too enthused about either possibility."

"I'm not, but my money is on cop, probably federal considering your military background. And since it seems to matter to you, I consider that the lesser of two evils."

"I'm FBI."

She lifted a brow and crossed her arms.

He read her skepticism loud and clear, digging in his back pocket and coming out with a leather bifold wallet. Norah took it and flipped it open. She didn't have to study it long; she'd seen enough FBI badges to know it was authentic. And she'd been questioned enough times to know what he wanted. "You're here about Lucius."

"Which you knew going in, so how accurate can your character assessment be?"

Her first reaction was to let it go. Then she glanced over at him, and decided a point needed to be made, so he didn't think she was a fool. And so she wouldn't make a fool of herself over a man who appealed to her far too much for her own good.

"You laugh a lot," she began, interpreting the lines on his face, "which means you are easygoing. Probably why you didn't make a career of the military, and why being a federal officer appeals to you. You're still working within the same set of rules, you feel like you're contributing, but there's no set schedule, and that suits you better. It also means you're not interested in stability, and you don't do long-term relationships. Your parents are likely divorced or—"

"My parents died in a car accident when I was twelve."

"I'm sorry," she said, and she truly was. She understood how it felt to lose parents, even though one of hers was very much alive. "It explains a lot. You were old enough to know what you lost and remember it, young enough for it to mark you permanently. You're afraid of that kind of loss, so you don't let anyone close." And she needed to remember she was talking to a person, not writing a case study. No matter how annoying that person was.

"You don't pull your punches," he said.

"You invaded my life, and you expect me to handle you with kid gloves?"

"It would have been nice."

She gave him a look, but there was a smile at the end of it.

"How much do you know about your father?"

"So we're being honest now?"

"Only if you answer the question."

She bumped a shoulder, pulling open the door to the stairway and starting up. "Lucius MacArthur," she said, trying not to think about him following her up the stairs, his eyes level with her butt. All of her butt. She curbed her embarrassment. He wasn't interested in her butt. He was interested in her family connections. Nothing new there, except her regret over it. And wasn't that troublesome?

"He's nicknamed Puff for Puff of Smoke," she said, putting away her attraction and getting back to the reason Trip Jones was there. The sooner she answered his questions, the sooner he'd be gone. "He can con even a true skeptic out of their life savings and disappear before they begin to realize they've been scammed. He hates that nickname, by the way. I could tell you his favorite color, but you can ask him yourself in a few weeks, when he gets out of jail."

"For?"

Norah sighed. She didn't like to revisit it, but she obviously wasn't getting rid of Trip until she played his game. And really, it wasn't her father being a criminal that haunted her, it was his crime. "My father was a very successful con man, and a failure as a bank robber."

"That all depends on your definition of failure."

"He's been in jail for fifteen years. I'd say most bank robbers would consider that an epic failure."

"But the loot was never found."

"No," Norah said, "the loot was never found. Instead of fading quietly into the past, my father had to become a criminal legend, and his crime is one of the most infamous of the twentieth century, right up there with the Brinks Robbery and D.B. Cooper."

"Of the original three conspirators, he's the only one who's still alive and that's only because he's safe in jail."

Norah sighed. After being verbally attacked, not to mention almost run over, dealing with memories of her father left her feeling a little defeated. Ignoring the truth, however, was never a solution.

Her father, Lucius MacArthur, was a federal inmate, but before that he'd been a con man. One of the best. And a sucker for a challenge. He'd been tapped by a trio of petty thieves, moving up the criminal food chain by pulling their first bank heist. Lucius's job was to charm his way into the bank and case the joint. He'd done his part, the others had done theirs, and then they'd died, one by one. All but Lucius. The proceeds

of the robbery had never been found, which brought
her to the infamous, and haunting, part of the story, at
least for Norah. "You're here about the loot."

Trip shrugged. "My job is to find out where Puff hid
it, and recover all the stolen goods."

"That's a pretty tall order," Norah said, "since they
emptied all the safe-deposit boxes, and there's no way
of knowing exactly what was stolen."

"I didn't say it would be easy."

No, but he acted like it would be a piece of cake
when really it would be next to impossible. First of all,
her father hadn't given up the hiding place, even after
nearly fifteen years in prison—not that she'd had contact with him in all that time, but Trip's invasion into
her life meant Lucius had outlasted the FBI. And then
there was the problem of even knowing what to recover. "Not all the people who rented those boxes had
made accurate disclosures," she reminded him. "Some
of them refused to report anything at all."

"The final tally is now estimated to be more than
fifty million dollars, and that doesn't include the personal items of unknown value," Trip added, smiling. "I
have to hand it to your father and his friends. It was a
nearly perfect crime."

"Sure, right up until the moment they got caught."

"Hence the *nearly* part."

"Hence?"

"I'm a fed, not an idiot."

"You know what they say." She glanced over at him,
smiling slightly. "If you have to point it out . . ."

"Hah, funny."

"Look, Trip," she said, turning serious, "I know it's
irresistible." Especially to a guy like him. Bank robbery was a sexy crime to begin with. This one was a

legend, even before you added in the unrecovered loot and topped it off with the legendary crime. "The agent who solves this will get a gold star."

"I'm going for a little more than a gold star. And you're going to help me."

Norah snorted out a laugh. "In your dreams."

He gave her a look that said in his dreams she was naked, which gave her a flash hot enough to make her wish she was. And not just naked, naked with him, in a room with a bed, or a wall, or a table. A really strong table . . .

And some really strong drugs, ones that wouldn't burn off in the heat so that before she tested the table legs she'd remember that James Aloysius Jones, III was just that kind of guy. The kind of guy who poured on the charm for any woman unfortunate enough to come into direct contact with him. Hell, he probably didn't even know he was doing it. The charm just oozed out of him. Well, she'd spent enough of her life being oozed on; best to remember she'd hated it.

Still she didn't imagine she starred in all that many naked male fantasies, so it was kind of a kick to get that feeling, even when she knew it wasn't real.

"Resistance could be construed as obstruction of justice."

She laughed again, softer this time. Trip's kind was so predictable. "Your charm didn't work, so now you're threatening me?"

"Charm? I kissed you because there were two guys in the audience this morning who looked hinky."

Norah felt a chill, and it wasn't because the temperature dropped as they exited the stairwell. Then again, maybe he was dipping into his repertoire of tricks again. "You're only trying to scare me."

chapter
3

"SCARE YOU? SOMEBODY JUST TRIED TO RUN you over."

"It was probably those two 'hinky' guys. Why don't you go arrest them instead of wasting time with me?"

"I don't know who they are."

Norah stopped walking, half turning so she could zero in on his face while she talked to him. Trip didn't like it. Then he reminded himself he wasn't spinning the story for her, so it was okay.

"Let me get this straight," she said. "There were two guys in the audience you thought were suspicious."

"Yep," he said, thinking she was just laying out the situation, getting her mental bearings, so to speak.

"And I was sitting on the stage, in front of three cameras, where my biggest danger was humiliation at the hands of a blond mouthpiece."

"Um, yeah."

"So those guys probably wouldn't have tried anything, not in the studio, anyway."

"No."

"So instead of staking them out or calling for backup, or any of the other law enforcement tactics, you kissed me."

Trip decided not to answer this time. He was only playing into her hands.

"And when we got outside, they tried to run me over."

Trip heaved a sigh, wondering how the hell it happened. One minute he was in control of the conversation, and the next he felt like an idiot.

Psychologists, he thought darkly, that's how. But this situation wasn't about mind games. "I don't know if those guys were in the Lexus. In fact, I bet they weren't. They didn't have time to get out of the studio, retrieve their car, and come after you. Which means it was somebody else."

She looked over her shoulder, seeming to realize for the first time what had just happened.

"This won't be the last time you're targeted," Trip said, "and that probably won't be the only guy who comes after you. Your father has a pretty big fan club— treasure hunters, insurance investigators, and your basic nutcases, just to name a few—and they're all about to go into a treasure hunting frenzy. They all know he's due to get out of jail soon, they'll all be after the money, and they'll all see you as a possible avenue to getting it."

"And you think you can protect me."

"Not unless you let me stick around, and that means at work and in your house, all the time. Night and day."

"Really? Is that what *all the time* means?"

"It means there's nothing you can do about it. I'm your shadow."

"Gee, I feel all warm and fuzzy now."

There, he thought, that snippy, sarcastic, pissed off tone. That was how he knew she understood what he was saying and she was on board with it. "I just want it to be clear."

"It's clear. And stop looking at me like that," she said, heading off in search of her car, "in fact, stop looking at me, period. And don't touch me, either. And switch to unscented soap."

Trip chuckled, hooking his thumbs in the pockets of his jeans. "My soap is unscented."

"How about your shave gel?"

"Nope."

"Deodorant?" She waved that off. "Never mind, I'll have to deal with your aroma, especially since scent is one of the biggest . . . never mind," she finished. "Just keep your distance."

"Because I smell?"

"Yes. No, because you're blowing this all out of proportion. I don't think the guy in the Lexus missed us because he didn't want to scratch the car. If he'd wanted us dead, we'd be splattered all over the sidewalk."

"Nice visual. But you're right. He didn't want you dead. He wanted to kidnap you and use you as leverage to get your father to give up the loot. Then he'd kill you."

"And you can stop with the scare tactics."

He blew out a breath. "Since we've already had this conversation how about I fast-forward? I think it ended with me saying 'night and day,' and you getting snotty about it."

"You remind me of my father—handsome, charming, and deceitful as all hell." And there was the added complication, the *huge* complication, of her physical reaction to him, Norah admitted. And with her, it was a short trip from physical to emotional. "I'm sure I'll be fine by myself."

"I'm sure you won't. And you're not leaving."

He put his hand on her elbow, a gentlemanly gesture. And a statement of his intentions.

She pulled free, then put a foot of space between them, sending a message of her own. "You said all I had to do was listen to you, and then I could send you away."

"I didn't say I'd go."

"ARE WE GOING TO MAKE THE ENTIRE DRIVE TO South Chicago in silence?" Trip asked her about five minutes after they'd pulled out of the parking structure.

Norah concentrated on midday traffic. It wasn't exactly "are we there yet?" but she still found it annoying. She didn't want to talk, she wanted to process, to let the events of the past hour and the snippets of information she'd dragged out of Trip thrash around in her brain until the truth beat the crap out of the lies and the spin spun itself off into oblivion.

"We're going to be spending a lot of time together. It'll be easier if we make an effort to get along."

"If you're looking for sweet and agreeable you might want to cut your losses and move on."

"Hmmm, I wonder what a psychologist would make of this level of hostility?"

"If it were me I'd take it as intense cynicism toward the person on the receiving end, based on an extensive past history of dealing with men with your brand of insincere charm and propensity for obfuscation."

Trip just stared at her.

"I don't trust you," she translated.

"You don't have to trust me. You need me."

"So you keep saying." Then again, he had come in handy several times already. And she was including The Kiss. She couldn't begin to gage the cost to her personal and professional life, but the look on Hollie's face? Priceless. "Look, I appreciate you risking your life and everything, but like you said, that car was just a scare tactic. I don't think—"

"So you haven't gotten any hang-up calls."

"Everyone gets hang-up calls."

"But you've been getting a lot more than normal."

"I broke up with my boyfriend, too. Is that indicative of anything?"

"Good taste?"

Norah had to smile over that. "Raymond wasn't a bad guy, really, just . . . I don't know why I stayed with him so long."

"Sure, you do."

Laziness, she thought, although that wasn't it, exactly. More like she'd chosen him for all the wrong reasons, chief among them being he was the exact opposite of her father. Staid, settled, reliable, comfortable . . . boring, which was exactly why the relationship had stagnated. No spark. Of any kind, really. She and Raymond Kline, dean of the Midwest School of Psychology, had always been more like friends than lovers, and once they'd stopped struggling with the lack of chemistry it hadn't been a bad relationship. Especially since he was one of the few people she'd run across who knew about her father and didn't care. "You don't think he—"

"No," Trip said, "he's an idiot, but we didn't find anything linking him to the crime—or anyone involved with the crime."

"You had him checked out?"

"Yes."

"How many others—No, don't answer that."

"It was necessary."

"Right. You're worried about the people in my life, but you're the one who invaded my privacy, not to mention the privacy of my friends."

"And neighbors."

"You're not helping your case."

"No, but you value honesty."

Norah glanced over at him. He had a stunning profile, classic, strong, handsome as sin. And he was playing her with every word he uttered through his even, white teeth.

"You're giving me just as much as you think is necessary to get what you want," she said.

And there was that jaw flex again. He didn't like that she'd pegged him, but he didn't value her preference for honesty enough to say it outright.

Trouble was, he had the upper hand, not because he was stubborn and devious and prepared to stick to her like a staph infection. Because he worked for the FBI. She had issues with Trip Jones, but she definitely didn't trust the FBI. They had Lucius under lock and key somewhere. If it wasn't for the fact that all America knew of the crime and the deadline for his release, he'd probably be in FBI hell until he decided to tell them what they wanted to know.

As it was they wouldn't let her visit him, for his safety they'd told her. That she believed. The kind of people he must be incarcerated with wouldn't hesitate to torture him for the whereabouts to a fifty million dollar stash of goods, most of which could be easily broken up and fenced, and all of which had already been settled by the various insurance companies. She hated that he was alone, that she'd been denied even fleeting moments with her father, but it was worth it if it kept him safe—safe from criminals, but at the mercy of the FBI.

The lesser of two evils, she reminded herself, glancing over at Trip Jones with his handsome face, mouthwatering body, and tendency to bend the truth to suit his needs. When Lucius was released from jail in a few weeks, the whole lost treasure aspect of his crime was going to blow up in his face. And hers. Considering the morning's events, Norah knew she wouldn't be able to protect herself, let alone her father. She didn't trust the FBI, but they were supposed to be the good guys, right? They wanted the loot, but they wouldn't hurt or kill her father to get it like the criminals would. She really had no choice.

"Earth to Norah."

"We need rules."

"Rules," he repeated, like he'd uttered another kind of four-letter word.

"Before I agree to let you stay with me, I'll need you to promise to obey some rules."

"Promise?"

"Do I need to get you a dictionary?"

He slid her a look, just the corners of his mouth tilting up. "I'm listening."

And that, she decided, was a start. "First, you won't do anything to harm my father."

That surprised him.

"Lucius has his faults, and he's definitely a criminal," Norah said, "but he's never done anything to hurt me intentionally. He can't help who he is."

"Neither can I."

"Yes, you can. You've already proven that you're very good at controlling yourself. So. No harm comes to my father."

"Or what?"

"Look, we both know I can't do anything to prevent you from hanging around, but I can make it difficult, or I can make it easy."

"So I listen to your rules and you'll cooperate?"

"No, you promise to abide by my rules and I'll cooperate."

"What makes you think I'll keep my promise?"

"You value your word." But she knew he'd crawl through loopholes, bend the rules as far as he could, and if it came down to life and death, he'd break them. But if it came down to life and death, and breaking the rules made a difference, she'd want him to. That didn't mean she wouldn't make an effort to establish those rules, if only to protect herself. "Second," she said, "I want the truth."

"There are all kinds of truth."

"Never play mind games with a psychologist."

"If someone comes at you with a gun you won't have time to psychoanalyze them, Norah. Not that you'll need to. *Shoot first and ask questions later* is a pretty straightforward concept."

"You said they want to use me as leverage, not to kill me."

"Yeah, but after a few seconds of conversation with you they'll probably change their minds."

"NICE," TRIP SAID WHEN THEY PULLED UP IN FRONT of her house, a Queen Anne perched between a Greek Revival mini-mansion and a half-timbered Tudor on a street of architecturally diverse homes, in a neighborhood inhabited by families who could trace their roots back street by street and parish by parish for over a hundred years.

"It's kind of like you," he said, stepping out of the car and stopping to take a good long look at the house, fronted by gray stone embellished with ornate gingerbread on the eaves and porch surround, painted in shades of white, peach, and dark gray. "Straightforward and serviceable stone, but then there's all that lacy woodwork." He turned to give her a once-over, much as he'd done with the house, only . . . more. "Makes me wonder what you're wearing under that ugly suit."

A heat rash, Norah thought, but said, "Plain white cotton."

"I went to parochial school."

"Nun fantasies? Does everything come back to sex with you?"

"Hopefully."

"And you wonder why I'd rather be alone." He opened his mouth, but she held up a hand. "I know, it's more fun with a partner. I should know better than to play word games with a sex maniac."

He laughed outright. "I've been called a lot of things, but *sex maniac* isn't high on the list. Probably because I'm not hanging out with senior citizens. Or nuns."

The heat Norah felt was all in her face this time. She wasn't a prude. Okay, she wasn't exactly porn star material, but she wasn't a nun, either. And who was she trying to convince? A dozen retorts ran through her mind, but in the end she did the only smart thing. She walked away.

Trip put his hand on the wrought iron gate before she could open it. "I'm sorry if I hurt your feelings."

"I don't have any feelings where you're concerned. Except irritation and the vague urge to stock up on disinfectant and antibiotics."

"Ouch."

"I'd apologize for hurting your feelings, but I don't think you have any above the waist."

"Ouch again."

And she might have felt bad if he hadn't been grinning the entire time. "Aren't you afraid if we stand out here someone will try to kidnap me?"

"I'm afraid if we go inside you'll try to kill me."

"Now there's an idea." And she brushed his hand off the gate and walked up the bricked walkway and the seven steps to her front door.

She unlocked the door and stepped into the foyer, open and sunny, with twin Victorian parlors to either side, the doorways embellished with carved columns and finials. She turned to the right, intending to put her purse in the parlor she'd converted into a home office, but Trip wrapped an arm around her waist and put his other hand over her mouth.

She struggled, automatically, mindlessly, not really sure what, or who, she was fighting.

He put his mouth close to her ear and said, "Listen," and she froze, but not because of his whispered warning.

It was the feel of him hard at her back that stopped her, his breath hot in her ear, his grip easing from hard to gentle as her pulse thickened and her head spun. Need blossomed low in her belly, spread through her until her breasts ached and her breath sighed out. Her eyes fluttered closed and she fell into the sensations, his hand, loose now, over her mouth, just his palm touching her tingling lips, his arm snug around her waist, and the whole, solid length of him pressed to her from shoulder blades to knees. All she'd have to do was turn, press her lips to his neck, his jaw, his mouth—

"Okay?" he breathed in her ear.

She nodded. *Just as soon as you stop touching me.* But she prayed he never would.

"Stay here. And don't be afraid."

Norah realized she was shaking and made an effort to steady herself as he moved away, toward the stairs. It was then that she heard the soft footsteps overhead, and the creaking of someone moving around over hundred-year-old wooden floors, and suddenly she had no trouble getting a grip. Not that she wasn't scared for real, but she was angry, too, and her anger was a hell of a lot stronger than her fear, especially when Trip came down the stairs, his hand fisted in the collar of a shirt topped off by an all too recognizable face.

The house had been left to her by her mother, because, the will had read, Norah was the only thing Lucius had loved more than the grift. He'd never do anything to risk his daughter's home. She'd grown up there, managed to hang on to it even through the lean college years. It was her family, all she had left, and to have it invaded, even by someone she knew, robbed her of a little of that security.

"Bill?"

Bill Simonds was forty years old, lived with his mother next door, and dressed like a reject from the seventies, long hair and sideburns, hip-hugging bell-bottoms, polyester shirt with a lot of graying chest hair sprouting out of the neck. Bill also considered her an idiot, since he said, "I thought you were out of town," as if she were the one in the wrong place at the wrong time.

"I always tell you when I go out of town," Norah said. "You're here about the bank robbery."

He ducked his head, his cheeks turning red.

"Your family has lived on this street as long as mine. You've known about the bank robbery forever."

"Well, yeah, but it was on the news at twelve. They showed clips of your interview with Hollie Roget, and then they interviewed her and she said how she wasn't allowed to ask you any questions about the robbery or what happened to the loot, and how it meant you probably knew something because you couldn't possibly support this house on a teacher's salary . . ."

He kept talking, but Norah turned and went into the parlor that also served as a living room. She remoted on the small television, flipped through the cable news channels, and there Hollie was, recapping her report and calling Norah's home "the treasure house."

"Oh. My. God. Who else has seen this?"

"Everyone," Bill said from the doorway. "But I have a key," and he held it up like a trophy.

"About that," Norah said.

Bill backed off as she crossed the room, but Trip was there behind him, and for once she was grateful because he plucked the key out of Bill's hand, and Norah could tell by the way Bill fought to keep it that he'd been in too much of a hurry to have it copied.

"Not that it would be a problem," Trip said, still reading her mind. "We're having the locks changed tomorrow. And if I see you around here uninvited again—"

"Which will be the case, since you're not welcome here anymore, Bill."

Trip didn't finish his threat, but Bill didn't contemplate the implications for long. Bill decided, in the interests of his continuing health, to beat a hasty retreat.

"Every locksmith in the city has heard about the treasure house, too," Norah said. "Whoever you call will probably set up a booth on the street corner selling copies of my front door key."

"Not the locksmith I have in mind," Trip said.

Norah decided not to dwell on the possibilities. She

went back into her office and called the number on the
crawl at the bottom of the screen inviting interactive
audience participation.

"That's not a good idea," Trip said from the doorway. She glanced over at him, but he was on his cell
and she was too overwrought to think about the potential repercussions of her actions.

Of course they put her through immediately. Hollie
smiled evilly from the safety of her perch beside the
news anchors, and Norah realized she'd played right into
her hands. As a psychologist she should have known
better. She really ought to hang up, she told herself, but it
felt good to take her anger out on the person who deserved it.

"Hello," the noon news anchor said, after he'd informed Chicago and every affiliate and national news
producer in America that Norah MacArthur, daughter
of the last surviving conspirator of the Gold Coast Robbery, was on the phone. "It's a pleasure to have you with
us today, Ms. MacArthur. What can you tell us about
the missing money?"

"Nothing. I don't know anything about any money.
I didn't call to talk about that. I want to set the record
straight about my appearance on *Chicago in the Morning*. Hollie was never told she couldn't ask questions
about the bank robbery. She chose to focus on my dating history instead."

Hollie looked surprised, but then she always looks
surprised. There was nothing slow about the mind behind the wide eyes and freakishly smooth forehead. "All
I know is that I was told to confine my questions to the
book, which was a real challenge since it was neither
well-executed nor properly researched. In my opinion,"
she added with a smile that only Norah would label
nasty.

Before she could find a comeback that was more than a spiteful commentary involving Hollie's focus on the exterior at the expense of real character substance, the anchor said, "We have another caller," and put an interested expression on his face as he stared into the camera. "This one's from Stu Enwright from WGXQ. Go ahead, Stu."

"We at WGXQ would like to apologize to Ms. MacArthur," Stu said, "and assure her that Ms. Roget was never told to avoid questions about the Gold Coast Robbery. She did not clear this interview with us, and any comments made by Ms. Roget about Ms. MacArthur's personal and professional life are strictly Ms. Roget's opinion as she is no longer a representative of WGXQ."

The anchorman kept smiling, just his eyes cutting to Hollie. Who was not smiling. She looked a little nauseous, as a matter of fact, and more than a little homicidal. Norah had no trouble guessing at who headlined Hollie's hit list.

Trip took the phone from Norah and said, "It would help if you ran the footage from fifteen years ago, especially the part where the FBI and the Chicago Police Department determined there was nothing at the MacArthur residence. Unless you want to be responsible for Ms. MacArthur's safety as well." And he disconnected, nodding when Stu Enwright informed Chicago and the world that the footage would be released as soon as it could be located.

"I guess you aren't the only one concerned about litigation," Trip said.

Norah looked over her shoulder, just in time to see him fold his cell closed and slip it into his pocket. "You had her fired?"

"She got herself fired. I called my handler, and explained the problem. He decided it was a bad idea for Hollie to have a big soapbox."

"She may not have her own program, but every news network in the country is going to want to interview her."

"I don't think so."

Norah sank back against the desk. "You got her blackballed, too? Jeez, Trip, she's going to complain to anyone and everyone she can. And she'll blame it on me."

Trip shrugged. "Let her. It will blow over soon enough."

"Not until the loot from those safe-deposit boxes is found."

"Which will be soon. I've been talking to your father."

If she hadn't already been leaning against the desk, she'd have needed to sit down. Normally she would've said her father was the last person who'd fall for a line, but Trip really knew how to deliver, and he'd be telling Lucius exactly what he wanted to hear.

"What if I told you Lucius is on board?"

"Lucius is in jail."

"He thinks it's a good idea for me to hang out with you the next couple of weeks. Once he's out he's going to tell me where the money is."

She laughed, instantly relieved. "He's conning you. He made a vow to see that everything gets back where it belongs. All of the partners are dead, so it's up to him."

"And you believe that? Maybe you're the one he's conning."

"He swore on my mother's grave."

That shut Trip up, which didn't mean he was convinced. "You don't think there's any chance he's playing you?"

"He wouldn't lie to me. Not about that."

"How about we go ask him?"

"Sure," Norah said, not believing for an instant that Trip would take her to see her father, and grateful for it. Lucius MacArthur was her only living relative, but she'd spent her entire adult life trying to live down his crime. She couldn't even begin to imagine what she'd say to him, but she had three weeks left to figure it out, and she wanted those weeks. "Have a nice trip. Let me know how it turns out."

chapter
4

"MIND IF I TURN ON THE TELEVISION?" TRIP asked Norah that evening.

They'd had dinner, which had taken less time to eat than to agree on where to order it from since he'd wanted real food, and she'd wanted something without grease, calories, and, apparently, taste. They'd settled on pizza—Chicago-style, of course, since he didn't get to the city all that often—with a side of antipasto salad which she'd stripped of meat and cheese and ignored the dressing completely.

Immediately after cleaning the kitchen to within an inch of its life, Norah holed up in her office, and left him to wander the tomblike depths of her house. It didn't take him long to work his way back to her.

"Television," he repeated because she hadn't looked up from her book, or even acknowledged his presence, and he'd been lurking in the doorway for at least a half hour. "It's that antique box sitting in your living room—"

"Parlor. And it's not antique."

"It's not plasma or flat screen."

"Yes," she said, not looking up but sounding huffy about being interrupted.

It was just too irresistible—childish, maybe, but irresistible. "Yes, I can turn on the television or yes, you mind?"

She looked at him over the tops of her glasses, black rimmed, cat's-eye glasses that gave her face a whole other character, one he found sexy, the way her eyes zeroed in on his, focused and intent, one eyebrow inching up along with the corners of her mouth because he was staring, he realized, and it was no longer comfortable or about poking fun at her because she was being so stuffy. And he'd completely forgotten what they'd been talking about, so instead he rattled around the room, lined with bookshelves that were filled with biographies, textbooks, and reference manuals. No fiction. "What do you read for enjoyment?"

"Shampoo bottles, road signs, cereal boxes," she said, poker-faced.

"Let me guess, wheat germ, granola, and fiber." He grinned at her. "Lots of fiber."

"What's wrong with fiber?"

"You're too young to eat fiber."

"No one's too young to eat fiber." And she went back to her book, stopping to type a note into her laptop.

"What are you doing?"

She sighed and looked at him, taking her glasses off first, to his disappointment. "I'm researching a new book."

He circled the room again, checking the titles on the

spines of her books, and just as she turned back to work he said, "What's it about?"

"Attention deficit. I have a perfect research subject in mind."

"There's nothing to do," he said.

"There are eleven other rooms in this house."

"I know. I've been in them all. I peeked in your closets, snooped in your medicine chests, and poked around in your bedroom."

"You forgot to mention my underwear drawer."

"I resisted that urge. The house is depressing enough. Getting a look at your unmentionables would kill the last bit of mystery, and if I found white cotton I'd have to shoot myself before I dropped dead from sheer boredom."

She smiled. He figured it was the mental picture of him with a bullet hole in his head.

"Some of those rooms you snooped through have televisions. With cable. No porn channels, but you can probably find some gratuitous nudity. Or maybe a Victoria's Secret commercial."

Trip shrugged. "I'm not really a TV watcher."

"What do you do for entertainment?"

"Solve crimes, catch bad guys, rescue damsels in distress."

She opened her desk drawer and rooted around, saying, "I think I saw some kryptonite in here."

His grin widened. "No Lois Lane complex?"

She rolled her eyes. "Go away and let me work."

"What do you expect me to do? This house is like a museum. You probably haven't moved a stick of furniture in fifteen years."

"Twenty," she said, "since my mother died. It's comforting to keep things they way they were. Everyone clings to something from their childhood, good or bad. For me, it's my home, and it's not hurting anyone, including me."

Trip kept his expression flat, but the way she was studying his face told him he wasn't good enough to fool her. "I don't like pity."

"It's not pity. I'm sorry about your parents, that's all."

He didn't like talking about his parents. He didn't even like remembering them, but it gave him something in common with Norah—or rather it gave her something in common with him, and he wasn't above using it. "Don't psychoanalyze me," he said, intending to do exactly that to her, in reverse.

"All business now, huh?"

"You better hope so, because the people coming after you, the ones who are serious, will be all business."

She laughed a little, but there was an edge of nerves. "Why do you feel a need to set boundaries for me? You kissed me."

"It seemed like the best course of action."

Norah shook her head. "There was any number of ways you could have gotten your message across. Just walking out on that stage and claiming to be my boyfriend would have been enough."

"It was impulse."

"You don't do things by impulse."

"Not very often." And he couldn't tell her he took one look at her in that ugly suit, all cranky because of Hollie, and all his protective instincts rose, along with some not-so-protective ones. Norah MacArthur got to him in a way he didn't want to understand, let alone explain to her. "I like to make a big entrance," he said.

"I guess I should be grateful you didn't pull your gun."

*　　*　　*

BY TWO A.M. NORAH WAS WISHING SHE HAD TRIP'S gun. Shooting herself in the head was probably the only way she'd get any rest. He'd insisted on sleeping in her bedroom, with her or without her. *With* wasn't an option, especially if she expected to get any sleep. *Without* was no better. The bed in the spare room was comfortable enough, the room was dark and cool, and the blankets were a warm, cozy weight on her, and the house was quiet, secure. And she was still awake. She could all but feel the bags under her eyes growing.

She'd tried several different relaxation exercises, she'd meditated, and she'd run case studies—boring case studies—and there she was, still wide awake, still staring at the ceiling and thinking she'd give just about anything to shut her brain off for an hour, to stop thinking of James A. Jones, III, sleeping right down the hall. In her house. And she wasn't doing anything about it.

As if she could.

He refused to leave voluntarily, and it wasn't like she could physically remove him. And if she called the cops he'd probably get some FBI connection on the phone and have them all fired, and honestly? It was comforting having him there, and, okay, no matter how much she'd like to believe otherwise, her attempts to get rid of Trip were half-hearted at best. It wasn't all about that kiss, though.

Lucius wanted to get the loot back to the original owners, but if the day she'd just had was any indication, he wouldn't get the opportunity, not with all the kooks coming out of the woodwork. Bill Simonds and Hollie Roget were no real threat, but the guy in the Lexus was a different story. Having Trip—having someone—in the house helped make her feel secure. And left her mind free to obsess about him, in her bed . . .

She heard a sound, just a whisper, really, then another and another, footsteps moving softly down the hallway outside her bedroom door. Her heart began to pound, but not because she suspected it was the man from the Lexus. Her brain took her in a whole other direction, led there by her body, and she heaved a sigh because she'd just managed to forget about Trip and there he was, creeping to her room in the dead of night. Except it couldn't be him. He was trying to win her trust; sneaking into her bedroom would be counterproductive.

That meant it was someone else.

She sat up, clutching the sheets to her chest, battling through the first wave of blinding terror, which didn't take that long because under the terror was anger. There was another stranger, in her house, uninvited, because of that stupid robbery. How much was she expected to take? she wondered, tossing off the covers and flouncing out of bed, pushed to action by the frustration pent up in her—all kinds of frustration, but this was one place she could let it out.

She eased her door open and peeked out, of course in the direction of Trip's—her room—which was how she spotted the shadowy figure inching open that particular door so he—or she—could tiptoe through. She probably ought to do something, but what? Yelling might wake up Trip, but she'd become the Primary Target, which didn't seem prudent. Rescuing Trip was nice and all, but putting herself in harm's way didn't seem like the best way to go about it. She couldn't call Trip because she didn't have his cell phone number, and it didn't feel like the police would be all that much help, seeing as they were miles away and the intruder wasn't.

She wasn't feeling all that threatened. Maybe it was the tiptoeing. Tiptoeing was a lot like mincing. She doubted the guy driving the Lexus would mince around if he broke in to kidnap her, and Trip definitely wasn't a mincer. Trip was the kind of guy who'd sneak up on you using every inch of his size twelve's without making a sound, and catch you totally unaware. Heck, he was the kind of guy you saw coming and never realized he was trouble until it was too late. And she was stalling.

She ducked back into her room, grabbed the first thing that came to hand, and before she could talk herself out of it, she raced down the hall, burst through Trip's door, and swung, two-handed, whacking the figure bending over him across the back of the head. The guy grunted and whipped around. He was wearing some sort of mask, but she got the distinct impression he wasn't happy with her. The impression was confirmed when he barreled by her, swiping an arm out and knocking her sideways on top of Trip.

"Son of a—" Trip dumped Norah off him and onto the floor, struggling free of the bedclothes and taking off after the intruder.

She got to her feet and raced down the stairs in time to see Trip fling himself at the intruder, tackling the man before he could get to the front door. They went down in a tangle of arms and legs, and in the complete darkness of her foyer, the only way to tell them apart was Trip's bare chest reflecting what little light there was. Norah raised her weapon, but they were rolling around so much that she missed.

Trip apparently felt the whiff of air and traced it back to her. "I swear—" he said before he had to duck a punch from the bad guy, "if you hit me"—another punch ducked—"with that, I'll"—the intruder got in a punch to Trip's ribs. Norah swung and hit Trip square in the chest because he'd chosen that moment to Hulk out. His breath whooshed out, the intruder scrambled up, knocking Trip ass over teakettle, and made his escape out the front door.

Norah went to the door and watched him run through the pool of illumination under the nearest streetlight, glancing back toward her house as he did. "Was that guy wearing a Robin costume?" she asked Trip.

"Robin?"

"Robin. As in Batman's sidekick."

Trip peered over her shoulder just as the guy hit another streetlight. "Yellow cape, green jockeys, orange top with a big yellow *R* on it. Not to mention the mask. Definitely Robin."

"Huh," Norah said, thinking it was appropriate since the rest of his face was chubby and pasty, and she got the impression he was just a kid, late teens, early twenties. "I wonder if Batman is around here somewhere."

"Why don't you and your book take a look around the house and let me know if the coast is clear."

Uh-oh. Norah shut the door and flipped on the foyer light.

Trip scowled at her, eyes narrowed, jaw locked, no smoke coming out of his ears, but she still took a step back when he came at her. She wasn't fast enough to evade him completely, but he only reached out and disarmed her.

"*The Gender Bridge*," he read off the front cover, his eyes already glazing over. "This thing only causes unconsciousness if you read it," he said.

"It was handy," Norah said.

"It was useless."

"It did a pretty good number on you."

"Yeah, and I'd be questioning the Boy Wonder right now if it wasn't for you and your literary efforts."

"Excuse me? I saved your life. That guy was so close he practically had his hands around your throat."

"I was faking it. And I was at a disadvantage since I was lying down, so I had to wait for him to get close enough for me to grab him."

"Oh," she said, cranky with guilt and lack of sleep. "You might want to clue me in on your plans next time."

He snorted. "Why can't you cower in your room like a good little girl, and let me handle the dangerous stuff?"

"Cower—girl—dangerous stuff!" she sputtered. "You're lucky I don't still have that book."

"And you're lucky you're still here. You did everything but paint a target on your back."

That put the whole episode back in perspective. So Trip was a misogynist; he was also willing to stand between her and possible death. It sort of cancelled out his bad traits. Except the one where he twisted the facts to suit his purposes. "I thought the news reports would keep idiots like that from invading my house."

"The news reports only keep the harmless kooks away. The guys who are serious still think you know something, and they're willing to do more than invade your house."

"You told me they weren't serious," she reminded him. "That guy certainly didn't try very hard."

Trip went silent. And pissy. "It would have been nice to ask him some questions," he grumbled.

"We already know it's about the robbery."

"And that's a great starting point, but I have about a million other questions. And I know where we can get the answers."

"No."

"We have to talk to your dad."

"No." She tried to walk way, but Trip caught her by the wrist.

"What do you think your chances are of winning this battle?"

She looked down at his hand on her skin, her suddenly heated skin, which was conducting very dangerous feelings of other parts of her body. If Trip wanted something from her—anything—she didn't think her chances of resisting him were very high.

But she was going to fight like hell anyway.

chapter
5

"SHE'S NOT EXACTLY WHAT YOU WOULD CALL cooperative," Trip said into his cell phone. He was leaning against the wall opposite Norah's lecture hall. He could see her through the door. She didn't look happy. But then, she never looked happy. Resigned, exasperated, irritated, mulish, and downright pissed off? Sure. The closest she came to the other end of the emotional spectrum was cautiously amused. And at the moment she looked like she was about to face a firing squad.

"Her old man's a famous criminal who knows where a shitload of money is hidden—she's treasure hunter catnip. And you're hanging around," Mike Kovaleski said in his usual blunt manner, "what's to be happy about?"

"We have a hit-and-run driver and a home-invader to track down. What could be more fun?"

"Not everyone has your sick sense of humor. 'Sides, her happiness isn't your objective."

Trip bit back the instant defense that sprang to mind. Mike was his handler, and yeah, he had a penchant for stating the obvious, but he was also ex-Marines, and he saw everything as a nail. In this particular situation, Trip was the hammer. And Norah was impeding his aim.

He lifted his gaze and there she was, wearing one of her ugly suits, this one the color of mud. She met his eyes, sizing him up. Every time she looked at him she studied, measured, quantified. And sometimes it had nothing to do with the Gold Coast Robbery—

"Run it down," Mike said.

"Not much to tell," Trip began, turning his mind from Norah's hot stares to Norah's danger as he ran through the events of the last twenty-four hours.

"Nothing there," Mike said when he was finished. "You got a stolen car and a doofus in a Halloween costume. One spells pro, the other screams nutcase."

"Sometimes the kooks are more trouble."

"You let him get by you. Next time, take him to school. Secret Agent 101."

"I'll try to remember that," Trip said, but he was smiling. Couldn't help it, since he'd flashed back to Norah and her textbook-slash-weapon, not to mention the fierce light in her eyes. Dangerous, he thought, adding it to the list of Norah's moods he'd compiled earlier. One of the expressions he'd forgotten to list before—and the only one he actually enjoyed. "Gotta go," he said to Mike, "class is about to start."

"Class?"

"Puff's daughter teaches college psychology. She has a lecture this morning."

"And you think it's a good idea to let her stand in

front of a big room full of people she probably doesn't know by sight? Unless you're using her as bait."

"She refused to call in a sub," Trip said. "Gotta go, the lecture is starting."

"Pay attention," Mike said in a tone of voice that went along with a headshake. "Maybe you'll find out how to make her behave."

"There's not that much knowledge in the world."

NORAH DEFINITELY WAS NOT ENJOYING HERSELF. Not that unusual a circumstance in Trip's short acquaintance with her, but at least it wasn't his fault this time. At least not entirely. She'd asked him to stay outside the lecture hall. He'd refused, and while the number of resentful glances she sent his way told him how she felt about his presence, the real trouble came from the student body. Or rather bodies, as in college-age female bodies, most of whom, it was clear from their questions, expected to discover how to "Create Your Mate." The few male bodies were interested in the female bodies, and the word *mate* was definitely involved. The two concepts, however, were far apart. As far as the distance to any church altar.

Norah's lecture unfolded like a mini war. She stepped up to the lectern, armored in her suit, a firm, authoritative demeanor, and her glasses. The students fought back with rampant curiosity and the desperation to avoid any actual knowledge on which they could be tested later. Norah answered their questions about her TV appearance and ignored anything pertaining to the Gold Coast Robbery. When she got down to actual teaching, just about everyone else in the room checked out, including Trip, but at least he stayed awake, which was some accomplishment considering he'd gotten as little sleep as Norah had. But if she could stay awake, he sure as hell would. He didn't need to be a psychologist to know what that would do to the balance of power in their relationship . . .

Shit, there was no balance of power in their relationship. He was hanging on by sheer obnoxiousness, hoping to wear her down enough to quit opposing him at every turn. Not to brag or anything, but he'd never had this kind of trouble with a woman before, on or off the job. It never took him long to worm his way into someone's trust, partly because he was trustworthy. Hell, he was an FBI agent, but was that enough for Norah MacArthur? No, she had to have issues with authority figures, thanks to her old man.

It didn't seem to matter that he'd saved her life— okay, maybe not her life, but she'd probably be tied to a chair somewhere if not for him—and was she grateful? No. She should be kissing the ground at his feet by now, but where was he after the longest twenty-four hours of his life? Tired, bored, bruised, and even when he did have a lucid moment all he could do was mentally undress her with his eyes because about four in the morning he'd started to wonder what might have happened after that kiss if they hadn't been on a G-rated television show. Not that he was an exhibitionist, but being on camera hadn't seemed like such a big obstacle when he was back in bed, remembering her in that little tank and shorts she slept in, wielding her book like a battle-axe. All she'd been missing were the glasses . . .

Trip sat up a little straighter in his chair and put that image out of his head. Not difficult since the class had ended and there was a mad rush. About two thirds of the audience made a beeline for the exit, more than one of the coeds giving him a smile on her way by. The rest dashed to the front of the room, surrounding Norah in a clamoring mass of insecure human flesh that made him understand why it was called a *crush* of people.

Trip had put himself between her and a couple tons of Japanese engineering without a second thought. No way was he taking on a bunch of college-aged girls with romantic troubles. They'd probably take one look at him and go into a homicidal frenzy. Hell, the lone male was smart enough to stand back and wait for the others to disperse.

Norah had taken refuge behind the lectern, which didn't provide much cover but seemed to represent an unassailable wall to the students, since none of them tried to cross that invisible barrier. "I'm not giving any relationship advice," she began.

About half the crowd of young women slouched off in various states of disappointment.

"And if you want to know how to get published, sit down and write something."

All but a couple of the other girls slouched off. Norah answered a couple of questions that actually seemed germane to her lecture, then turned to look at the kid who'd been lurking behind the female hoard. He just stood there, stringy hair hanging in his face, looking more like a gamer than a psych major, tall and gawky and soft around the middle. Then again, looks could be deceiving. Who knew that better than Trip, with his job, or Norah, with her father?

About the time Trip decided he'd been creeping the crowd of young women, he plucked up the courage to step forward and actually speak.

"I know my grades aren't great, Professor MacArthur," he mumbled from behind his curtain of hair, "but all I need is some tutoring. I want to be a psychologist, just like you."

Want and *psychologist* were the operative words there, but judging by the way the kid was invading Norah's personal space he wasn't making a career path so much as trying to make time.

"I could come to your house," the kid said, clinching Trip's opinion of his ulterior motives. "You wouldn't even have to talk that much, just help me when I have a question about the reading."

"You are . . ."

"Uh, having a hard time with, like, the big words, and—"

"I was asking your name," Norah said with a perfectly straight face.

"Oh, right, my name. Bobby," he said, nodding the entire time. Or maybe he was just bobbing his head out of habit, which gave his name a whole new meaning and made Trip laugh.

Norah shot him a look. Bobby didn't notice.

"Bobby," Norah repeated. "I don't tutor. If you're having this much trouble with a one hundred level course, perhaps you should be rethinking your educational path."

"Man, you're, like, cold, Professor MacArthur."

"I find it saves time."

"Yeah, but, like, a little sympathy wouldn't hurt, y'know?"

"Sympathy is highly overrated," she said, patting him on the arm. "Directness is often the best course when I feel someone can handle the truth."

"Okay then." Bobby turned around and shambled up the aisle, mumbling to himself and shaking his head.

She had that effect on him, too, Trip thought as she strode past him, that little annoyed frown on her face, and all he could do was jump up and trot along behind her like a puppy.

Balance of power, hah.

"That kid has a crush on you," he said as they walked out of the lecture hall.

"I didn't get that impression."

Trip shrugged. "You'd be the expert."

"He probably doesn't have a very good home life," Norah said. "So many of these kids are a product of divorce or single-parent homes, and psychology seems to offer a way to understand what they've been through."

"Is that the voice of experience?"

She shot him a look, not amused.

"You can't cure the problems of the world."

"I can't even solve my own at the moment," she said, clearly identifying him as a problem by the way she was glaring at him.

Trip just grinned, getting the point but not taking it personally. "The parking lot is this way," he said, trying to steer her in that direction.

She slipped around him and continued on her way. "I have a couple of appointments."

This time he took her by the elbow. "Reschedule."

She shook him off. "I'm booked for six months, and with my other commitments—" She stopped walking. "You can't be in session with me," she said. "Patient confidentiality, not to mention having an audience makes people uncomfortable talking about their problems."

"I get it," he snapped, and just before she turned away he saw her mouth quirk up, just a little, and he caught on to her game. Stupid of him not to see it before, but then he was dealing with a lack of sleep and an overabundance of testosterone.

"I'll be busy for a while. You should take off."

"Got nothing else to do."

Her frown intensified, but she only said, "Fine, you can wait in my outer office."

"Sure, I could use a nap. We have a long drive ahead of us." And who was smiling now, he thought, but when they got to her office a couple stood up from the sofa and Trip wasn't so amused anymore. "Did Mike send you?" he asked them, referring, of course, to Mike Kovaleski, his—their—handler, since they all worked for the Bureau.

"We came because Aubrey is intrigued," Jack Mitchell said, referring to his partner, Aubrey Sullivan.

"You're an FBI agent?" Norah asked Aubrey, taking in her outfit, which even Trip could tell was high fashion, a flirty little wool suit in fuchsia—hardly an unobtrusive color—and pointy-toed stiletto-heeled shoes that he was already picturing on Norah. Just the shoes.

"Jimmy Choos, right?" Norah said, her voice low and breathy, which did amazing things for the fantasy, even if it was only the shoes winding her up.

Aubrey smiled, transforming her plain features to pretty, if not compelling, which seemed to be of more interest to Norah than the expensive feathers. "I think of myself as an agent," she said around that wide smile. "So does the FBI. Jack—"

"I think Aubrey's a pain in the ass. I was saddled with her on a case last year—"

"I saved your job," Aubrey reminded him. "And your ass. Jack got burned," she said for Norah's benefit. "The Bureau thought he was a mole, and I was targeted for death by Pablo Corona."

"The drug lord?"

"The insane drug lord," Aubrey said, "but it all worked out in the end."

"I think she gets that, since we're not corpses," Jack said.

"And you're here about the robbery," Norah said, "but my usual clients seem to be missing."

"Your twelve o'clock canceled." Jack handed Norah a note. "Your secretary left you this."

Trip leaned over her shoulder, read the note in what he assumed was her secretary's handwriting, telling her the noon clients had been cancelled, then filled with a last-minute call in.

"Convenient," Norah said, ranging herself opposite the three of them, tapping foot, arms crossed, waiting for an explanation.

Trip refused to cave in to her body language; no point in letting her get used to having her own way. On the other hand, he was still walking a fine line between tolerance and banishment, and presented with another pair of agents, one of them a woman, he wasn't sure she'd choose him . . .

And she had him second-guessing every word and every action he took, Trip realized, worried about how she was reading him. Well, the hell with that. He needed to treat this like any other case—and bottom line? It was *his* case. "Don't tell me Mike sent you," he said to his competition.

"Aubrey heard about the missing loot," Jack said, shooting his partner a long-suffering look that Trip took to mean she'd nagged him into coming. "She got bit by the treasure-hunting bug."

"Take your butterfly nets and run around in someone else's garden," Trip said.

Jack shrugged. "No skin off my nose."

"If you need any help," Aubrey said to Norah.

Norah slid a glance in Trip's direction. "Well . . ."

"Honey, I read your book," Aubrey said with a small chuckle. "Chapter four."

"What?" Trip looked from one woman to the other, feeling his face heat even though he had no idea why. "What about chapter four?"

Aubrey and Norah burst out laughing. Even Jack was smiling.

"What are you grinning about?" Trip grumbled.

"They're just poking fun at you."

"Is that what you think?"

Aubrey popped up an eyebrow, leaned close to Norah, and whispered something. Norah's eyes widened, as her gaze shifted to Trip's face, then slipped down.

"What?" Jack asked Aubrey, who said, "Just rumors, nothing for you to worry about."

"Aren't there any rumors about me?"

"Of course, although not the same kind."

"What kind are they?"

"I'll tell you later."

"I hate this shit," Jack said as they walked off. "You know I hate this shit. Tell me what the rumors are or there won't be a later."

"Now, Jack," Aubrey said, reaching up to pat his cheek, "you should never withhold sex to make a point."

"Who's withholding sex? I was talking about my gun."

"They're adorable," Norah said once they were out of earshot.

"Don't let Jack hear you say that."

"Aubrey has him wrapped around her little finger."

"Maybe in this kind of situation, but when they're on a job, they make a hell of a partnership."

"That's what every woman wants in life," Norah said, sighing. "Someone to have amazing sex with, and someone to talk to after sex."

"They seem kind of . . . contentious." Trip exited her office, Norah following along absently as she took the verbal bait.

"It's banter, Trip, and banter is really just another way of saying I care for you. Jack clearly isn't the kind of man who talks about his feelings easily. When Aubrey teases him, it's just like the eight-year-old boy on the playground who pulls the little girl's braid and runs away because he wants her to notice him. Aubrey knows Jack very well, I'd say, and she's careful to poke fun at him without crossing any lines. He gets the kind of attention he's comfortable with from her, and she gets attention back from him. It's a win-win.

"And you've checked out of the conversation."

"I'm listening to every word," Trip said as they passed the dean's office, "just keeping an eye on the surroundings. That's my job.

"You have a real knack for translating psychobabble into English," he added nonchalantly. "Maybe I should read your book."

"Maybe you should find out what the dean's secretary wants first. Since you're keeping an eye on our surroundings."

Trip halted a couple of steps past Norah, huffing out a breath and wondering when he was going to get his shit together on this job. He held up a finger for the benefit of the dean's secretary, a thin, washed-out slip of a woman who looked like the first stray breeze would float her off to bank against the nearest curb with the last of the fall leaves. She shrank back into a doorway, just her head peeking around the frame and all but vibrating with apprehension.

No threat there. "You and I need to get some things straight," he said to Norah.

"If you're about to tell me you're in charge, you can save your breath."

"My first responsibility is staying alive and keeping you alive. I can't do that if you won't listen to me."

"Professor MacArthur?"

"I have a perfectly sound mind—"

"Which doesn't do you any good when you have to act without thinking, like last night when you tried to coldcock me."

"Professor MacArthur?"

"*What*," they bellowed in unison, both whipping around.

The dean's secretary froze, but only for a split second before her eyes landed on Trip, her cheeks glowing the slightest shade of pink. "The dean would like to see you, Professor MacArthur," she said, apparently forgetting her shyness.

"I'll wait for you out here," Trip said.

Norah hooked him by the arm and towed him into the dean's office. "Maybe the dean and his secretary are conspiring to kidnap me."

"I doubt it."

Violence was not the first impression Raymond Kline, dean of the Midwest School of Psychology, made. Tall, thin, pale, sandy blond hair smoothed back from a receding hairline, and the sort of superior attitude that came from spending a lot of time in a self-made ivory tower. Dean Kline gave the impression that the mere suggestion of physical violence would make him faint dead away. He was also responsible for the safety of the entire student body, both character flaws Trip had used against him. And Norah. Which she was about to find out.

"Trip," Dean Kline said, smiling his thin, ascetic smile, his hand flaccid and just a bit damp when Trip shook it.

"Raymond," Trip said, squelching the urge to wipe his palm on his jeans. How Norah could have dated this guy was a complete mystery, Trip thought, which was beside the point.

"You two know each other?" she said, which was

obvious since they were on a first name basis, but she was just getting on board with reality, her expression boding ill for Trip. Hell, her expression would have boded ill for the *Titanic*.

"Norah, why don't you sit?" Kline suggested.

The withering glance she sent them both was really just overkill for Trip. Kline didn't get it. Kline thought he was in control of the situation. Trip lounged back against the wall, prepared to enjoy the verbal evisceration. Then she looked at him and he remembered his guts were in her sights, too.

"Let me see if I have this right," she said, pacing the length of the room and back. "The two of you got together and discussed the situation and decided what I should do."

"Now, Norah—"

She whipped around and glared at Kline.

He took a step back, caught himself, frowned, and stepped forward again, popping his chin up so he could stare down his nose at her. *Moron.*

"My. Personal. Business," she said, not raising her voice but enunciating each word very carefully.

Trip couldn't see her face, but this time when Kline stepped back he stayed there. He wasn't smart enough to keep his mouth shut.

"Since you're going to be difficult about this," Kline said, "I'll get right to the point. I've decided it's best if you take some time off. For the good of the student body."

"Time off?" Norah went so pale she was practically transparent, except for a spot of hot pink in each cheek. She held it together, though. Faced with losing what she treasured the most, she held it together.

"You must see the logic in my decision," Kline said.

"Must I?"

"In cases such as this I have full discretion. The board—"

"You went to the board?"

"Not yet, but I will if you make it necessary. Look, Norah, it's for your own good. Considering our relationship—"

"Our relationship is over."

"But—"

"Over. Done. Finished. History."

"Like your job," Raymond said coldly.

Norah seemed to falter a bit.

Without thinking, Trip sidled a step closer in case she needed his support. "How long?" she asked, stiffening her spine and lifting her chin.

"Until this issue is resolved," the dean said. "Of course, if you were inclined to share your father's story, and anything that results from it, with the college . . ."

"You're blackmailing me?"

"Of course not. It's just that the publicity is so disruptive, and if the treasure were found that would stop."

"You were happy about the publicity from my book, and all the attention it brought the college."

"Yes, but you don't want anyone hurt on your account."

Norah looked over at Trip. "No one is going to get hurt."

"Well, now, we don't want to take any chances."

Norah digested that for a moment. "And what are the *chances* my position will still be open when this . . . stupidity is over?"

Dean Kline gave her a slight smile. "I'll do everything in my power to see that you have a place here to come back to, once you've dealt with your personal unpleasantness."

Trip fielded a look from Norah, pure fury. "Thank

you," she politely said to Kline, then whisked out of the office, rounding on Trip the second they were in the hall again. "You went to that ass behind my back."

"Actually, my boss called that ass behind your back, then he sent me to see him."

"I'm not tenured. I could lose my job."

"Kline assured Mike you wouldn't."

"Did he also mention that we dated for three years?"

"And he slept around."

She frowned. "Actually, he didn't, not that I could ever find out. He did a lot of looking, and he wasn't really *in* the relationship for the last year, but I can't say there was someone else. In fact, he wants"—she smiled faintly—"wanted to get back together. I doubt he still feels that way. Silver lining. Which doesn't absolve you." Norah hefted her briefcase and started walking, this time heading for the faculty parking lot.

"You don't need that job."

"I like that job. And don't tell me what I need."

"You don't want to know what I think you need."

"Does it include you going away?"

Trip chose to ignore that remark.

"That wasn't a rhetorical question."

"I'm not going to explain why I'm here again. You're stubborn, not stupid."

She glanced over at him, so angry that Trip wondered why she didn't burst into flame. "You seem to be quite intelligent, and yet you have a real problem figuring out when you're not welcome."

"You're a pain in the ass. A wordy pain in the ass."

"Here are two more words for you. *Interfering jerk.*"

"Stubborn idiot."

"Government patsy."

"Bookworm," Trip shot back, and then he had her up against her car, his mouth on hers, his hands on her body, taking as much of her as he could get. She came right back at him, curling her hands into his shirt, trying to drag him closer, which was impossible since the only thing between them was a couple of thin layers of clothing and enough heat to cause spontaneous combustion.

And then she was pushing him away. Trip surfaced enough to hear the catcalls and whistles of a group of students passing by. Instinctively he shielded her from them, telling himself he'd caused her enough trouble for one day.

If not for the taste of her still lingering on his tongue, the feel of her body against his, the need pounding through his bloodstream, he might actually have believed it.

chapter
6

"I TRIED. TWICE."

"Tell me." *And make it fast*, he added, but he kept his impatience to himself. Time was at a premium, but pushing the kid only discombobulated him, and then it would take twice the time to get the facts.

"I just got out of Professor MacArthur's lecture," Bobby said. "I asked her to tutor me at her house."

"You what?!"

"It's okay. She blew me off, like, completely. Jeez, she barely even looked at me. That guy was sitting in the back of the room and she was hot to get out of there."

"You must be mistaken."

"Nope. I broke into the house last night just like you told me to, Dad."

"Don't call me Dad."

There was a short, hurt silence.

"Someone could overhear." And there was no way

this kid could be his son, but he stayed mum on that subject, too. He needed Bobby. For the moment.

"Oh, right, I forgot."

"So, you broke in."

"Yeah."

He rolled his eyes. "And?"

"That guy was there. That guy you said is an FBI agent. He woke up, so did Professor MacArthur, but he didn't, like, pull a gun on me or anything. I could've taken him if not for her. She hit him with a book, and I ran away. Are you sure he's a cop, 'cuz he didn't even chase me."

He didn't say anything but his blood pressure rose so fast he was afraid the top of his head might blow off. You were out of the picture for a little while and some *guy* moved in on your turf. It was damned inconvenient. But not exactly unexpected. Norah was a woman who deliberated, who made decisions based on reason and logic. She didn't jump into things. Lucius MacArthur, the last living member of the Gold Coast Robbery, was about to be released from prison, and that would bring out all kinds of treasure hunters, and Norah might feel safer with a Fed squatting in her house. "You were disguised, weren't you?"

"Yep," Bobby said proudly. "I wore my Halloween costume. Robin."

"You went as a bird?"

"Robin. You know, 'Holy breaking and entering, Batman.'" The kid was laughing. It took him a minute to realize he was the only one. "The TV show," he said. "Batman and Robin."

The caller lifted his eyes heavenward, wondering what he'd done to be saddled with this doofus of a kid. "I'm familiar with it," he said. "It was a little before your time, though."

"They play it on TV Land all the time. It's really cool, how they walk up walls and stuff. I wonder how they did it."

Another eye roll. He would have explained it, but what was the point? "Maybe you should actually attempt to learn something in those college courses you're taking."

"What for? I'm gonna be rich, right?"

"Only if you do your part."

"You want me to break in again?"

"No." They'd be prepared for it now. "Go keep an eye on the house, let me know what they're up to."

"But . . . the neighbors all know each other. If I park on the street, they'll notice my car. And I can't lurk in the bushes for two days."

Hallelujah, he wasn't so stupid after all. "Go in disguise."

"But you said—"

"Not Robin," he said with another eye roll. "Try being a meter reader or the cable guy. Nobody ever notices the cable guy."

"Then I must be the cable guy all the time."

Okay, now he felt bad. But only a little. "I'll call you in a couple days, see how it's going. And stay away from Norah." No point in pressing their luck. She was too observant—when the FBI wasn't around to distract her. And apparently Hell had frozen over; it was the only way he'd be thanking the federal government for putting a man in Norah's house.

THE UNITED STATES PENITENTIARY AT MARION, Illinois, sat nine miles outside its namesake city and over three hundred miles from Chicago. From 1906 to 1963, the worst of the worst criminals were sent to

Alcatraz. After The Rock closed, they were relocated to Marion, USP. Two guards were killed in 1983, sending Marion into permanent lockdown, meaning the inmates, including the likes of John Gotti and Pete Rose, spent twenty-three hours a day confined to their cells. It was the perfect place for an aging bank robber whose true identity would earn him a one-way ticket to the afterlife his particular religious beliefs threatened him with.

The prison had converted to medium security a few years before, but by then nobody would guess they were sharing close quarters with an infamous criminal who was keeping a multimillion dollar secret.

Norah and Trip were shown to a tiny, depressing private interview cubicle, industrial gray walls, furniture bolted to the floor, and Lucius MacArthur, the single bright spot—not for his orange jumpsuit, for his attitude. Lucius lounged in a cracked plastic chair at the dented metal table, looking for all the world as if he wore a velvet smoking jacket and puffed on a twenty-dollar stogie. As a bank robber he'd proven to be a complete failure. Paying his debt to society didn't seem to have dampened his enthusiasm for life.

"Still think you're lord of the manor?"

He looked up from his newspaper and unleashed the wide, open, I'm-you're-best-friend-I'd-never-do-anything-to-harm-you smile he was famous for. The smile that put anyone on the receiving end instantly at ease. Heck, it took Norah a minute or two to fight off its effects and remember what was going on, and even then she crossed the room and hugged him, hard and long. Whatever else, he was her father, and she hadn't seen him for nearly fifteen years.

"Let me take a look at you," he said, holding her at arms' length, nothing in the way he studied her making her feel self-conscious. She chose not to take it as a con; it was just part of his charm that he could make anyone feel like they were absolutely perfect just the way they were. "You're all grown up, but you're still my little girl."

And just a few words to make her heart ache. "I hate seeing you in here."

"Darlin' Norah," he said with the slight Irish accent he got so much mileage out of, "I am, as you know, a veritable Houdini when it comes to locking mechanisms. Were I so inclined, I would leave this wretched island behind. Federal prison, however, is not completely without merit. I have gleaned all manner of interesting tidbits from my unfortunate incarcerated brethren, innocents all."

Trip nudged her. "Now I see why you talk like that."

Norah ignored him. "You're supposed to be rehabilitating yourself, not expanding your criminal knowledge."

"A day you learn nothing is twenty-four hours wasted," he said piously, his eyes sparkling as he added, "I don't need rehabilitating."

"That's a matter of opinion."

Lucius's eyes flicked over Norah's head, but his reaction surprised her. He seemed to take an instant dislike to Trip, which was really unlike him . . . "You've met before?"

Her father's smile turned brittle, his eyes taking on a warning glint. "The boy has come to see me a few times. I didn't know he'd made your acquaintance as well."

"*Acquaintance* is too mild a word. He moved into my house." Lucius's expression notched down to threatening, with a contemplative edge that made Norah think he might be canvassing his new store of criminal knowledge and deciding how it might apply to Trip. She wanted Trip to go away, but not in a manner that would earn her father more jail time.

"If you hear me out," Trip said, "I think you'll agree—"

"And how will you be getting me to agree, boy?"

"Because I assume you want her safe. Puff."

"I object to that scurrilous nickname."

"Then don't call me boy."

Norah rolled her eyes, but they were too intent on one another to notice her disgust.

"Take yourself off, and I can call you gone," Lucius said to Trip.

"I'm not going anywhere until you tell me where the stolen goods are hidden."

"Or else what?"

"Or else Norah will be targeted again, and this time they may not miss."

Lucius straightened, losing the studied nonchalance in his posture and most of his Irish accent. "What happened?"

Norah took the seat across from him and, keeping her voice low, recounted the scare tactic hit and run, their late-night visitor, and Trip's theory that she might be kidnapped to use as leverage to gain the loot.

"You're going to be dead," Trip said to Lucius when she'd finished, "and so is Norah if you don't cooperate."

"It won't come to that," Lucius said. "As soon as I'm released from this country club, I intend to return everything to its rightful owner or their heirs. They're entitled to their own personal items without the government playing middleman."

"And what about the money?"

"Well, now, money isn't exactly a personal item, if you take my meaning."

Trip snorted softly. "Meaning you get to change the rules whenever it suits you."

"I'm not changing the rules. There wasn't all that much money to begin with, and the rest of the boys used up most of it in hiding. Not that it did them much good," Lucius said, launching into his own narrative, none the less dramatic for being softly spoken. "By the time I arrived at the meeting place, the Hanes brothers had killed Noel Black, squabbling like beggars over the split. The cops arrived not long after me, and they made little pretense at negotiating. When the shooting was over Rickey Hanes was dead, and Mickey was well on his way to joining his brother. He whispered the hiding place to me with his dying breath."

Lucius stopped to reminisce, shaking his head after a moment. "I was arrested, of course, and tossed into this den of iniquity, but by then I'd already promised the Almighty that if he got me through that cowardly hail of bullets and let me live long enough to walk from this veritable Hell on earth, that I would right the wrongs I'd committed."

"The FBI can help you with that."

"The FBI help me? Balderdash. The FBI wants to get their hands on the contents of those boxes. A city like Chicago, there's always a lot of shenanigans going on, and chances are some of it landed in those boxes. The boys in Washington want to get a look. They'll use whoever they can to that end, and give little thought to repercussions."

"That was fifteen years ago," Trip pointed out. "Unless there's proof of a murder in one of those boxes, any information we find is likely past its expiration date."

"There's no statute of limitations in the game of politics. And our new, young president, wouldn't he be from the grand state of Illinois, now?"

"Don't let your love of drama lead you to creating a story where there isn't one."

"Don't let your naïveté lead you to judging a book by its cover."

"My job is to follow orders."

"I believe you, more's the pity. You're a tool, boy."

Trip's jaw clenched once before he replied. Lucius might have missed it. Norah did not.

"Is that supposed to piss me off, Puff?" he said his voice low and cool, "because I've always been a tool, from the day I joined the Marines to the moment I finish this case and move on to the next one."

"And you're all right with that?"

"I'm a damn good tool, and the way I see it, there's no shame in what I do."

"How about the way you do it?" Lucius shot back, his glance flicking to Norah.

Trip slammed his hands on the table, practically went nose to nose with Lucius. "If I'm using her, I'm not the only one. And at least I care what happens to her."

"Be careful, boy, one word from me and she'll send you packing."

"Wait a minute, both of you," Norah snapped out. She'd been willing to sit there and listen—listen and learn while they bandied words and sniped at each other. But they'd overstepped. "I'm *not* a tool, and I'm not going to be a pawn, either. You," she said, pointing a finger at her father, "stop acting like you're the only one involved in this. And you"—her focus swiveled to Trip—"stop making decisions for everyone else. We're in this mess together," and she couldn't quite believe she was saying it after resisting Trip so inflexibly. But seeing them play tug-of-war with her life made her realize that if she didn't play an active role in this lunacy, decisions would be made for her. That was unacceptable.

"Unless we start to cooperate," she finished, getting to her feet, "it's going to end badly. And then who are you going to blame?"

"Well, I guess she told us," Lucius said, his gaze switching to Trip. "Any more questions, boy?"

Trip smiled slightly, easing back. "Have you read her book?"

"I have."

"You don't happen to know what's in chapter four, do you?"

"GOING OUT IS JUST AS HARD AS GOING IN," TRIP observed as they waited at the last checkpoint before exiting the prison. But at least they'd gotten Lucius to promise to include them. Once he got out. Now all he had to do was keep Norah safe for three weeks, retrieve the loot, and get his ass back to D.C. with another successful op under his belt. Simple, right? He slid a glance Norah's way and lowered his expectations. *Simple* was not a descriptor that applied to her. And three weeks seemed like an eternity.

"It's difficult to see him in there," Norah said, "and it's difficult to leave him in there."

"Not much longer now, and he'll be out for good."

"But he won't be safe."

"He would if he'd reveal the hiding place. We could recover the loot, and he'd truly be a free man when he walked out of here." He looked at her expectantly.

"Once his mind is made up there's no changing it."

Trip heaved a sigh. "I figured as much when he found out you weren't safe, and he still wouldn't come clean."

"He has an unshakable optimism. And you're protecting me."

"Yeah, but who's protecting me?"

Norah gave him a look, not amused. "Suppose we said we found the loot? Everyone would back off then, right?"

"Except the press, and they'd want proof."

And when they couldn't provide proof, it would be open season on anyone by the name of MacArthur.

The gate clicked open and Norah stepped through and collected her purse from the guard. Trip followed her out. Or tried to. She stopped dead halfway out the door; he clapped his hands around her waist and stopped just short of full frontal contact, looking over her head.

"Hold it together," he said, stepping up beside her and coming face-to-face with Hollie Roget.

Hollie was flanked by a cameraman who looked like he spent his off-hours in a cardboard box under I-94, greasy black hair, clothes that could have been culled from Dumpsters, and mismatched shoes. Trip was thankful they stood upwind. The guy kept his eyes downcast, and his expression was set to Lurch, like any minute he'd let out a groan and shuffle off to fetch some bubbling, smoking potion for Morticia Addams. But he looked well-fed and strong, just the kind of man Hollie would prefer, tall, muscular, and stupid.

She gave him a little shove, and he put the camera up to his face. Trip assumed he'd turned it on. Hollie didn't.

"Get this or you're fired, Loomis," she said, then shoved her microphone in Norah's face. "Ms. MacArthur," she continued, looking and sounding the part of a reporter on location—as long as the camera didn't pick up the nasty glint in her eye. "You've just come from visiting your father, Lucius MacArthur, the last living member of the gang responsible for the Gold Coast Robbery."

"I have no idea what you're talking about."

"Neither did the guards I spoke with, but I have my sources."

"Jesus," Trip said, laying his hands on Norah's shoulders, "did you tell the guards?"

Hollie's smile started to fade off, but he left her with one last hard look as Norah said, "Trip," and turned blindly into his arms.

She didn't stay there long, trying to claw her way free and go after Hollie. Trip held her back.

"You better pray nothing happens to my father," she shouted over her shoulder as Trip towed her back toward the prison entrance.

"Is that a threat?"

"Do you want me to repeat it for the camera?"

"You've already destroyed my career," Hollie yelled back, "what more do you think you can do to me?"

"I have a very good imagination. I'll come up with something."

"Okay, now you're scaring me," Trip said.

She wasn't, unfortunately, having much of an effect on Hollie. Hollie crowded close, still asking questions.

"Did your father tell you where the loot is hidden?"

Norah tried to climb over Trip to get to Hollie, red hazing her vision. Trip wrapped an arm around her waist, lifted her feet off the ground, and toted her back inside the jail, putting her down once the door closed behind them.

"We need to see the warden," Trip said to the guard.

"That's convenient," the guard said as he buzzed them back in, "because the warden wants to see you."

* * *

NORAH STOOD BY HER FATHER'S BED IN THE
infirmary, looking down at his bruised face and battered
body and trying not to cry. She had nothing against
sorrow, but her tears weren't for her father—at least not
completely. There was a lot of anger and frustration
mixed in. Tears would be cathartic. She intended to hang
on to all that hot emotion for the next time she came
face-to-face with Hollie Roget.

"He's going to be fine," Trip said from the other
side of the bed.

"He was lucky."

Trip chose not to respond to that observation, and
really, what could he say? The both knew the only
reason Lucius was still alive was because whoever
had attacked him wanted the location of the loot, and
Lucius couldn't give it up if he was dead.

"Where the hell were the guards?" she wanted to
know, letting just a little of her frustration out.

"There'll be an investigation."

"Which will go nowhere."

"You have no faith in the system."

"After this you want me to have faith in a government institution?" Not to mention she was enough of
her father's daughter to be wary of law enforcement
agencies, from the local deputy sheriff all the way up
to the director of the FBI. There might be people who
couldn't be corrupted, but everyone had an agenda, and
she was pretty sure the Bureau would pursue its goals
even at the expense of her life.

"Norah."

She met Trip's gaze across the bed.

"I understand what you're going through," he said.

Coming from a man who knew how it felt to lose

his parents, there was nothing he could have said to calm her more quickly than that one quiet statement.

"We'll find out who's responsible for this."

"I know who's responsible for this. Hollie—"

"Norah."

Her name was spoken so softly this time, she'd have thought she'd imagined it if her father's hand hadn't tightened around hers, just for a second.

She leaned down to him, afraid she wouldn't be able to hear him over the pounding of her heart. "I'm here, Dad."

"Nice . . . to be . . . called Dad."

She glanced up at Trip and smiled. "Trust you to get mileage out of something like this."

"Always play the angle, darlin'."

"I'm glad you said that, because the angle here is to tell me where the loot is hidden."

"Dangerous."

"We'll be fine," Trip put in.

Lucius cracked his one good eye open. "We? No. Tell Norah."

"You expect her to go after the loot by herself?" Trip said. "Alone? No way."

"Her decision."

Trip looked to Norah, but he already knew she wasn't going against her father.

The infirmary occupied a long, narrow room with a row of hospital beds along each wall, not even curtains to offer privacy. A guard and a nurse flanked the door, with a prisoner cuffed to the two beds closest to them, on opposite sides of the aisle.

Lucius was at the far end of the room, sans the cuffs since he wasn't going anywhere—not under his own steam, anyway. Trip took himself to the middle of the aisle, about halfway between her and the door, back turned, arms crossed, looking like he should be wearing fatigues and army boots, and standing a post with a rifle in his hands. Comforting. And a little scary.

Lucius's hand tightened slightly on hers, and Norah bent down so he could whisper in her ear. "You're kidding," she said, then listened some more, shaking her head. "I promise," she told him when she was done.

She tried to let go of his hand, but he clutched at her. "Go to sleep. I'll be here when you wake up."

Once he'd drifted off Norah joined Trip, perching herself on the end of the nearest bed. He must have had a dozen questions, but he kept them to himself, giving her a chance to get herself under control. It took an embarrassingly long time, and thankfully he didn't offer sympathy. That would have put her right over the edge.

"He gave me the location," she said, keeping her voice down. "I promised him it would be handled exactly as he wants."

"There are conditions."

"Mine," she said, "not his. First, get my father out of here."

"Done," Trip said so fast she knew he'd been expecting that.

"And have Hollie Roget killed."

"You don't mean that."

"Right now? Yes, I do."

He shrugged. "You're running the show."

Norah watched him pull out his cell phone, not saying a word while he talked, too quietly for her to hear.

"That's it?" she said once he'd disconnected. "She's dead?"

"Regretting your decision?"

"I wanted to watch."

Trip grinned. "There's a federal warrant keeping her away from you—"

"Which she'll ignore."

"Then I'll have her arrested. No reputable TV station, radio station, magazine, or newspaper will touch her. Being in jail will ensure that even the tabloids keep their distance."

"She'll hate me even more."

"What can she do about it? Besides, I'm pretty sure you can take her. Especially with a book in your hands."

Norah smiled faintly. "I told you I wouldn't be a tool or a pawn," she said, getting back to the matter of the robbery. "I'm in this, 100 percent, or I tell the world where the hiding place is."

"Playing the angles?"

"Absolutely." For the highest stakes there were.

"You're not leaving me much choice," he said.

"I'm not leaving you any choice."

Trip rubbed the back of his neck, but like she'd said, he had no choice but to agree, which he did.

Norah clammed up.

"You promised to tell me where it is."

"Yes, but I didn't say when."

Trip smiled, if reluctantly. "Payback?"

"Self-preservation."

chapter
7

HOLLIE HAD THE GOOD SENSE TO BE GONE
when they came out. Of course, it was morning by then,
and Trip figured she hadn't left for good. She wasn't
smart enough to stay away from Norah permanently.

He'd arranged for Lucius to be released, but he hadn't
even tried to budge Norah from the prison until the
agents and an ambulance had arrived to transport her
father. The sun was just cresting the horizon by the
time they followed her father's gurney out to an ambulance disguised as a linen delivery van, and saw him
off to his safe house.

"There's no one following him, is there?" Norah
asked, her breath steaming on the cold morning air.

"Just the guys who are supposed to be following him.
They'll make sure no one crashes the party."

Norah didn't say anything. Norah looked like she
was all done in. Trip had caught a catnap here and there

in the midst of the frivolity. Every time he'd surfaced Norah had been at her father's bedside, one of his hands in hers, her eyes on his face. The woman was stubborn, contrary, and exasperating. She was also brutally loyal to those she loved. Even if that person was a convicted felon. Sure, she'd been a pain in the ass for most of the two days he'd known her . . .

Two days.

He forgot where he'd been going with the previous thought, stunned by the brevity of a relationship that felt like it had lasted a lifetime.

"Are we leaving?"

Trip opened the passenger door of Norah's Ford Escape hybrid, and held out his hand. She took a step back and clutched her keys tighter.

"You're exhausted," Trip said.

"I slept on and off."

"Not that I noticed."

"You mean while you were sawing logs on the bed across the aisle?"

"I woke up often enough to know you didn't sleep."

She shrugged. "It's only three hundred miles to Chicago, and I can sleep when I get home. It's not like I have to work."

And she was blaming him for that. Which he fully deserved since he'd gone behind her back and gotten her kicked out of school—for her own good, sure, but she wasn't ready to admit that yet. "This is ridiculous. Give me the keys."

Norah lifted her chin and headed for the driver's side of the Escape, and Trip thought, wrong approach. He should have reasoned with her. Not that he'd ever had much luck reasoning with a woman who could find a way around any argument. Even the logical ones.

Take now, for instance. She knew she was exhausted,

she knew he'd gotten a lot more sleep than she had, and she knew there was an even better reason to let him drive. But did she hand over the keys like a rational adult? No, she got behind the wheel, her expression sulky, no doubt full of energy fuelled by anger over Hollie Roget's irresponsible journalism and the attack on Lucius.

He sighed heavily and climbed into the passenger seat, banking on the fact that anyone coming after them would stop short of harm, since whatever Norah might know about the proceeds of the robbery would be lost if she was. "Let me know when you want me to take over," he said as she settled herself into the driver's seat and fastened her belt.

"Just sit back and enjoy the ride."

"I can handle the sitting part," Trip said.

Enjoying was another story, especially since, moments after Norah picked up Interstate 57 north out of Marion, Illinois, she also picked up a tail.

Norah thought five miles under the posted limit was a reasonable speed. A black Cadillac Escalade SUV paced them a dozen car lengths back, bigger, faster, having trouble with the pokey pace but not trying very hard to go unnoticed. No doubt they already knew where Norah lived. Which could mean only one thing.

"Too tired to drive the speed limit?" he said to Norah.

She looked over at him, then back at the road. "Is there a reason you're trying to goad me into driving faster?"

Trip sighed heavily.

"You do that a lot," she observed.

"It's a new habit I've picked up since meeting you."

"There's a simple remedy for it."

"Sure, you could cooperate once in a while."

"It's not cooperation if I'm the one making all the compromises."

Trip let his head fall back against the seat, suddenly worn out. "Just once it would be nice if you followed directions without all the time-wasting discussion."

"It's not logical to expect blind trust from someone you've only known for two days."

Trip made a sound that definitely wasn't a sigh. It came from the back of his throat, for one thing, and there was a lot more frustration than exasperation involved.

"You haven't answered my question" was Norah's reaction.

He caught himself before he sighed again. "There's a black SUV behind us. Last I checked he was one lane over and two cars back."

"We're out of Marion. The traffic is thinner." Norah sat up straighter, giving the Escape a little more gas while she checked out the road behind her in the rearview mirror. "But the SUV is still there."

"They won't be content to hang back once there are no other cars on the road."

"What does that mean?"

"It means we can keep driving and wait for them to make a move, or we can pick the time and place, get a little control over the outcome."

"I'm all for Door Number Two," she said, glancing over at him, looking a little frightened and a lot open to suggestion.

And here he was with a completely empty suggestion box. The terrain didn't offer much help either. Marion USP sat about three hundred miles from Chicago, at the southern end of the state, about halfway between the Missouri and Kentucky borders. It was a fairly straight shot down Interstate 57, and the adjective that best described the terrain was *flat*. There was a hill here and there, a stream or small river to keep things from being completely boring, and towns of various sizes were peppered along the route, but Trip preferred to keep the innocent bystanders innocent, and unharmed. As far as topographical features that might work to their advantage in the current situation, it was pretty much a bust.

To make matters worse, they were in a smaller, slower vehicle with a novice at the wheel. A novice who might be pissed off enough to pull off a miracle. As hopes went it was pretty lame. And their only one.

"Do exactly what I tell you to do exactly when I tell you to do it," Trip said.

"But—"

"No questions, no discussion. You're going to have a split second to maneuver, starting now. Swerve right." And to help her he grabbed the steering wheel and jerked it—a little too hard since the Escape might not be fast but it was maneuverable, going up on two wheels in an attempt to make a ninety degree turn at seventy miles an hour.

Norah wrestled it back under control, shooting him a look that went from cranky to panicked when something crashed into their rear bumper. "I think you should drive," she said, taking the *no discussion* rule at face value by clambering half over the console into his lap without giving him a chance to say more than "Wait" and "Stop," or point out that the guys in the SUV might not want to kill them, but changing drivers at a high rate of speed might do the job anyway. Then again, the car slowed drastically with her foot off the gas pedal.

The SUV shot ahead, brake lights flashing as it slowed to block them in behind a minivan just merging onto the highway.

Trip grabbed Norah's long-handled ice scraper from behind the driver's seat, jammed it between the gas pedal and the seat bottom, and the Escape leapt forward, slamming her against him. He gasped for air, managing to get his hand on the wheel with absolutely no idea what to do with it because he was fighting to see around her. "Dammit, Norah," he said, dragging his other hand out from underneath her and putting it on her backside.

She jackknifed, twisting sideways, which solved his visibility problem but left her with her face against his stomach—distracting—and jammed her left foot into one of the openings in the steering wheel. Disaster. The Escape accelerated, the Escalade and the minivan still serving as moving roadblocks, and the steering wheel wouldn't budge.

"Move your foot," Trip shouted.

"It's stuck."

The Escape hurtled down the road at the SUV, the driver flashing his brake lights like they were too stupid to know that slamming into the back of an Escalade would be tantamount to impersonating crash-test dummies. Trip blew the horn, hoping the guy didn't actually want them dead. He must have gotten the picture because the SUV sped up, passing the minivan with barely enough room for the Escape to squeeze by. If they'd been able to steer . . . "Lift your leg," Trip yelled.

"What!?"

"Just do it."

Norah lifted her leg up, and the wheel turned enough to save their asses, bumpers just brushing as the Escape scooted into the next lane and shot by the Escalade.

"Okay, you can relax," Trip said, a little calmer but still aware that they were running out of options, and

as intriguing as it was to have Norah's head in his lap,
the timing wasn't all it could be.

"There's a curve coming up."

"I think we should worry about the SUV," Norah
said, hands braced on his thighs so she could see over
his shoulder. "It's coming up behind us. Fast."

"Either way we need to go left."

"You need to—"

"Twist your foot—no, like pigeon toes—A little
more," he said when the Escape didn't quite make the
turn. "That's it. Now back. Good," he finished as they
came around the curve and saw no traffic, except the
Escalade, which took the opportunity to come up alongside them.

They were on a straightaway, coming up on Rend
Lake. The lake sat about twenty miles north of Marion,
a long, narrow body of water with an even narrower
section that jutted out at a forty-five degree angle to
the rest of the lake. I-57 passed to the east of the main
lake over that narrow finger of water. In summer Rend
Lake saw a lot of visitors, hiking, boating, camping,
even during the week. Late fall weekday mornings
meant no traffic, except the Escalade, pulling even with
them. The rear passenger window motored down. Trip
didn't figure they wanted a better look at the scenery.

Sure enough, a .38 eased out, the wielder clearly
wanting to remain hidden behind the tinted windows.
And while Trip was pretty sure it was meant to incapacitate the Escape and not its occupants, the awkward
position and the high speed made for a pretty wobbly
grip and an uncertain trajectory.

He tried to dislodge the window scraper, but it wouldn't
budge, and instead of losing speed they gained, Norah's
arms and legs flailing for balance, including her foot still

jammed into the steering wheel, which sent the Escape swerving all over the road.

Trip threw caution to the wind, letting go of the steering wheel, pushing Norah as far forward as he could and managing to get his legs underneath him, then jamming them across the console and into the driver's seat. The top of his head and the edge of the sunroof became painfully familiar with one another, the rest of him getting less painfully intimate with Norah, rubbing against her breasts, belly, thighs as he slid his body between hers and the seat backs, while the Escape slalomed down the road and the Escalade alternated between chasing them and avoiding them. And then things went from bad to worse.

"I'm stuck," Trip said.

Norah tried to push him, not having much luck until she brought up her free leg, planted her foot on Trip's butt, and shoved for all she was worth.

Trip dropped into the driver's seat, the window scraper popped up, and he jerked the wheel in an effort to block it from delivering an accidental crotch shot, but with no consideration for Norah's ankle, still stuck there. She jerked her foot out of reflex—and pain. The Escape veered sharply to the right, cutting across the shoulder and screeching against the old-fashioned steel guardrail.

"*My car,*" Norah wailed, apparently forgetting her life was more important than her vehicle, not to mention they were just moving onto the bridge over Rend Lake.

She tried to sit up, sending the Escape careening back into the right lane to crash against the Escalade. The gun went off, taking out the Escape's rear passenger window, and apparently scaring the crap out of the Escalade's occupants since Trip heard a lot of high-

pitched shrieking coming from the other vehicle, which
sped up and swerved violently left, then even more violently to the right as the driver overcorrected. The heavier, larger vehicle smashed through the guardrail and
dropped out of sight.

"I think I saw a splash," Norah said, bracing herself
on the empty passenger seat so she could see out the
back window. "And there . . . Two people just surfaced."

Trip nudged the steering wheel so the Escape coasted
to a stop at the side of the road past the lake. He turned
in his seat, but he didn't have the same line of sight as
Norah. "Can you make out faces?"

"No, but I bet they're mad."

"It's not their expressions I'm after."

"Oh, you want some physical characteristics." She
peered out the back window again, "Sorry, they're just
blobs."

Useless specks. He considered getting out of the
vehicle and hiking back, but even if he'd been comfortable leaving Norah alone, they weren't just going
to swim over for a little chat. Hell, they'd probably
shoot him since he was only an obstacle to what they
wanted. Considering the adrenaline popping through
him and the urge to burn it off in the fastest way possible, shooting him could be seen as a favor.

"A little help here," Norah said. "Can you work my
foot free?"

"This position has some potential," Trip observed,
"but I like it better when the other end of you is in my
lap. Maybe we should try again when we have a little
more time to experiment."

Norah wrenched her foot free and crawled out of his
lap, not exactly careful where her knees and toes
landed. He suspected that might be on purpose.

"I'm a psychologist, not a scientist," she said as she

dropped into the passenger seat. "I already know where experimentation of that kind will get us."

Trip didn't need the benefit of formal training to get her gist. His knowledge was more experience-based, and his experience told him that sex with Norah MacArthur would be a huge mistake. Potentially mind-blowing if that kiss was any yardstick, but still, a mistake. He could write off that kiss to misjudgment. Sex with her would be a conscious decision made for reasons he couldn't begin to understand because he refused to examine them. Best they stay a mystery. And unrealized. He needed his mind intact if he was going to get them both through the minefield this operation had become.

chapter
8

"OH, FOR PETE'S SAKE," NORAH SAID WHEN they pulled up in front of her house in her battered Escape and saw a man standing half in-half out of her front door. "This is getting completely out of hand."

"We reached out of hand at the paparazzi swarm," Trip said. "Once there's vehicular assault and gunfire we've officially crossed over into life or death. But that guy isn't a problem. I called him."

Norah peered through the passenger window. "Why am I not surprised?"

The guy resembled the Hulk, without the green skin and low forehead, but intelligence in a man was always dicey. They either wanted to run your life or they wanted you to run theirs. The first wasn't bad; a lot of women made peace with it, letting the man think he was making all the decisions when in reality they listened politely and then did what they wanted anyway, as long as what they wanted didn't rock the boat too much. It was a perfectly viable relationship mode, so viable whole books had been written about it.

The second involved more work and less delusion, but it wasn't bad either. Norah just hadn't found a man who could inspire her to take either road. Maybe she never would, but she liked her life the way it was. Sure, she had trust issues, but then, who didn't?

"He's okay," Trip said, misinterpreting her hesitation, "he just looks scary."

No, Norah thought, scary was a man she'd only known for three days, but who appealed to her so much there were moments she wanted to throw herself at him, knowing he'd catch her but not caring how long he held on. Not that she actually thought Trip Jones was capable of a lifelong commitment, but she ought to at least be concerned about how hard the fall would be when he dropped her.

Trip was oblivious to the morbid direction of her thoughts. He was already out of the vehicle and halfway up the walk. The Hulk stepped down the porch stairs to meet him on the brick walkway. Norah braced herself and joined them, surprised when Trip introduced them and Robert Lawrence took her hand gently in his, the look in his eyes just as gentle.

"You don't look like a Bob," Norah said. "Or a Rob."

"What do I look like?"

"Trouble." All those muscles controlled beneath that soft touch and those soft brown eyes—not to mention the intelligence behind them? Definitely trouble. For some other woman, thankfully.

"You can call me Law," he said, his eyes taking on a more humorous glint before he shifted his gaze to Trip. "She's direct. I like direct women. You never have to wonder what they're thinking."

"Yeah, aren't I lucky?" But he took her hand from Law's and tucked it in the crook of his arm.

Norah untucked it. And sidled a step away from him.

Law found that vastly amusing. So amusing a flock of seagulls in the park two blocks away took to the skies, shrieking. Law's laugh was just as big as he was. "You make your own luck, Trip. Isn't that what you always say?"

"You're here to upgrade security, remember?"

"Really?" Norah glanced over her shoulder at her wreck of a vehicle. "Is he going to take you away with him when he goes?"

"I'm not the one who decided to drive after twenty-four hours without sleep," Trip shot back. "I'm not the one who crawled out of the driver's seat when things got rough."

Norah didn't have a response to that. Trip was right, and she was wrong, and worst of all, she understood why she was wrong, and why she was making such bad decisions. She kept trying to exert a little control in her life, fighting against Trip because he brought out feelings in her that were scary and worrisome and confusing. She ought to be focusing on the robbery, remembering that while there were a lot of kooks out there, at least one person was willing to beat up an elderly man to get access to a cache of loot hidden for fifteen years.

No matter what Trip's personal impact, she needed to concentrate on his professional reasons for insinuating himself into her life. She didn't have to trust him, per se, but she had to keep in mind that protecting her was in his best interest at the moment, and he knew what he was doing. If it took a million reminders, hell, if she had to write it on the back of her hand with a Sharpie, she'd get it through her thick skull that Trip was on her side before someone else got hurt.

Rather lowering, she admitted, to have her confident, independent self-image shattered by the first handsome face and killer body to come along, but she couldn't hide from it, either. Sometimes it sucked being a psychologist.

"I'm sorry," Trip said into the silence, "that was out of line. True, but out of line. And stop grinning at me," he grumbled in Law's direction.

Law held up both hands. "Just changing locks, here."

"I should be apologizing to you," Norah said, the words sticking a little in her throat until she pictured that black Sharpie, and how stupid she'd look walking around with the words "trust Trip" written on her hand.

"Apology accepted," Trip said, even though she hadn't technically given him one, which made her feel like she should apologize for not apologizing, and that made her head hurt.

"I'm going to get some sleep," she said, hoping a little rest would get her thoughts back on a nice, logical course, and that she hadn't completely lost her sanity due to a combination of adrenaline and hormones. She stopped on the second step and looked at Law, now eye level. "It's okay to go inside, right? I won't set off alarm bells or booby traps or attack dogs when I go through the door?"

"Well, there is a big net that comes down from the ceiling to trap intruders."

"After the last two days it wouldn't surprise me to be tackled by Ninjas."

"That's some imagination you've got there."

"You have no idea." And her gaze flicked to Trip, which was exactly what she'd been trying not to do.

The two men grinned and exchanged glances that should have included waggling eyebrows.

"It doesn't take—Never mind," she finished, because she'd been about to tell Law it didn't take imagination, that she'd been almost hit by a car, intruded on last night, and had he totally missed her wreck of a vehicle sitting at the curb? How the heck did he think the sides of her Escape had gotten crumpled like used tinfoil? So finding out that her house had been secured by the Three Stooges branch of the FBI seemed like no big stretch.

And yet she knew he'd apply her "it doesn't take imagination" to Trip, which was mostly true, since she'd seen him in boxers last night, and there was the whole thing about him being just like other men, except she had a feeling if she did a test drive she'd find out he wasn't like all other men. Hell, he'd probably ruin her for all other men, and when this fiasco was over he'd disappear from her life, the jerk, leaving her with a wildly unrealistic yardstick—

"She looks like she's considering violence," Law said to Trip. "You don't usually have that effect on women."

"She's not like other women."

"Men," Norah muttered, climbing the steps since she didn't seem to be necessary to the conversation anymore, at least as far as verbal interaction went. But she was smiling as she skirted Law and his tools to get to her front door, their laughter floating behind her, deep and hearty and cheerful. And protective.

"Hey, before I forget," Law said, which made her turn back in time to take the small box he held out, about the size of a hardcover book and as heavy as one. "FedEx dropped this off for you."

Norah read the label, then tucked it into the crook of her arm. "Thanks," she said to Law. "For everything."

"Something wrong?" Trip asked her.

Norah looked at Law and his alarm system, at her

crumpled escape, then at Trip. "Everything," she said, and went inside.

"DON'T YOU EVER GIVE UP?" NORAH SAID TO HOL-lie Roget four hours later when she found the woman on the other side of her front door.

Then the alarm went off, and since Norah didn't have the code, she took off her shoe and beat the little keypad next to the door until it was a pile of plastic shards and broken circuitry on the floor. More impor-tantly, the sound cut off.

Trip had told her not to open the door—by way of a Post-it stuck on the doorknob—but honestly, if he wanted her to follow instructions he should have stuck around, right? Or left Law to babysit. But they were both gone, she'd spied Hollie through the little peep-hole, and she'd gotten enough sleep to be able to keep her wits. And there were things she wanted to say to Hollie. None of them were nice. Some of them, it turned out, weren't even verbal.

Hollie opened her mouth, and Norah took a step for-ward and popped her in the face. It wasn't a very hard punch, she didn't put her weight into it, and Hollie had a pretty bony face so it probably hurt her hand more than Hollie's chin. But it felt damn good.

"I should have you arrested for assault," Hollie said, rubbing her jaw.

"Assault? How about we take a trip to Marion and compare your injury to my father's? You're lucky he isn't dead, or I'd be suing you. As it is I think my law-yer could make a case for stalking."

Hollie started to say something defensive, judging by the way she jammed her hands on her hips. Then she stopped, took a deep breath, and said, "I'm sorry."

"Wow, that actually sounded sincere."

"I truly am sorry," Hollie said, "See? No camera, no microphone, no recording devices. You can frisk me if you want."

"Uh, no, thanks."

"I really didn't intend for your father to get hurt. Sometimes I get so focused on a story that I forget real people with real lives are affected."

"And what do you have to gain by apologizing?"

Hollie smiled faintly. "I guess I deserve that."

Norah didn't return the smile, but she didn't slam the door in Hollie's face either. She was curious.

Hollie didn't keep her waiting. "I want to work with you on the treasure," she said.

Norah did try to slam the door then. Who knew Hollie had such amazing reflexes and big feet? A lot of nerve, that Norah was already familiar with.

"Please hear me out."

Norah stared pointedly at Hollie's Manolo through the size ten crack in her front door. Hollie slowly removed her foot. She hesitated once or twice, but the foot finally retracted all the way. It was the second time she'd done something almost respectable. If not for that pesky ulterior motive.

But damn it, Norah was still curious. "I've already wasted ten minutes on this," she said, opening the door just wide enough to see Hollie with both eyes. "Make your case." Even if it would still be no.

The defeated look on Hollie's face told Norah she got that, but she was going to try anyway. "I want to make a documentary about the robbery. I think it would help your father if people knew his side of the story. We could spin it—"

"My father was guilty, he was convicted, he's done his time. It doesn't need spin."

"Okay, but giving the loot back to the victims is pretty amazing. I'd love to be a fly on the wall while it happens."

Norah thought of her more as a rodent, but the fly image was pretty good, too, and ready-made. All she had to do was superimpose Hollie's face over Jeff Goldblum's and there it was.

"You're smiling. Is that a good sign?"

"Not for you." But she held the image another few seconds. Childish but oh so amusing. "Making a documentary will take a pretty long time," she pointed out. "Too long to fix your career."

"Look, my career is toast. There's no going back to the news, but somebody is going to make a documentary about this. Why not me?"

"Well, you have all the right answers, I'll give you that."

"What are the questions?" a deep voice said from the walkway behind Hollie.

She swung around, Norah looked past her, and there stood Law, a bag from a local electronics store in his hand, and Trip, carrying takeout.

"One of them better be about why the alarm went off," Law said, holding up a small device about the size of a cell phone, a blinking red light on the face of it.

"You weren't supposed to open the door," Trip said.

"I wouldn't worry about her so much if I were you," Hollie said. "She punched me in the face."

Trip climbed the steps and took a good look. "You didn't do any damage, Norah. Remind me later to show you how to throw a punch."

"She doesn't have the heft for it," Law said, giving Hollie a wide berth as he walked around her and into the house. "I vote you get her a nice little handgun and take her to the range. It'll save the wear and tear on the alarm pad, too," he added with a sigh, dropping his bag and heading back out the door, to the electronics store, presumably. "Next time, Norah, take your aggression out on her, not the alarm," he tossed back over his shoulder.

"Bloodthirsty lot, aren't you?"

"*Bloodthirsty*?" Trip said, considering Hollie's choice of words for a second or two. "Doesn't have exactly the right ring to it."

"I'd say *vengeful*," Norah said, "but it smacks of righteousness and well, my father is a criminal, so I'm not sure how righteous I can be. How about *vindictive*?"

Trip shrugged. "I've been known to be vindictive on occasion. So, did she tell you what she wanted after you punched her?"

"Yes. She's got staying power, and a good amount of self-delusion. She wants us to let her come along so she can film a documentary."

Trip walked by her into the house, laughing the whole way.

"I think that's a no, but I appreciate the apology." And Norah shut the door.

"You don't really believe she wants to do a documentary," Trip said when she turned around.

"I think we should take a good long look at the list of safe-deposit box owners and see where Hollie fits in."

"I'm already on it," Trip said, taking out his cell phone. "We?"

Norah shrugged. "My father isn't going to be safe until this thing is settled."

"So you're going to tell me where the loot is, right?"

"Do I have any choice?"

chapter
9

HAGGARD, THAT'S HOW SHE SHOULD HAVE looked after yet another sleepless night, Norah thought, puzzled by the face looking back at her from the bathroom mirror. It was her face, sure enough, but she looked . . . definitely not haggard. There were no bags, for one thing. Her eyes were sort of . . . *sparkling*, she labeled them cautiously. And her skin was definitely brighter. Even her hair, which was usually well-behaved, was unmanageable—in a good way. The bathroom lights picked up the red that normally only made itself apparent in the sunlight, and it was curling, just a little wild, around her ears and at her nape.

And then there was her attitude. She ought to be dreading the next two days, being cooped up in the Escape—ironic—for hours on end with Trip, not to mention there'd be a hotel room involved. That was a lot of alone time with a man who wound her up on so

many levels. Yet here she was looking forward to the
adventure. The fact that she could even consider it an
adventure amazed her.

She'd spent so much time planning her life, and there
was a lot of satisfaction in ticking those accomplish-
ments off her list, but that planning took a lot of time
and energy, she realized. And it was stressful, agonizing
over the goals and the timetable, then fretting about
whether or not it was doable, and if she'd made the right
decisions. All because it was the rational, stable thing to
do. Rational, *hah*.

Who knew she'd have so much fun walking into the
unknown, that it wouldn't matter to her to have people
invade her life in strange, and sometimes violent, ways.
Heck, that made it even more of an adventure.

"You're beautiful," Trip said, appearing in the open
bathroom door.

Norah turned to look at him, her heart in her throat.

He was checking his watch.

She turned back, met her own eyes in the mirror,
and thought, Of course. What made her pulse stutter
was just a toss-off compliment to him, aimed at getting
her moving. Just like that, her mood went from optimism
to cynicism. She was going on an adventure all right, a
real-life treasure hunt, complete with people who'd do
whatever was necessary to get a piece of it. Unfortunately one of those people was Trip Jones. Working for
the FBI didn't make him a hero. In her world, it meant
just the oppo—

She jumped, heart pounding, slapping her hands over
her ears as the house filled with the deafening *whoop-
whoop-whoop* of a siren, lights flashing, just like red
alert on a submarine. All that was missing was a sweaty
Matthew McConaughey shouting, "*Dive*."

Trip made a more than adequate replacement for

Matthew, not sweaty and not shouting, but the visual was better, as far as Norah was concerned, and his re-action reflected hers, swearing under his breath and tromping down the stairs.

She grabbed her jacket and raced after him, freaked as much by the siren as by what it announced. She ought to be used to the idea that people kept trying to break into her house, but it never seemed to get old, and Trip, like it or not, represented safety.

"That friend of yours takes his work seriously," she said when the cacophony died down.

"All I wanted him to do was scare off intruders," Trip grumbled.

"Maybe he was worried about some of them being hearing impaired."

"We're going to be hearing impaired. And sleep-deprived."

"It's better than dead."

"You really have no faith in my abilities, do you?"

"Ask me that question again after we find the loot, and people are *really* trying to kill me."

"Whoever it was is gone." He opened the door, set the alarm, and shooed her out, barely waiting for her to collect her purse, scarf, and gloves.

"Finding the loot will get you out of danger."

He started down the steps, still talking. Norah stayed where she was, and all she heard was blah, blah, blah because there, sitting at the curb, was a Harley-Davidson. The most amazing Harley she'd ever seen—not the Hog kind of Harley with the long front fork and the Biker Mama jump seat. This motorcycle was trim and sleek and powerful-looking, jet black, including the wheels and exhaust, and definitely built for speed and per-formance.

"We're going on that?" she asked Trip.

"Give me a chance to explain," he said, misunderstanding the awe in her question for fear, probably because her voice had cracked when the word ADVENTURE flashed across her mind again, this time in big, yellow, Indiana Jones-style lettering.

She wasn't about to disabuse him. It would be embarrassing, for one thing, and she had no intention of giving him the satisfaction of knowing he'd just made her day. She took her eyes off the bike so she didn't drool, and walked down the steps, saying, as casually as she could manage, "Now I know why you asked me if I had a leather coat."

He looked at the fitted hip-length jacket in her hand. "That's not a leather coat, that's a fashion statement for an art gallery opening."

He, on the other hand, had on a scarred bomber with a sheepskin collar. They were both wearing jeans and boots. Hers had set her back almost a week's salary. She would have gladly traded them for his beat-up and broken-in black motorcycle boots.

"I'm going to freeze my backside off," she said.

"It's warm today, and you're wearing a sweater thick enough to qualify you for honorary sheephood. You'll be fine." He opened the gate and gestured her through.

She didn't go. Reality was crashing the party. "Do you really think a motorcycle is a good idea? It's not much protection."

He sighed, shot her the we've-been-through-this-already look, then explained anyway. "First of all, they won't harm you. You know the location to the treasure. And they won't harm me because I'll be driving the motorcycle, and harming me will harm you. They will follow us, and the motorcycle is a lot faster and a lot more maneuverable, which means we can lose any tails."

"Not much cargo space," she said, noting there wasn't

so much as a leather saddlebag, let alone the storage compartments some motorcycles sported. Her small overnight bag was strapped behind the seat, along with Trip's.

"We won't need space if someone takes the loot away from us."

"Kind of a catch-22, isn't it? The motorcycle gets us to our destination alone, but it makes the return trip problematic."

"Let me worry about the return trip."

She gave him a look. "Do you want to pat me on the head and call me a good little girl, too?"

"Will you just get on the damn bike?"

Norah tried to comply, but her feet stayed frozen to the ground, and her features tightened into the kind of expression mothers warned their children to avoid if they didn't want their faces to freeze that way. This is what I wanted, she reminded herself, eyeing the motorcycle but still not making any move toward it, even when she tried to remind herself this was an ADVENTURE. Problem was, she wanted movie adventure. She wanted car chases and gunplay and treasure hunting all from the safety of her La-Z-Boy, with a bowl of popcorn in her lap. She wanted, Norah thought in bitter disgust, to be a spectator.

Fuck that, was her next thought, the *fuck* part startling her a bit because she never allowed herself to think like that. Thinking that way might lead to talking that way, and she'd spent her entire adult life keeping up appearances, atoning for the neon sign she was sure everyone could see on her forehead, the one pronouncing her the daughter of a con artist/bank robber. Trip already knew who she was and where she came from, and he didn't care. Of course, Trip thought of her as a means to an end, first and foremost, so the rest of it didn't matter to him, as long as she served her purpose.

But it damn well mattered to her. He might be okay with blind servitude; she wasn't. She'd made her position clear to him at the jail yesterday; now all she had to do was convince herself that she meant what she'd said. Watching from the sidelines would be counterproductive to that goal.

"Look, I know you don't trust me," Trip said, mistaking the reason for her hesitation.

"You're FBI—"

"And your father drummed a distrust of authority into your head, starting at an early age. But you are authority, Norah."

"Not the kind that can send you to prison for life."

"Are you planning to break some laws?"

"Not intentionally."

"Then I'm no threat to you."

Yes, he was, and not just because of the effect he had on her personally.

"Your concerns are valid, Norah. I'll admit the suits at the Bureau don't let me in on the high-level decisions, but I'll do my best to look out for you and your father."

"Telling me what I want to hear?"

"I'm making you a promise."

"Those *suits* you mentioned don't give a damn about your promises. You know that as well as I do."

He met her eyes. "So where does that leave us?"

Right where she'd been yesterday, facing the same truth and coming to the same conclusion she'd come to at her father's bedside. If she left his fate, and her own, in the hands of the FBI—and Trip was the FBI—she was a fool.

She stepped toward the bike.

"Hi, there!"

They both sighed this time, the voice enough to demoralize them even before they saw Bill Simonds speed-walking over from his house next door. He was coatless, his hands in his pockets, braced against the chill in the air but more worried about catching them than pneumonia.

"Where are you off to?" he said with excessive cheerfulness.

"We're going to jump off a bridge," Trip said, deadpan, "want to come along?"

"Well, now," Bill said, his face folding into no-call-for-sarcasm lines, "I thought maybe you'd need someone to pick up your mail, Norah, take in the paper, that kind of thing."

"I thought you got the message when she took her spare key away from you," Trip said. "And changed the locks."

"You're right, you're right, I overstepped. But I'm really sorry, like I told you the other day, *Norah*, and I promise not to do it again."

"You were watching the news the other day, right Bill?" she said. "The part where I reminded everyone how the Chicago PD and the FBI searched my house fifteen years ago and found nothing?"

"Oh, well, sure I saw that."

"But you didn't believe it. Look, we're going to find the loot today. My father told me where it is, and we intend to retrieve it and turn it over to the FBI."

Trip caught her by the elbow and hauled her up next to him. "What are you doing?"

"Letting the neighborhood know there's no point in breaking into my house. By this time tomorrow it'll all be over, Bill."

Trip thrust a helmet in her direction. "What she really means, Bill, is run along and spread the news."

Norah opened her mouth. Nothing came out because she did want him to run along and spread the news, and if she said anything else, it wouldn't have been sincere, and a jerk like Bill Simonds would pick up on that in a heartbeat. Taking her key back and telling him never to darken her door again he misunderstood, but the least amount of insincerity in her voice and he'd be all hurt and insulted— Just like that, she thought as he took himself off in a huff, closing the window of opportunity on her chance to defuse his hard feelings.

It didn't help when Trip laughed.

"Don't put words in my mouth." She shoved the helmet back at him with enough force to get a little *oof* out of him. "Especially nasty ones."

"He's a putz."

"A putz I have to live next door to," she said, winding her scarf around her neck and jamming her arms into her jacket. She took the helmet back, only to have her cell phone ring. She shoved the helmet back at Trip—he stopped it short of his solar plexus this time—and took out her cell.

He slid up next to her and peeked over her shoulder.

Norah flipped the phone open and said, "Hi, Myra," sidling away when Trip tried to lay his head next to hers so she could hear the call.

Having his head next to hers meant there'd be no conversation because having his head next to hers meant having the rest of him right there, too, and that would be totally discombobulating and probably rob her of the ability to talk. And now she'd completely lost the conversation. "What?" she said to Myra. "I'm getting some interference."

"The interference wouldn't be named Trip, would it?"

Trip was coming to the same conclusion, judging by his grin.

"What's going on, Myra?" she said, ignoring him and his ego.

"I saw Hollie's stunt yesterday. Are you okay? I mean, it seemed to end on a high note, since people will stay away from your house."

"Yeah, it actually worked out in my favor." For a change.

"I thought I'd come over later, bring a couple of dates."

"Dates?"

"Ben and Jerry."

Norah huffed out a laugh, her eyes shifting to Trip. "Jack Daniels and Jose Cuervo might be a better idea."

"I could swing that. We'll order Chinese."

"You don't know how good that sounds, Myra, but I'm going to need a rain check."

"You're busy?" Myra asked, her voice sounding bright and hopeful. "With that yummy man, I hope."

"Sure," Norah said, sending Trip a sidelong glance. "Yummy."

"You're not still with him?"

"Yes."

"But you don't want to tell me about it. After we've been friends for all this time?"

Norah was a bit startled by that. They'd known each other a couple of years, and they were friendly, but not morning-after-spill-the-intimate-details kind of friends.

"Never mind," Myra said, "we'll have lunch when you get back and I'll martini the truth out of you."

Norah couldn't help but smile. Maybe they weren't bosom buddies, but Myra was irresistible.

"And before I forget, I'm sorry."

"Sorry about what?" Norah asked her.

"I heard Raymond put you on hiatus. He's a putz."

"I couldn't agree more. Listen, Myra, can I call you later? We need to talk about the book anyway."

"Fine," Myra said, a shrug in her voice. "Listen, I got a call from the *Sun Times* this morning. Are you available tomorrow for an interview?"

"How about Monday? That would work better."

"I have to wait until Monday? You're killing me, Norah. Can't you give me just a hint of what's going on?"

"I'll just say the next book better do well. Talk to you later." And she disconnected before Myra dragged the truth out of her. She hadn't quite come to terms with losing her job, even temporarily, herself. The last thing she needed was somebody else second-guessing her decisions.

"You ready?"

No, she thought, then took another look at the motorcycle and changed her mind. She was looking forward to the adventure, damn it, because it would be over soon enough, Trip would take off, and she'd be left in her own boring world again. Nothing new, except this time she'd be aware of it. Every day for the rest of her life.

AS SOON AS SHE GOT ON THE BIKE THE *ADVENTURE* was back. The sun shone, the motorcycle thrummed, and Trip was between her thighs—not in the way she might have preferred, but she held on tight, her arms around his waist, her front pressed to his back, living in the moment, in the feel of his muscles rippling and flexing as he shifted and balanced, working his way through rush-hour traffic on I-94 heading north out of the city. The horns blaring behind them, however, had nothing to do with his driving.

"We've got company," Trip said via the Bluetooth

earpieces he'd insisted they wear so they could keep in touch, even on the bike. "Hell, it's a damn parade. There are at least three vehicles following us."

Norah looked over her shoulder. It wasn't hard to pick out the offenders. Bill Simonds's white and rust minivan, a black Honda Pilot, and a maroon BMW X3. They were all bigger than a standard sedan, and they were having a lot more trouble maneuvering around the other vehicles than Trip was having. "Hollie Roget is driving the BMW."

"What is it going to take to stop that woman?"

"A wooden stake." Norah watched the three vehicles jockey for position. Hollie seemed to be aware she had company, but even though Norah could see her homeless camera man riding shotgun in the front passenger seat, he made no effort to film. "She's awfully persistent for someone who has no connection to the robbery."

"The Bureau's background check didn't pick up anything," Trip said. "There wasn't time for a really deep dive, but if she was after the loot why would she publicize it and put herself in competition with half of Chicago?"

"You have a point," Norah said grudgingly. She wanted to believe Hollie was in it out of greed, but what Trip said made sense. "So what do we do about the people following us?"

"Did you ever see the *Matrix* movies?"

"No."

"Good." And Trip punched it.

The bike leapt forward, Trip working his way through the gears and taking bigger risks in traffic. Norah clenched her hands at his waist and stared over his shoulder, paralyzed by fear and morbid curiosity. If her cinematic repertoire hadn't been so sadly lacking, she'd already know what a top-speed motorcycle escape in heavy traffic looked like. Probably not from the back of the bike, with the wind rushing by and an overwhelming feeling of complete exposure and incipient disaster.

Trip shot the Harley between a semi and a sedan, laying the bike over so far Norah could see beneath the SUV in front of them, her peripheral vision filled with the blur of pavement whizzing by. The driver of the sedan laid on the horn and the brakes, giving Bill Simonds' aging white minivan an opening to slip through and take up a position behind them, fenders rattling, motor sounding ready to explode.

Hollie's BMW crowded through after Bill's minivan, and the Pilot lumbered around behind the sedan to come up on their left. Suddenly Trip had nowhere to go, the SUV's driver communicating with Bill Simonds through some sort of criminal telepathy to box them in against the semi, still on their left. The vehicle in front of them was at the mercy of traffic, hundreds of weekday commuters juggling hot coffee, putting on mascara, eating breakfast, and talking on cell phones. The ones who weren't multitasking were running late and fighting road rage.

"This isn't good," Trip said.

"How would they get out of it in the movies?"

"Keanu Reeves would lay the bike on its side and slide it under the semi."

"I don't suppose that works in real life."

"Maybe for a stuntman wearing leather who doesn't have to worry about a passenger."

"I'll take that as a no."

"You don't have any ideas, do you?" Trip asked her.

She'd wanted him to treat her like an equal partner, and here she was, completely devoid of helpful suggestions. "Not at the moment," she said, watching Bill's minivan shudder up on them, "but if I survive this I'm going to watch more action movies."

Trip laughed grimly. "I'll give you a list," he said, the last word all but drowned out by the blare of horns.

Norah looked over her shoulder and saw Hollie's maroon X3 straddling the lanes behind Bill and the SUV, her bumper against his, her motor roaring as she stepped on the gas. At first glance it appeared she was hell-bent on crushing them between Bill's grille and the vehicle in front of them. Instead, she backed off, eased over a few feet, and sped up again, crashing into the side of the minivan, which was no competition for German engineering. Bill and his minivan had a close encounter with the side of the semi's trailer. The semi driver tried to stop on a dime, the squeal of air brakes and the smoke of his tires burning on the roadway and sending the rest of the commuters into a tizzy.

The bigger vehicles were unable to evade the sudden snarl of traffic. Trip took advantage of it, guiding the bike through gaps and between cars, leaving the scene of the accident and their pursuers far behind.

"Not exactly *The Matrix*," he said.

"It worked."

"Thanks to Hollie."

Yes, Norah thought, thanks to Hollie. And her ulterior motives, whatever they were.

chapter
10

THEY SPENT ABOUT TWO HOURS ON THE ROAD
between Chicago and Milwaukee, with no visible indication there was anyone following them. Trip took his
time, seeing as the ferry across Lake Michigan didn't
leave until 12:30, and since it was the only car ferry they
were at its mercy. Trip chose to kill their extra time at
a restaurant on the outskirts of the city, well away from
the docks.

"Tell me again why you chose this place?" Norah
said, keeping her voice down and talking behind her
menu. Even then her eyes shifted to the locals, a couple of grizzled old-timers nursing coffee at the Formica
counter and a trio of teenagers at a table across the
small dining room.

"We have a clear view of the parking lot," he said.

"Good thing. There's not much to look at in here.
And I'm including the menu."

"Are you kidding? Places like this usually have the best food."

"Even the menu is greasy," Norah said, closing it and slipping it back into its slot behind the condiments.

"It's a long ride, and I'm not stopping between here and there except for gas. I guess you could get a hot dog at one of those convenience stores."

"Okay, Dad."

"Reverse psychology working?" Trip said.

"Reverse psychology is unnecessary. I was making a commentary on the food choices here, not stating my intention to boycott."

"Save the commentary, at least while the waitress is around, or you're likely to get an added bonus."

Norah thought about that a second then made a face. "Great, now I won't be able to eat at all."

"Neither will I if that waitress doesn't get her act together."

Said waitress glanced their way and completely ignored Trip's we're-ready-to-order smile. So he gave her a little wave. She shifted so she was leaning against the back counter, lifting one hand to lazily chip at the nail polish on her thumb. Trip opened his mouth—

"Spitting," Norah reminded him, "in your food."

"I don't understand this," he said, honestly puzzled. "I never have this kind of trouble with wo—waitresses." Then he smiled because the waitress in question was meandering her way to their table.

"OMG," a voice shrieked into the uncomfortable silence, cutting off Trip's route to lunch.

The voice was followed by a teenage girl, tattooed, pierced, and wearing black—including her nails, lips, and hair—who skidded to a stop by their table.

"You wrote that book, right? The book that, like, explains, like, *everything* about men."

Men was a relative term, considering her two friends were similarly garbed and not even close to adulthood by anyone's standards but their own.

"I'm Jillian," the girl said, pointing to her friends in turn, "that's Tommy and that's C Clip. His name is really Calvin Clipper, but he thinks C Clip sounds cooler. I tried to tell him you have to *be* cool, not just come up with a cheesy nickname, but he's a guy, and you know guys."

Norah smiled at the kid. "I don't know cool, but C Clip sounds like one of those rappers." The red in his face went from embarrassment to a hot kind of vindication, and while he was giving Jillian a snotty see-there look, Norah winked at her.

"Oh, sure," Jillian said, completely mollified before she could even take offense, "right, sounds like a rapper."

"Nicknames are really just a way of reflecting our true personality," Norah continued, Jillian nodding like a bobblehead the whole time, "a way to honor the name your parents gave you while establishing your own identity."

"Anyway," Jillian said, reclaiming the center of attention, "I saw you on TV the other day. That Hollie Roget's a bitch, right? But you got the last laugh."

Norah looked at Trip. "Yeah, I got the last laugh."

"So what brings you to Milwaukee?" Jillian wanted to know. "Nothing going on here, and I mean, like, *nothing.*"

"There's beer," Trip observed.

Jillian's friends perked up at that notion.

The women ignored him.

"I'm . . . researching a new book," Norah said.

"Man, can I be in it?"

Norah laughed a little. "I think you have to be. But of course I'll need to change your name."

"Oh"—Jillian's face fell—"oh, sure."

"I'll tell you what," Norah said, pulling out her cell phone, "give me your number, and I'll call you if I have any questions. I imagine your name will show up in the acknowledgments."

"Really? That's, like, amazing." And Jillian reeled off her number, stumbling to the door behind her friends, and only because C Clip grabbed her by the arm and pulled her along.

"That was, like, amazing," Trip said, "how they all walked away feeling good about themselves. Except Tommy. I'm not sure he talks."

Norah looked pretty pleased with herself.

"That's some smile."

"Just remembering how it feels to be young."

"Sure, you're all of what, thirty-two?"

That seemed to startle her. "The operative word there is *feel*," she said.

"Isn't that your choice?"

"Yes," she squared her shoulders, "yes, it is."

"You'll have to tell me how to do that someday."

"Do what? Make those kids feel good about themselves? It's just basic psychology."

Trip snorted. "Psychology is just a con masquerading as science."

"Everything I said to them was absolutely true. It's all in the way you say it."

"Like a con. Don't lie to the mark if at all possible."

"You'd know," Norah said, then clamped her mouth shut when the waitress, her pink plastic name badge identifying her as Polly, sidled up to the table.

"You a celebrity or something?" she said, curiosity overcoming her taciturn nature.

"Not really," Norah said. "I wrote a book. On relationships."

"Not . . . You wrote *How to Create Your Mate*." The woman's face lit up and she turned in circles, trying to find someone in the place she could tell about it. She came up empty, so she proceeded to chatter on about the book.

Trip had stopped paying attention after the word *Mate*, but Norah listened attentively, not able to get a word in edgewise, but nodding now and then and making what must have been the appropriate face at the appropriate time since it kept Polly's verbal diarrhea flowing.

"Can we order?" he finally broke in.

Both women looked at him, Polly's mouth clamping shut. Finally.

"I'll have a burger, medium, American cheese, fries, Coke," Trip said.

Polly didn't write it down, but he figured it couldn't be that difficult to remember.

"No salad on the menu," Norah said glumly as Polly turned to her. "I guess I'll go with the grilled cheese and water, with a slice of lemon if it's not too much trouble."

"No trouble at all." Polly glared at Trip again, walking around the counter to the window. She had a short, pithy conversation with the cook on the other side, filled their drink order, then returned to the table and picked up the conversation where she'd left off. At least that's what Trip surmised since he spent the time running over his plans for the rest of the day.

A little bell dinged, and Polly hustled back to the window to retrieve their food, Trip already salivating by the time she slid the plate in front of him.

"Wow," Norah said, "thank you, Polly."

Trip looked across the table and threw his hands up. "I don't believe it. You got them to make you a salad."

"The grilled cheese is on there, too," Norah pointed out.

Polly sidled over to Norah's side of the booth and leaned down a little. But her eyes were on Trip. "Chapter four," she said to Norah. "Right?" And everyone in the place laughed.

Except for Trip.

THE FERRY LEFT AT TWELVE THIRTY. DESPITE THE goings-on at the diner, Norah and Trip made it to the dock in plenty of time, Norah standing by while Trip secured his bike personally, then following him to the premium seating on the uppermost deck.

"Nothing but First Class for the feds," Norah said, taking a seat across the table from Trip.

"They only had premium tickets left," Trip said. "They'll probably reject my expense report."

"Maybe I should offer to pay my own way."

"They'll probably take you up on it."

"Tell them to deduct it from the haul—"

"Ixnay," Trip said.

"I'm sorry?"

"Didn't you ever speak Pig Latin?"

"I grew up with a father who spoke English right to my face and still managed to make it so I couldn't understand him until it was too late."

"No wonder you're old beyond your years."

"Ouch."

"Okay," Trip allowed, "*old* probably wasn't the right word, but since the other choices were *inhibited*, *boring*, and *repressed*, I decided *old* was the least objectionable."

"I was wrong about you," Norah said. "I accused you of being a con man, but a con man would never stoop to that level of honesty."

"Did you just insult me?"

Norah smiled. "So what does it mean, *ixnay*?"

"It means be careful what you say because you never know who's listening."

Norah didn't bother looking over her shoulder. She knew who owned that voice. "How did you know where to find us?"

"Some girl named Jillian plastered it all over the Web that you were having lunch at a greasy spoon near the ferry terminal in Milwaukee."

Hollie plopped down at the next table, Loomis shuffling along to lurk behind her chair. "Sucks to be famous, doesn't it?"

"Right this moment? Yes."

Hollie just laughed. "You can't be surprised to see me."

"I understood the ferry was sold out. We only got tickets because of the bike."

"It wasn't hard to convince someone to sell me their ticket and take the next ferry," Hollie said with a shrug. "The up side of being famous."

"Don't you mean infamous?"

"Really, Norah, it's going to be a long trip if you insist on being unpleasant the entire time."

Norah looked at Trip and relaxed. She didn't have to give Hollie the satisfaction of objecting because Hollie wasn't going to get away with stalking them. Trip was already on it.

"I mean," Hollie was saying, "isn't it convenient that there are two of us and two of you, and even the same sex. And it's such a small boat—"

"Ship," Trip inserted.

"That there's really no way for us to avoid each other anywhere, even the bathroom."

"Head," Trip corrected her again.

Hollie looked startled, but then that word probably had a whole other connotation in her world. "Convincing" someone to sell her a ticket, for instance. Maybe an ungenerous thought, but it made Norah smile, and it had the added bonus of shutting Hollie up while she tried to figure out why Norah was smiling. Unfortunately, the silence didn't last long, Hollie resuming her attempts to get a rise out of them. Trip crossed his arms and went into some sort of half doze/zen-looking state. Norah had psychology on her side. She knew it would drive Hollie crazy that she didn't react.

Ninety minutes into the two-and-a-half hour trip Norah was on the verge of strangling Hollie and shooting Trip. She settled for kicking him under the table. He slitted one eye and peered out at her for a second or two. Then the other eye opened, he got to his feet without saying a word and wandered off, Loomis tagging along behind him.

Norah, annoyed, watched him go.

"Men can be so . . . inscrutable," Hollie said.

"Wow, congratulations on the correct use of the word *inscrutable*."

"Oh, the claws are coming out. Really, Norah, if you would just let me come along this wouldn't have to be so unpleasant."

"You should get a life of your own, Hollie," Norah said, not completely out of spite. "You just need to get some perspective."

"Perspective!? It's your fault—" Hollie stopped, throttled back on her anger, impressing Norah again. "I'm trying to get a career," she said. "Then I can worry about having a life."

"Suit yourself," Norah said, wondering where in the blazes Trip had gotten to.

Hollie sat forward just then, a frown on her face.

Norah looked over her shoulder and saw him ambling their way. Hollie's lackey was nowhere to be seen.

"Where's Loomis?" she wanted to know.

"I left him in the head. I think he's seasick," Trip said, taking his seat.

"After two hours?" Hollie said, angry and suspicious, and rightly so considering Trip's smug grin.

"He was doubled over the toilet, groaning. Sounded pretty bad to me."

"And he had no help getting that way, right?"

Trip put on a sympathetic face. "I wanted to help, but there really wasn't anything I could do for him."

Hollie stewed about it for a minute, then crossed her arms and huffed out a breath, arriving at the inevitable conclusion there was nothing she could do about it.

Trip met Norah's eyes, one side of his mouth quirking up into a smug little grin. "Don't you want to . . ." He tipped his head toward the bathrooms.

"Why yes," Norah said, getting to her feet and not bothering to hide her smile. "I was just about to do that very thing. It's cold out there," she said to Hollie, as if the woman didn't already know that, "and then there's the motorcycle—all that vibration. Not to mention the coffee, and, I don't know, all that water out there just naturally gives you the urge to—"

"I'm going," Hollie grumbled, beating Norah across the room.

Norah dawdled in the restroom, combing her hair, straightening her clothes, brushing imaginary lint from her sweater. She had no idea what Trip was up to, but she figured it would take some time.

When they returned, though, he was sitting in the exact same place they'd left him, in exactly the same position. When the captain announced they'd be docking, Trip sat up, that little smirk returning to his face.

Norah frowned at him, but he only popped up an eyebrow as the ship slowed drastically and there was a bunch of banging around down below, along with shouts from the crew.

"What the hell?" Hollie jumped to her feet, going for one of the life preservers stowed under her seat and taking it to the nearest steward.

Norah stayed where she was. "What did you do?" she asked Trip quietly.

"I don't think Hollie is going to be a nuisance," was his response, "at least not for a little while."

The nuisance in question came back. "Some of the cars came loose, and they're bashing into the other ones," she said, giving Trip an accusatory stare. "It's a mess."

"That's terrible," Trip said.

"Hmmmm . . . I'm getting the impression you have a different role in Norah's life than boyfriend."

"Why? Wouldn't you want your boyfriend to protect you from stalkers?"

Hollie didn't take the bait. "I'd also be willing to bet my BMW is one of the vehicles rolling around down there, but your bike is perfectly fine."

"There are some nice casinos in Michigan," Trip observed, "since you like to gamble so much."

"Is that a commentary on my chances of following you?"

"I'll bet you're going to have some time on your hands."

"We'll see," Hollie said and took off.

"Are you crazy?" Norah asked him when Hollie was out of earshot. "Someone could have been hurt."

"They never let anyone in with the vehicles when they dock for just this reason," Trip said. "Besides, I only unhooked a few of them, and I made sure there are secured vehicles all around the loose ones."

Norah sat back. "I'm still not happy about this, but there's a little part of me that wishes I'd thought of it."

"There may be hope for you yet," Trip said, grinning.

"Not if I turn into my father."

He shrugged. "It could be worse."

Norah looked at him and thought, It already is.

chapter 11

THE CITY OF MUSKEGON OCCUPIED A STRETCH
of Michigan coast where its namesake river met its
state's namesake lake. It had sent fur pelts across the
ocean to Europe, tank engines to fight world wars, and
wood to help rebuild Chicago after the great fire of
1871. It had lived a brief but successful life as an oil
boom town. To Trip it was just a jumping-off place for
what he hoped was the last leg on his race to lunacy.

Race, however, was a very loose term. Nobody was
following them—and it would have been obvious since
the rural, northern Michigan roads were pretty deserted—
but Trip felt a sense of urgency to finish the op and get
away from Norah. To get away from himself, he admitted, from the warm, comfortable way it felt to have her
arms around his waist and her body pressed against his
back, the way her voice in his ear made him smile one
minute and want her the next. She was a means to an

end, he reminded himself. She knew it, so why did he have trouble remembering the score?

The answer, of course, was obvious. She was pressed against his back, her hands firm on his belly, and her voice sounded in his ear, soft and relaxed. And he seemed to have a finite amount of resistance where she was concerned. It was a dangerous combination.

The solution was just as obvious, he thought, pouring on the gas. They made it to Ludington, seventy-five miles north of Muskegon, Trip fighting like hell to remember Norah angry and verbally abusive instead of *oohing* and *aahing* like her pleasure came from a whole different source than the beautiful fall scenery.

By the time they got to Petoskey, another two hundred and fifty miles, the parts of Trip that weren't numb from the cold were on fire. Night had fallen hours before, it was pitch-black, and Trip had a mean case of blue balls. He wasn't looking for a place to stay, though. Not yet. He figured they'd stop late and get up early. The less time they spent in a room with a bed the better.

According to the research Trip had done the night before after Norah had finally come clean about their destination, they had two choices from Petoskey. Mackinac City or one of the smaller towns dotted along Lake Michigan's shore, Cross Village being the northernmost. They were going to need a boat come morning, and while Mackinac City was the center of tourism for that part of the state, with any number of charter companies, large and small, it would also be the logical destination for anyone on their trail. Hollie, for instance.

In the end he opted for Cross Village. Sure, it was small, and a small town was hard to disappear in, but it had that unexpected angle, and it turned out to be another hour past Petoskey. Less time in a motel room, alone, just him and Norah. And that bed.

Reluctantly, he headed for the VACANCY sign he spied on the far side of Cross Village. When he found it he could see why. The place was all but deserted, and he was including animal and insect life. The Cross Inn had passed run-down at least two decades ago and was fighting off *derelict* with its last gasping breath. It was also the only motel around. The downside of choosing small town America.

"Do you think it's safe here?" Norah asked, taking her helmet off and leaning even closer.

No. "Perfectly."

"Then I should have my own room."

Great, she was feeling it, too. "No."

"But—"

"I'm not letting you out of my sight." The trick would be to keep his hands off her. It didn't help knowing she was worried about spending the night in the same room with him, and it didn't help that she wasn't arguing more. "No objection?"

"I'm freezing. I just want to get warm."

Trip chose not to think of the ways he could help with that. He went into the office and made the arrangements, then walked down the row of rooms until he found their door about halfway between the office and the end of the building.

The last time they'd stopped for gas there'd been a sandwich shop at the gas station. Trip had picked up dinner, but even though it had been hours since lunch, Norah didn't even look at it. She rubbed her arms and paced the room while he fired up the wall heater, keeping her coat on until some of the chill was off the air. She hadn't complained about the cold at all, but he realized now that she'd stopped talking entirely a couple of hours before.

"You should have told me you were freezing," he said.

"I figured the temperature was no surprise to you."

"Sarcasm works better when your teeth aren't chattering."

"Are you kidding? The chattering is how I knew I was alive for the last two hours."

Trip rolled his eyes and stripped off her coat, wrapping her in a blanket from the bed.

"I'm all right," Norah protested, and when he began to chafe her arms anyway, she tried to shove him off, just as he stepped back. She tipped forward, off balance, heading for a face-plant with her arms trapped in the blanket.

Trip caught her and hauled her against him, including her mouth, since it was right there. Her lips warmed beneath his, softened as she gave a breathless murmur and sank into the kiss. Her body relaxed against his . . .

Just as a knock sounded at the door. Norah stumbled back, fighting one arm free to press trembling fingers to her lips as she turned away.

Swearing under his breath, Trip went to answer the door. He turned back, the tray the manager handed him enough to kill the awkwardness. Norah dropped her blanket and flew across the room, wrapping both hands around one of the steaming mugs.

She took a sip, groaning with pleasure. "Chicken noodle," she said, adding, "thank you," with enough surprise to piss Trip off.

"Replaced by a mug of soup," he said, going for levity and not quite pulling it off, judging by the searching look she sent him.

Her phone chimed, saving him from the question

she'd been about to ask. One he wouldn't be able to answer without lying, and she'd probably see through that, too, which irritated him all the more. It was bad enough to be stuck with a civilian, let alone a woman, on a dangerous op. Why the hell did he have to get saddled with a psychologist who'd just happened to grow up in con artist boot camp? Not only did she see through whatever spin he tried to put on the situation, she knew why he did it better than he did. Hell, the woman was practically walking around in his brain. He didn't want her in his brain, or anywhere else, for that matter. She was trouble, plain and simple, and he needed to stop letting his emotions run away with him. So it stung that she thought he'd ignore her discomfort, not to mention the fact that she didn't complain once, just hung in there like a real trooper. It would only bother him if he let it, and at the moment it was distracting him from a conversation he ought to be listening in on.

Norah had gone to the other side of the room with her phone and her mug of soup. Trip ambled over, surprised when she said, "Wait a minute, Raymond," and put the phone against her shoulder to block the sound.

Raymond Kline was no threat. He should have walked away, but damn it, he wanted to know why she was talking to her ex-boyfriend. "Put the call on speaker," he said, no-expression, including his eyes, which she studied for a second before she said, "You want to listen in? Because you don't trust me?"

"Because it might mean something, and you have to filter the conversation through the relationship. I don't."

She shrugged and did as he'd requested. "Hello, Raymond? I'm back."

"You sound funny."

"I have you on speaker phone."

"Oh." There was a pause while he wondered who else was listening and came to the conclusion it was Trip. From the sound of his voice wasn't happy about it. "I just wanted to see if you're okay."

"And?"

"And you didn't leave a lesson plan," he said, sounding put out.

"You told me to stay off campus until this business with my father is settled."

"I could come over and pick it up. I've got this bottle of wine, from a rather new vineyard in Michigan, but it's quite good, and I've been wanting to get your opinion."

"I'm not home."

Another slight pause, then, "Where are you?"

"None of your business."

"Looking for the loot?"

Norah met Trip's eyes.

"I see," Raymond said when he'd concluded neither of them was going to answer. "So we're not even friends now."

"Guilt isn't going to work," Norah said.

"You're still angry. You're punishing me for putting you on sabbatical."

"I won't be put on the defensive either. Honestly, Raymond, this isn't about you. I'm still hoping I have a job, but I understand why you did what you did, and I'm sure I'll be fine either way." And she sounded surprised enough, Trip decided, to really mean that. "I have my practice and my writing—"

"Now, Norah, of course you have a job here." He paused for effect, Norah feeling no need to fill the silence. "If you still want one."

"We'll talk about that later, all right?"

"Really, Norah, the board wants you to come back,

and of course, so do I, but at the moment I'm worried about you. Please tell me where you are."

"I'm perfectly safe, Raymond."

"But—"

"I have to go, Raymond, my dinner is getting cold." And she disconnected.

"You played that well," Trip said.

"I didn't play anything," she said, and she was looking him straight in the eye. "It just occurred to me that I don't need that job as much as I think I do, and I won't be an emotional hostage. I've been supporting myself since I was a teenager, and I have a lot more options now than I had then."

Trip crossed the room to pick up his sub, but really he was mulling the change in Norah. Somewhere between Chicago and the middle of nowhere she'd done some thinking, and some concluding, which could be really good. Or it could be trouble. "A lot of people are suddenly interested in your whereabouts," he said, deciding to concentrate on the op, where he had some control. Or so he told himself.

"I noticed that," Norah said, "but if you're talking about Myra, you can relax, or stand down, or at ease, or whatever FBI agents do."

"I'm undercover. It depends on the situation." And since the situation involved Norah, *at ease* was not an option.

"Myra is my agent and my friend. She's just worried about me because you showed up out of the blue and she doesn't have any idea who you are."

"It didn't seem to bother her when we met."

"That's because she saw you and, well, you're you."

Trip grinned. Her directness had its perks at times.

"Ted Bundy," she said, and he lost his grin because Ted Bundy was good-looking and smooth and seemingly harmless, right up to the moment he became a murderer.

"Once you were gone she remembered that you're a stranger," Norah continued on the subject of Myra Newcastle. "And Raymond is only worried about the college. It's all he cares about."

"Then he's an idiot," Trip said, turning to unwrap his sub because her eyes were already on his face.

He glanced back and knew it was too late. She held his eyes, and there was no confusion in hers, no expectation, either. She'd not only found herself, she'd made some decisions, and he was involved, judging by the way she was looking at him.

Then the look turned hot, and he didn't give a damn about consequences, because he was across the room, kissing her, his hands framing her face, then slipping around to bury in her hair as the kiss went deeper, wilder. She tasted like chicken soup, salty and hot, scorching when she kissed him back, putting her whole body into it. And it was some body. He found that out firsthand because they were both peeling off clothes as they backpedaled to the bed, and fell on it.

Trip dragged his mouth from hers to drop to his knees, tearing off her boots, then her jeans, leaving her in a bra and panties because her sweater and shirt were already gone.

"White cotton," he said, her laugh trailing off into a moan as he laid his mouth on the inside of her thigh, inching down white cotton so he could take his mouth to her.

She bowed up, hands fisted in the bedcover, so responsive he nearly lost it. Watching her, enjoying the way she came undone, was too much to resist. So he stood the pain and pleasure, let them burn in his blood until his skin tingled and every breath he drew was fire in his lungs, until she collapsed bonelessly, so wrung out she could barely breathe. But she reached for him anyway, and he went to her, fumbling at his jeans like a teenager desperate to get them off, never mind his boots.

"Condom," she said, and had him jerking his wallet out of his back pocket, ripping out the condom and fumbling with it, the little foil package beyond hands that were suddenly all thumbs.

Norah took it from him, tore it open, smoothed it on. And had his eyes rolling back in his head, the heat and softness of her touch sending him over the edge. He caught her hips and surged into her, stopping when she cried out, so damn glad to discover it was pleasure, not pain, on her face, pleasure as he slipped her bra straps down and took one hard peak into his mouth. She bowed up again, her hips meeting his in an ever-faster, more desperate rhythm until her breath caught in the back of her throat as he felt her constrict around him, once, twice, again and again before he buried himself in her, and let himself go with her.

"ARE YOU ALL RIGHT?"

Norah floated back down, found herself wrapped in Trip's arms, and thought, Oh yeah. Since she was still fighting to regain her breath, she only nodded in answer to his question, but the concern on his face pushed her to say, "Why wouldn't I be?" When his expression didn't change, she smiled. "I'm fine, Trip. Better than fine." She stretched a little, loving how deliciously used her body felt, how relaxed. Even the stress she carried around constantly in her neck and shoulders was gone.

Her head was on his shoulder. If she stretched, just

a little, she could have kissed him. But it would be a kiss that conveyed more than she wanted it to, and definitely more than he'd be comfortable with. This was just sex. She'd decided that before she allowed herself to become intimate with Trip, and even if the decision to go there had been torn from her by a hunger she couldn't have resisted, it was still a deliberate choice. Trip was part of the ADVENTURE, a once-in-a-lifetime opportunity to let herself go, and she refused to have regrets.

Trip tapped on her forehead. "What's going on in there?".

"Honestly? Nothing."

"Why not?"

Norah leaned back so she could see his face better. "What do you think should be going on in there?"

"Nothing," Trip muttered, just sulky enough to make her smile.

"Do you want me to cry and make a scene? I can call your handler and tell him you took advantage of me, if that helps."

"You could have told me you'd already decided you were okay with this."

"It's not like we took the time to discuss it."

Trip laughed a little. It was a nice sound, as nice as the way his fingers trailed softly up and down her arm. "Maybe I can manage a little foreplay next time."

"The whole day was foreplay."

"Scoring one-o-one," Trip said, "get a woman on the back of a motorcycle and you're in."

Norah hummed in the back of her throat, part amusement, part contentment. "I think it had more to do with being wrapped around you, but the bike might have played a part. Tomorrow we get to see if it works on men."

"Because?"

"You're teaching me how to drive a motorcycle. Just in case," she added before he could argue.

He didn't, probably because he knew she was right. "Just in case," he repeated.

Progress, Norah thought, pushing herself up on one elbow. "Now about that foreplay . . ."

chapter
12

GOOD SEX TO MAKE UP FOR THE LAST . . . OKAY,
her entire adult life, an excellent breakfast to make up
for the dinner she hadn't had, and she was going to
spend a good part of the day wrapped around Trip on
the back of his motorcycle. What, Norah thought the
next morning, could be more glorious? Okay, the skies
were boiling like Shakespeare's cauldron, the temperature had passed arctic and was heading for deep-space
cold, and the motorcycle-driving lessons had been a
complete failure—she had to do what with her left
foot, left hand, and right hand all at the same time? But
she was looking on the bright side.

"Are you sure we should do this?" her practical-and
pessimistic side asked anyway, bolstered by the sight
of Lake Michigan to her left, with its white caps and
churning surf.

"Weather report says it will clear later this morning," Trip said back, via Bluetooth.

"Okay," she said, trusting him implicitly. "Ever think of becoming a meteorologist?"

"Everybody hates those guys."

Not in your case. If Trip said it would be beach weather in January, everyone in his viewing area would be walking around in swimsuits. Or at least all the women would be.

"Those guys are always wrong" was all she said. "That's why everyone hates them."

"That's just a cliché. Like you can't trust a federal agent."

"Clichés happen for a reason."

Trip chose not to respond, which made her feel a little guilty, but only for a second. After all, he'd brought it up.

"Where are we going to get a boat this late in the season?"

"Kizi."

"What's a Kizi?"

"I asked the manager of the motel when he brought breakfast, and he said Kizi can get me anything I want."

"What are the chances Kizi goes through legal channels?"

"Ignorance is bliss," Trip said.

Norah had to agree. She'd been getting quite the education since Trip had come into her life. About some things she'd have preferred to remain blissfully ignorant; other things had just been bliss.

They took 119, a stretch of road that alternated between views of Lake Michigan and a tunnel of trees famed for its fall color, but almost leafless now with the storm that had blown in overnight. 119 led them to

Cross Village, the last town on the shore until Macki-
naw City, which sat at the foot of the bridge connect-
ing Michigan's upper and lower peninsulas.

Cross Village had been founded where Father Jacques
Marquette, during his missionary travels, had planted a
cross on the bluff overlooking Lake Michigan. That
small cross had long since disappeared, but a large cross,
visible for miles out into the lake, had taken its place.

It was a quiet town filled with quiet people, a bas-
tion of the remaining Ottawa Indian population, and
home to Blissfest, a folk music festival that drew visitors from across the nation. The sun hadn't fought its
way very far over the horizon, but even at that time
of the morning the place seemed to be hopping, people
having breakfast, buying papers, or trading hellos as they
met on the sidewalks. They all stopped to stare at the
crazy people on the Harley. Not to mention they were
outsiders.

"So much for flying under the radar," Norah said.

"I didn't count on so many early birds."

"Be grateful it's not hunting season yet. Half these
people would be carrying rifles, too."

Trip didn't have a comeback for that, but she could
feel his relief. "Where do you suppose Kizi is?"

"Don't know, don't care," Trip said, and kept going
right through town.

"I thought we needed Kizi," Norah said. "He's going
to get us a boat."

"We'll find one," Trip said. "There'll be vacation
homes peppered all along the shore. Someone will
have a boat still in the water."

"You're going to steal a boat?"

"We're going to steal a boat."

"That sounds great in theory, but my job doesn't
come with a get out of jail free card."

"Do you have a better idea?"

"Wait until spring?" Which she knew wasn't an option. What she didn't know was why she wanted the delay. Was it because she was afraid of drowning, or of Trip leaving just when she'd begun to find this new side of herself? And there, she concluded, was a question that could wait until spring.

119 had ended in Cross Village. Trip kept to whatever roads he could find along the coast, taking the time at each one to check for a boat. Finally they came across a house with a tent-covered structure next to the dock. Trip guided the bike into the drive and left her there while he walked down to scope it out. He came back with a smirk on his face.

"Jackpot," he said.

"There's a boat in that tent?" Norah followed down the dock. A square metal structure had been erected beside the dock, white canvas covering the portion of the posts about a foot above the surface of the lake. Inside the tent a boat was suspended from the top of the frame. The boat was maybe fifteen feet from end to end, completely open with a semicircle of seats at the rear and a pair of swivel seats behind the windshield at the front. "It's pretty small."

"We don't have far to go," Trip said, "it'll do the job."

Norah glanced at the white-capped expanse of water, then back at the boat. "It looks like the waves will be higher than the sides of the boat."

"Have a little faith," Trip said.

He jumped into ankle-deep water at the shallow end of the tent, and began to turn a crank that lowered the boat slowly toward the water.

"You do that, and I'll start praying," Norah said.

Trip continued to crank, and in the end the possibility of what they might find was stronger than Norah's fear of the waves. Or maybe, she thought as she climbed into the boat without an argument, she was foolishly over-confident in Trip's abilities, but it just didn't seem like anything could go wrong... Okay, things had gone wrong, but not in a mortal injury way. And she was wearing a life preserver. It smelled like it had been soaking in mildew for a year, but if she went over the side she wasn't going to care. Once Trip had parked the motorcycle inside the garage with the miraculously broken door lock, they located some gas, the boat was underway, and the wind was blowing, she couldn't smell anything. She couldn't feel anything, either, but she'd spent two days on the back of Trip's Harley in the frigid wind, so being numb was hardly new.

"We're almost there," Trip said to her not much later.

Norah lifted her head out of the neck of her jacket and looked over the front of the boat, then stuck her face back into her collar again. One sight of Waugoshance Lighthouse was enough.

The lighthouse sat at the western end of a shoal stretching seven miles from the Michigan shoreline westward into Lake Michigan. The shoal consisted of a series of shallowly submerged gravel beds dotted with low, weed and evergreen-covered islands that appeared and disappeared depending on the water level of the lake. Waugoshance had warned ships off the shoal for the last half of the nineteenth century and the first dozen or so years of the twentieth, at which time it was replaced.

It had sat abandoned and derelict for nearly a hundred years. Its metal skin was peeling away, the stone structure beneath crumbling, the birdcage light at the top nothing but the curved metal framework that gave it its name. It was, however, stationary and it offered shelter from the wind.

Trip nosed the boat in as close as he could, then jumped out on the lowest course of stones in the lighthouse's base and tied off. He helped Norah out of the boat, then jumped back in, handing her their bags and scavenging beneath the seats. He joined her, his arms full of stuff, including a toolbox and a first aid kit.

"What's all that?"

"Everything I could find," Trip said. "You never know what you're going to need."

"We need to get our butts up to the top of the lighthouse," Norah said. "Before the whole place washes away."

They made their way up the stairs, careful of the crumbling redbrick walls and the debris already covering the risers.

"What exactly did Puff tell you?" Trip asked her when they reached the top.

Norah laughed a little. "He said there'd be a loose brick."

"Ha-ha."

"Yeah." Norah turned a slow circle. "That has to be the understatement of the century."

Trip started working his way around the room. "What bothers me more is there's no place big enough to hide fifty million dollars worth of stolen goods. There aren't even any empty spaces behind these bricks."

"Damn it." Norah headed for the stairs.

"Where are you going?"

"He conned us." *He conned me.* The possibility had always existed, but it still hurt like hell.

"Think, Norah," Trip said, stopping her before she'd taken the first step down. "Why would he send us here?"

She turned around, already grabbing on to that tiny ember of hope.

"Let me rephrase that," Trip said. "Why would he

send you here? He wouldn't hesitate to send me on a wild-goose chase, but he wouldn't do that to you."

Trip continued to work his way around the room, peeling loose bricks off the walls as he went.

The ember took fire, fanned into a flame that felt like the sun coming up inside her, filling her with warmth and light. Lucius was her father; she'd love him even if he'd conned her. But it felt damn good knowing he hadn't.

She set to work helping Trip, systematically stripping a section from the floor to as high as she could reach, then moving on.

"Don't worry about the ones down low and up high," Trip said when he noticed what she was doing. "He would have put it at eye level."

"Okay, but eye level for my dad is about halfway between yours and mine."

"Good point," Trip said, adjusting his focus down about half a foot.

But Norah was already there. "Eureka," she said, spying a bit of plastic behind the brick next to the one she'd just pulled out.

Thunder rumbled outside, she glanced toward the window, but stayed where she was, worrying the next brick out of its socket so she could pull free what turned out to be a small plastic bag about four inches by three, with a seal at the top and a folded piece of paper inside.

"There's something wrapped in the paper, but I can't see what it is."

"Put it somewhere safe," Trip said. "It's time to get the hell out of here."

Norah took a better look out the window. "Man," she breathed, watching the sky off to the west grow darker by the second, except when lightning forked down. She took a step closer to the open window, scared out of her wits but fascinated at the same time.

"Shit," Trip said, taking her by the hand. "It's going green."

She stuffed the note in the pocket of her jeans, trying to keep her feet as he towed her down the stairway.

"Kind of odd weather for this time of year," he said, slowing a little as they hit a particularly dicey section of the stairs.

"Not for the Great Lakes," Norah said, breathing a sigh of relief when they'd navigated the last step and started making their way out to where the boat was tied. "Early in the season, maybe, but there are some hellacious storms in this part of Lake Michigan, and Superior is even worse."

"Let's just get to the ... boat ..." Which was already half sunk, they discovered just then. They'd gotten there in time to watch a six-foot wave pick it up and slam it hull first into the shoal, the boat splintering into pieces while the storm whipped up the air around them and the sky opened up, pelting them with stinging particles of ice.

They ducked back inside the lighthouse, and even if they'd had cell phone service it wouldn't have done them any good to call for help.

"Nobody's coming out in this weather," she said. "Not even the Coast Guard." She took out her cell, checked it just in case. "The big question is, how are we going to get out of here when the weather clears?"

Trip didn't offer any suggestions, but he slipped an arm around her shoulders and pulled her close. "I've been in worse jams than this."

"Where?"

"Give me a minute," he said, "I'll think of one."

A bolt of lightning speared down into the lake, followed by a clap of thunder so loud Norah swore she felt the lighthouse quake.

"Jeez," she said, shrinking back against Trip and not feeling stupid about it because it was nice to have a strong man around at a time like this. "Did you feel that?"

"Like the earth moved? That was nothing." And he spun her around and took her mouth.

Norah sank in, pressed against him, forgetting herself in the heat and the flavor and the scent, a thousand sensations spinning through her. The storm raged wilder outside, wind and waves battered the lighthouse, rain lashed through the open windows, and lightning forked from the sky, lighting Trip's face, his expression so fierce she almost climaxed just from knowing how much he wanted her.

He put his mouth, that hot, talented mouth, on her neck, and Norah felt as if the electricity surged from the storm through Trip, spearing to her breasts and belly, bursts so strong she threw her head back and moaned. His hands slipped under her sweater to find her breasts, his skin cool on her heated, aching nipples.

She loved the feel of him, his palms rough against her sensitive skin, his muscles firm beneath her roaming hands. She loved the solid bulk of him, the shudder of his stomach muscles and the rasp of his breath catching as she slipped her hands down, one of them fumbling at the snap to the jeans, the other cupping him through the denim, rubbing until he tore his hands off her so he could tear hers off him.

"Stop," he said, catching her wrists and pulling them away from his body.

"You're right," she said struggling against the towering need inside her, so incredibly relieved when Trip said, "I didn't mean to stop *completely*," sounding just a little outraged by the suggestion. Outraged and in pain.

"Um, stone floor, really cold, and we're about to get soaked."

He kissed her again, deep and hot and just a little wild, and when she surfaced she was standing between the open door and the open window, crumbling brick at her back, Trip hard against her.

"Still cold," she murmured, but it didn't seem as much of an obstacle this time. Until he spun her around. "*Trip*," she protested, but before she could feel the cold rough brick against her palms his arms snaked around her, one going under her coat, the other slipping down, and even through her jeans she could feel the heat, that delicious heat.

She let her head fall forward, as he unsnapped her jeans and slipped them down, along with her panties, the air cold and sharp but only for a moment before he was in her and wrapped around her, his hand busy at her breast, his mouth on her neck. The storm was raging in her like it raged outside, building as her breath grew short, building as she rocked against him, building as his hands gripped her hips, as he thrust deeper, again and again, as she tightened impossibly around him. Releasing as every nerve overloaded and she climaxed, her body rolling in long, deep waves filled with impossibly bright pleasure, brighter because she knew Trip was with her.

"Christ, Norah," he said, holding her tight with his chin on her shoulder, his head next to hers, a kind of vertical cuddle. Or maybe he was holding on so tight because he didn't want to fall down.

She felt him wobble a bit as he let go, and while the practicality of it stung a bit, there was also the satisfaction of knowing she'd made him go weak.

"I'll never look at a brick wall the same way again," she said as she put herself back together, physically and emotionally. Trip left a hell of a damage path, but it was up to her to make sure she didn't get destroyed.

"If you were looking at the brick at all I did something wrong." He waited a beat, then said, "nothing to say?"

She turned around, grinning. "I could tell you that was amazing, but you already know that."

"Just amazing?"

"B-plus. Care to shoot for an A?"

"Yeah, but I'm going to need five minutes. Or so."

"How about I give you ten?"

chapter 13

NORAH WOKE TO TRIP'S HAND IN HER BRA.
But not in a good way.

"Cold," she protested, getting her hand batted away when she tried to stop him from shoving something into her cleavage. Something cold and plastic. Lucius's clue, which they'd never gotten to read yesterday before darkness fell.

"We have company," Trip said, pulling her to her feet.

"I just managed to fall asleep five minutes ago," Norah said, stooping to gather up the single blanket that had been on their stolen boat, and the life preservers they'd used as pillows. Then she realized there was no place to return them to. Not to mention the rest of the situation finally sank in. "Company?"

The sky was a pretty fall blue when she looked out the window, deeper than the pastel blue of summer, the air on the cold side of crisp. And there were boats all around

the lighthouse, big boats, small boats, boats made of
wood, aluminum, fiberglass, and combinations of the
three, each of them carrying at least two people. "Well, I
guess it's not going to be a problem getting back to the
mainland."

"I wouldn't be so sure of that. Unless hunting season started last night those guns are probably for us."

Norah looked closer. Sure enough, some of the boat-
ers had weapons she could see. "What are we going to
do?"

"The best defense is a good offense," he said, starting down the stairs.

"Football analogies? That's all you've got?"

"You're panicking, MacArthur," Trip said. "Get a
grip."

"I'll get a grip all right, around your neck."

"Take a number."

They came out at the lower level and stopped, taking a slow look around. "I don't think I can count that
high." Okay, so that was an exaggeration, but there had
to be at least twenty boats bobbing at anchor in a loose
semicircle around the doorway side of the lighthouse
where the shoal made the water shallow.

"Who's the admiral of this flotilla?" Trip called out.

"Kizi," was the response, shouted by someone Norah
didn't bother to locate because she was busy staring at a
man about seven feet tall who dominated the deck of the
nearest boat, an older wooden model with shiny brass
railings and a tall mast with a furled sail. Tattoos curled
over the backs of his hands and above the collar of his
coat, and he had big gold earrings in both ears. All he
lacked was a parrot and an eye patch.

"I have a sudden urge to say *Arrrgh*," Norah murmured for Trip's benefit.

"I have a feeling he'd take offense. See those tattoos?"

"It's the muscles that worry me," Norah said. "And the gun."

"He's an Ottawa Indian," Trip said.

"Is that good?"

"Probably not, considering I work for the government, and I haven't run across any Indians of any tribe that have a friendly outlook toward Uncle Sam."

"Don't tell him you're a federal agent."

"I wasn't planning to. I just wanted to make sure you understood why it would be a bad idea."

"All you had to do was tell me not to say anything."

"You tend to require explanations. I thought I'd save us both some time."

"You two keep talking to each other, we gonna think you trying to put one over on us."

They both turned to stare at the giant. Neither of them spoke.

"Saqwasikisi. Kizi for short," he said in a booming voice that completely went along with his physique. "Nice of you to wait while we took our boats out of winter storage."

"You can thank Mother Nature."

"The Earth Mother always protects her children, the Ottawa."

Not from the Europeans who'd almost wiped them out. But Norah kept that to herself. Messing with someone's religion was off-limits, even when that someone didn't come with a private army.

"She'd be the MacArthur woman," Kizi continued, "the one who knows where fifty million dollars is hiding," he said to Trip. "Who are you?"

"A friend."

"No friend of mine," Kizi said, accompanied by a low mutter of assent from the peanut gallery.

"He's a friend of mine," Norah said.

Kizi crossed forearms the size of hams across his
chest, his face stoic and his voice deep. Norah forgot
the pirate stereotype and thought of Sitting Bull. Especially when he spoke, not enough pattern to his speech
to make him sound like a cast member for a remake of
Last of the Mohicans, but enough so you still knew he
was an Ottawa. "He be a friend of mine, if he tell me
what you found."

"We didn't find anything," Trip said. He opened his
coat and turned out his pockets.

Norah did the same, helping when he dropped their
packs on the ground and set about emptying them.

"Maybe she's hiding the loot in her clothes," some
helpful man called out, everyone else laughing except the
lone woman, who added, "I'd rather check the nooks and
crannies." The men's laughter turned even more raucous.
So did their commentary.

Norah took a step back, or at least she tried, until Trip
slapped an arm around her waist and hauled her against
him, making it look like he was being proprietary but
muttering "relax" under his breath. She could have told
him just being pressed against him was enough to accomplish that, but she didn't want to seem weak and
pathetic. Scared out of her wits was okay, but it would
have been good if she'd handled it better.

"Don't kick yourself, professor," Trip said, startling
her, not because he saw what she was going through, but
because he had a lot of other stuff to focus on, and he
still took the time to gauge her feelings and reassure her.

She smiled up at him, just a little. "Maybe you
should be worried about them."

"I don't have to. Kizi is in charge. He won't let the
situation get out of his control, so I just have to worry
about him."

Sure enough, Kizi held up a hand and the laughter

died off, all but one brave soul who said, "I bet they hid the loot inside somewhere, thinking we're just hicks and we won't find it."

Trip did a Vanna White gesture to the doorway, nudging Norah to one side but keeping his arm around her. "Be my guest," he said.

Kizi held Trip's gaze for a second, then let his hand fall forward, the only permission his motley crew needed to rush the place, swarming over the sides of their boats onto the shoal and splashing through knee-deep water, crawling up the stone base like a tide of ants at a picnic.

Norah fielded more than one leer, but Trip kept his body between her and the treasure hunters, and the lure of fifty million dollars was more than her powers of allure could overcome. Not that she was trying to be alluring. Hell, she was radiating ugly as hard as she could.

"Okay," Norah said when they were gone, "which boat—ouch." Trip let go of her arm, stepping aside so she could see they weren't alone. "Oh," she said, rubbing her arm but glad he'd stopped her before she'd gotten to the part of her statement that included boat theft, especially since the guy they'd left on guard had a long gun resting across his thighs. He was also about eighty and a Santa Claus look-alike—if Santa had been armed to the teeth.

"He's old," she whispered to Trip, "probably can't see very well. And I really don't want to be here when those guys come out empty-handed," she added. Trip knew that, of course, but it couldn't be emphasized enough, since she figured there'd be a hell of an ugly scene and she didn't want to be the consolation prize.

"That's a shotgun," Trip said, not keeping his voice down. "I figure it's loaded with wide-pattern shot, and we have to go right past him. Even if he was legally blind he'd hit us."

"But you're thinking about it, ain't you," the old guy said with a smile—an oddly sweet smile since he also hitched the gun up higher. "What do you think your odds are of getting to me before I can shoot you?"

"Pretty good," Trip said.

"I'm inclined to agree with you," the old man said. "Name's Digger." He picked the gun up by the barrel and handed it to Trip.

Trip grinned. "Thanks." He dug his wallet out of his back pocket and took out a hundred dollar bill, handing it to the guy.

"Gun ain't worth that much, son."

"You want to give it back?"

"Nope." The bill disappeared into Digger's pocket.

"It's not for the gun anyway," Trip said. "It's for looking the other way."

"Don't matter," Digger said, winking at Norah, "eyesight ain't too good anymore anyway."

"Evidently your hearing is fine," she said, letting Trip help her down the stone base.

"Don't hold with hurting a woman," Digger said. "That thing's got all the pickup of a floating tub," he added as they headed for one of the larger boats. "Kizi's boat is the best of the lot, but you take that and he'll never stop coming after you. And what Kizi goes after, Kizi finds. That one there would stand you in good stead." Digger pointed to a smaller aluminum boat that was dented and dirty.

Norah couldn't see into the small cabin belowdecks, but judging by the rest of the picture, she didn't want to.

"Guy who owns it don't care about the outside, but he's a wizard with an engine . . ."

They heard a ruckus from inside the lighthouse.

"Maybe he won't be needing it," Digger finished as Trip slung the shotgun into the boat and boosted Norah over the side. "And just so you know, the gun's only loaded with rock salt."

"Thanks for the tip," Trip said.

Norah was making herself useful, hauling the anchor out of the water, but keeping her eye on the lighthouse, where the sounds of a full-blown argument spilled out of the door and windows.

"Relax," Trip said, "they're not finding anything so they're turning on each other. Let's get out of here before they decide the real culprits are getting away."

"Too late," Norah said.

Before they'd done much more than get the boat in motion, the treasure hunters piled out the door of the lighthouse, slung themselves into their boats, and set up pursuit. Digger was right, it turned out; the boat they'd taken was the fastest of the lot, but not by much. It had a fairly shallow draft, especially at top speed with the prow nosing up out of the water. But at about eighteen feet long with what sounded like two big, and probably heavy, engines, the reef must have presented a problem since Trip steered away from it, even with the other boats heading for them at top speed. In her limited experience, Trip was a daredevil; his preference for boats full of men with guns over the shoal told her a lot.

"As long as they think we know something they won't shoot at us," he yelled over the roar of the engines.

"All we have to do is not get caught."

"I'm working on it."

Not fast enough. But she knew he was doing everything he could. She did a mental rewind of the guys at the shoal, which only made her more desperate since she really did not want to find herself at their mercy, and while she trusted Trip, and after the book fiasco she knew he'd rather she kept out of his way, she couldn't

just stand by and do nothing. She went below, fighting
for balance with Trip turning the boat on a dime every
five seconds, trying to pick her way through a cesspool
of junk she chose not to identify, but making a note to
scrub herself with bleach later. Considering the amount
of random flotsam and jetsam there really wasn't much
to find, but in a small cabinet at the very front of the
cabin she came across emergency supplies. Including a
flare gun.

TRIP LET THE OTHER BOATS HERD HIM TOWARD
the shoal, watching for his opening, waiting while half
the boats set up a scrimmage line on the landward side
and the others drove him straight for them. Hard to feint
in a boat, but it was just as hard for his opponents to
move at a second's notice. He steered toward one opening, then cut the wheel hard left, laying his boat practically on its side as he poured on every last ounce of
speed, cut right again and shot through the narrow opening between two larger wooden boats. One of the occupants to his right started to climb onto the rail; Trip
lifted Digger's shotgun, and the guy had a change of
heart before he even brought the muzzle to bear.

"Thought so," Trip muttered, slaloming his way around
the rest of the boats and managing to get ahead of them
by sheer skill and the stupidity of the other skippers.
There was probably some pure dumb luck involved, too.

He headed southeast, toward the house where they'd
left the Harley. It was their only advantage, and not
much of one with Norah sure to be slower than some of
the men chasing them. Otherwise he spared little thought
to Norah and what she might be doing in the cabin.
Until she appeared at the top of the stairs clutching a
gun-shaped object distinctively yellow in color.

"Look what I found," she said, brandishing it as she stepped out onto the deck.

"What do you expect to do with that?"

"Shoot it at them."

"Which will do nothing but make them shoot back. That leaves us with no flares and a shotgun filled with rock salt."

"Maybe it will scare them."

"I've got everything under control."

"It doesn't look that way from where I'm standing," she said, staring off in their wake and looking worried.

Trip didn't need to review the situation. The shore loomed about a hundred yards ahead, but their pursuers were only about half that distance behind them, dangerously close. And then there was Norah with that damn flare gun, heading for the rear of the boat.

Trip caught her by the back of her coat, and then didn't know what to do with her since he had to keep one hand on the wheel. She twisted free, and he clutched wildly at her, somehow managing to grab her right arm and throwing them both off balance. They went down in a tangle of limbs. The flare gun went off, the flare plowing through the deck and into one of the engines, which exploded into a raging fireball as they hit shore. Literally. The boat plowed up about ten feet onto the beach, throwing them back toward the gaping hole in the deck with its burning engine.

Trip latched onto the base of the driver's seat with one hand, managing somehow to hook Norah with the other arm, then dragging her to her feet and boosting her over the side, just as the second engine blew.

"Jesus," Trip said, grabbing her hand and pulling her toward the house. The other boats were keeping a safe distance from the fire, but they weren't going to wait long. Already a couple of them were landing to the north and south. When they jumped out of their boats, they brought their guns with them.

Norah was stumbling, a little shell-shocked. Not used to getting blown up. Or shot at, which didn't seem to be a problem since she wasn't the main target. Trip went down halfway to the house, his right leg giving out at the same time he felt the burning pain of a gunshot. He took Norah down with him, rolling and boosting her back to her feet. "Go, Norah, get out of here," he yelled at her.

She didn't hesitate, reaching into his coat pocket for the key to the Harley, jumping to her feet, and racing off without a backward glance.

Trip fought his way upright just in time to meet the first of the guys from the boats. He braced himself on his good leg and ducked under the punch the first guy threw, striking him in the throat hard enough to put him down permanently without killing him. He heard the bike start up then stop, probably because Norah had let off the clutch without giving it enough gas. Worse, Kizi heard it, too, and he drew the same conclusion. He separated from the pack of men swarming off the boats, heading for the garage, not bothering to hurry. He didn't think he had to. Big mistake.

The Harley flew through the door with Norah hanging on for dear life. She zoomed past Kizi, past Trip, heading for the lake. Trip heard a splash, spared a glance over his shoulder and saw her stop in about a foot of water, then two more guys were on him.

He took the first man out with pathetic ease, but the second went right for his wounded leg, getting in a punch to his thigh that took him down to one knee, the guy jumping back suddenly because it was move or eat the front end of the Harley. Norah zipped between them, stopping a couple of feet in front of Trip and yelling, "Get on."

Trip got on, at least for a second before Norah did a jackrabbit start that stalled the bike and dumped him off the back of the motorcycle onto his ass in the sand. She restarted the bike, and Trip got to his feet, running and hopping on his bad leg, trying to get on the bike with it jerking forward as Norah fought the gears. He finally made it on just as two more guys were about to grab him.

Trip elbowed one in the balls; that one jackknifed and took his fellow treasure hunter down with him. Trip put his arms around Norah, found the handlebars, and gunned the bike enough to get away, giving Kizi, halfway down the hill, a wide berth. Once they made it to the road, he let Norah drive just long enough to put some distance between them and their pursuers. Since none of them had a car handy it only took a couple of miles.

"Let me look at your leg," Norah said once they'd stopped by the side of the road.

"It's just a graze." But he nudged her off the bike so he didn't have to move too much, slid forward, then waited for her to get on the back.

"You still need first aid," she insisted, slipping on the Bluetooth ear piece he gave her.

"It's not my leg I'm worried about, it's my ass. And yours."

"They'll be coming after us in a car," Norah said.

"It'll be bigger than a car. Most of these year-round snowbelt guys have something with four-wheel drive and off-road capability." He drove another five miles then pulled off the road and into the forest.

"Do you have any idea where you're going?" Norah

asked him after they'd been riding through the woods for a little while.

"South," Trip said.

"That's pretty vague."

"We have to hit a road or building sometime."

"Not necessarily, Trip. A lot of upper Michigan is state forest. Miles and miles of state forest. And you're bleeding."

Trip chose to ignore that, until he felt her hands at his leg. He looked down and saw her slip her scarf around his knee and shimmy it up to the wound on his thigh, wrapping it as best she could on the back of a Harley jouncing through primeval forest. When she was done, when her arms were wrapped around his waist again, he rested his hand over hers, just for a moment. It was only gratitude, and maybe a little camaraderie, he told himself, grateful she couldn't give him one of those searching looks. He didn't want to wonder what she was thinking. He didn't want to think at all.

Trouble was, he had to spend the next few hours alone with his thoughts. And his feelings.

chapter 14

ABOUT DINNERTIME THEY CAME ACROSS SIGNS of civilization, avoiding the small frame house with the tidy backyard carved out of the woods, to pick up the road that ran in front of it. They followed the winding two-lane road into a small town with no name. As far as Norah was concerned it could be called Convenience. A small hotel sat near the edge of town, with a modest strip mall and a couple of restaurants, one fast-food, one mom-and-pop, on opposite sides of that narrow road comprising the main drag of the town.

Trip pulled into the motel and stopped by the office, keeping away from the window. He handed her money without saying a word. He didn't have to. She was hardly at her best after a night in an abandoned light-house, a run-in with an angry mob, and an explosion, but she had Trip beat.

"Put your hair up," he said.

"Really?"

"Really."

Norah lifted a hand, ran it over her hair, then wished she hadn't. Her hair had to look like hell. It felt even worse, tangled and flat, and her scalp began to itch just at the thought of how dirty it must be. But considering how the rest of her looked, she doubted even such a gnarly case of helmet hair would seem out of place.

"Color's memorable," Trip said shortly. "Never hurts to take precautions." He dug through a compartment on the front of the Harley, handing her a bit of string.

Norah tied her hair back, not bothering with the brush in her overnight bag.

"Whenever you're done humoring me," Trip said, gesturing toward the office.

"I'm not humoring you," she said. But they both knew that was a lie. Trip probably took it for guilt; Norah felt only sympathy.

She'd gone over her actions. Repeatedly—heck, she'd had nothing to do but think. She'd decided she hadn't done anything wrong, or nothing more than Trip had. And sure, the flare wouldn't have been much of a deterrent, but it would have been better if they'd blown up one of the other boats instead of their own, and that was Trip's fault.

He tapped the spot right between her eyes, and she realized she was frowning.

"Don't think so much," he said. "It makes me nervous."

Norah wiped the frown from her face and went into the office. When she came out, she handed Trip the room key and headed for the road.

"Where are you going?"

"Shopping."

"Not like that."

She stopped, looked back at him. "We're hungry and filthy, and you need medical attention. I know you won't go to the emergency room, so—"

"Take a breath, professor."

She glared at him.

"You can't use your credit card."

"Those guys aren't exactly geniuses," she said. "I doubt they have the connections to track my purchases. I know"—she held up a hand—"precautions." And she figured she'd caused enough trouble for one day.

So, apparently, did Trip.

"She keeps helping me," she heard him say when she came back into the room an hour or so later. He was talking on his cell phone, probably with that Mike guy in Washington. Judging by the tone of Trip's voice, the two of them were commiserating over what a screwup she was.

"It was your fault, too," she muttered, which earned her a scowl from Trip. She stifled the gesture she wanted to make in his direction. Giving him the finger would be rude and childish.

They'd gotten away, hadn't they? After several hours of trekking through the forest, in the cold, with a wounded leg . . . She winced, imagining how much pain he had to be in. But it didn't stop him from pacing back and forth across the small motel room, shooting her a look every now and then but keeping his voice down for the most part.

She dumped her bags on the table, one containing a change of clothes down to the skin for each of them, one holding first aid items, the last a white takeout sack from the mom-and-pop place, filled to bursting with food.

Trip came over and pawed through the clothes, pulling out a pair of boxers and holding them up. They

were black, dotted with little pink hearts and one big
red heart right over the placket in front. "I'm a lover not
a fighter?" he read the white lettering on the backside.
"Wishful thinking?"

"It was a gift shop. The only underwear they had
were novelty ones." She whipped them out of his hands
and tossed them on the table. "Trust me, I didn't waste
my time hoping you wouldn't give me an earful, so go
ahead, get it over with. It's my fault the boat blew up,
it's my fault you got shot, I can't follow simple instructions.

"But if I'd taken off on the Harley like you told me
to, you'd probably be in really bad shape now, if not
dead, and the boat was just as much your fault as it was
mine. If you hadn't tackled me instead of treating me
like an intelligent human being—"

"If you warned me before you did things I wouldn't
feel a need to tackle you," he said, talking over her.

"What was I supposed to do? You had your hands
full driving the boat."

"Maybe you should stop beating yourself up, Norah.
Yeah, I'm not happy about how things played out, but
we got away and it was because you blew up the boat.
The explosion held those guys off and gave us time to
make a run for it."

"But I slowed you down."

"We were both cold and tired, and running in sand.
My getting shot was just bad luck. And you saved my
life," he added, which surprised her—not for the grudging way he said it but because he'd said it at all.

"At last," Trip said, lowering himself into the nearest chair with an exaggerated sigh, "peace and quiet."

"And all you had to do was agree with me." She
pulled him to his feet and unsnapped his pants. The thigh
of his jeans was stiff with dried blood, the whole thing

stuck to his injured leg. She dumped out the first aid supplies and found the small, cheap scissors she'd bought, cutting around the wound. Then she pulled him into the bathroom.

"A bath would be better," she said, "but there's no telling what's in that tub."

"You, if I'm lucky."

She might have taken him seriously if he hadn't been too tired to put much heat behind that suggestion—and if she hadn't been so freaked out at the idea that he'd actually been shot. She went to gather up the bandages and tape, and by the time she returned he was out of the shower and half-dressed.

Norah pushed him down on the closed toilet and took a good look at the wound, now minus its denim bandage.

"It's just a graze," Trip said.

Norah shot him a look, studying the two-inch long furrow on his thigh. It might be a graze, but his face was drawn with pain and he'd lost a fair amount of blood. "It's pretty clean," she said. "You could use some stitches, but—"

"There's a law. They have to report bullet wounds."

"Then I guess you're stuck with me." She slathered on antiseptic cream.

He sucked in a breath.

"Sorry," she muttered, laying gauze over the wound and taping it down on all four sides. "We'll have to keep an eye on it, make sure it doesn't get infected."

"It'll be fine."

She started to get up, saw that big red heart, and smiled.

"Impressive, huh?" Trip said with a ghost of his usual devilment.

"It's not you, it's those boxers. I'll have to use them in my next book."

"They weren't my idea," he reminded her.

They were every man's idea, Norah thought as she left him to finish dressing. It was an instinctual thing, and that heart sitting right over his testicles said it all. Men reproduced. Women nurtured. Both genders confused sex with love in different ways. It wasn't bad, it wasn't a condemnation of either men or women, and it wasn't to say they didn't love. But those boxers were a pretty spot-on illustration of the differences between them. Nor was it something she should forget. It was too late to keep herself from getting emotionally hooked, but she couldn't let her emotions put up a smoke screen for her intellect. Trip would go on his way when the loot was found, and while she'd been focusing on what that meant for her father, she needed to remember what it would mean for her.

He came up behind her and reached over her shoulder into her shirt. She smacked his hand away, and not because she thought he was overcome by her charms. He was after the clue.

She collected the new clothes she'd bought for herself and headed for the bathroom. "I'm taking a shower, and I'm keeping this"—she held up the plastic bag they'd retrieved from Waugoshance Lighthouse—"until I'm done. We'll look at it together."

"You're lucky I'm too tired and hungry to take offense."

She snorted softly. "It's not like you can chase me down, especially since I have the key to the bike. And your wallet."

"And I have your dad."

"He's not going to tell you anything."

"He's not going to tell *you* anything, either, as long as you can't get to him."

"So you've been holding him all this time in case you needed to keep me in line?"

"No, we've kept him in custody according to the terms of his sentence, at a secret location so he'll be protected while he heals. Using him as blackmail is strictly a bonus."

"The FBI doesn't do things by accident." She closed the bathroom door behind her and shot the bolt home.

"If I wanted to come in there, do you think a locked door would stop me?"

"Not if the loot was in here."

IF HIS LEG HADN'T BEEN THROBBING LIKE THE heartbeat of Satan, Trip would have been up and pacing the room. Instead, he had to sit there, burning—and not in a good way—as he listened to the water run while Norah showered. He wanted to join her. After last night he wouldn't have hesitated. If not for her parting shot.

She came out, cool, calm, keeping her distance—despite a T-shirt that read *Too Sexy For My Clothes*—and letting him know it. She'd been holding a part of herself back anyway. He'd resented it even as he'd acknowledged he was doing the same. Now she was back to the woman he'd met a few days ago, not trusting him, although he had to admit she had cause. The FBI would use whoever they wanted by whatever means were handy with no regard for the consequences to anyone but the Bureau.

The part she'd overlooked was that he was a tool, too. Then again, he'd chosen his path. He'd been fine with it, too, until now. Maybe it was the first time he'd been faced with a truly innocent person caught up in a criminal enterprise. Maybe, he allowed, it was Norah.

Trip took that idea out for a spin, looked at it from every angle he could think of, then put it away, into a little box in his mind. A man in his position didn't have the right to think in emotional terms, and a man who might have to use another person to complete a job had to know he was poisoning the well before he ever dipped into it. She was right to freeze him out. As long as she didn't shut him out where the Gold Coast Robbery was concerned.

"Let's get something straight," he said, "you're not going to work against me, right?"

"You have my father in custody." Her voice was even, matter-of-fact, but she wasn't looking at him.

He couldn't let it matter. "I'll tell you where he is right now, if you ask me."

"Because I'm the key to finding the loot."

"Yes."

Her eyes lifted to his. He held her gaze for a moment that felt like an eternity roasting over hot coals. Then she nodded and looked away.

"I appreciate the truth."

But she didn't answer his question. She didn't ask where her father was, either, so Trip decided to take it as progress toward closing his case and getting back to Washington, and eventually moving on to the next job. And if there wasn't the same sense of anticipation and exhilaration he usually felt, he'd deal with that when he had to.

Norah dug into the food bag, pulling out sandwiches and soup containers and sliding one of each across the table to Trip.

Trip cracked the lid on the soup. The scent of chicken noodle wafted out, lukewarm, but he was starving and hurting, and it was just like Norah to provide the kind of food that would satisfy every kind of hunger, both the physical and the emotional.

She ignored the food altogether and pulled out the clue bag, still pissed but keeping her word. She opened the small plastic bag and pulled out the paper inside. When she unfolded the paper a piece of jade, wafer thin, about three inches long and intricately carved into a flat elephant, fell out, along with some unset gems.

Trip flattened out the white plastic takeout bag, put the jewels and elephant on it, and took out his cell phone. "The jade piece is easily identifiable," he said as he snapped pictures. "My guess is it will be traced back to the robbery. My handler will verify it." He sent the pictures to Mike and snapped his phone closed.

"Gems are a compact, easy way to stash money, which means they wouldn't have been reported, and they were loose in one of the safe-deposit boxes."

"Are you sure they weren't broken down from one of the other pieces of jewelry?"

"There wasn't time."

"It wouldn't have taken that long. Gold is pretty soft."

"There's a bigger question we need to think about."

She looked up, both of them speaking at the same time, Norah saying, "There's a fifth partner."

"We're being conned" was Trip's take on the situation, and then he said, "The FBI would have known if there was another partner."

"How?" Norah demanded. "Their *shoot first and ask questions later* approach? My father was the only survivor, and he hasn't exactly been a font of information."

"Until now. Why do you think that is?"

"He's not running a con," Norah insisted. "Not on me."

"If you don't believe he'd use you to put one over on the FBI, you're seriously delusional."

Norah slapped both hands on the table and got to her feet. "After five minutes with you I can understand what he's got against the FBI."

"There's no reason to make this personal."

"You just did."

Trip stopped, took a deep breath, and tried to see around his frustration. "He's your father, Norah. There's no way to keep this from being personal to you."

She sighed and sank back into her chair. "You're right, and he's had a long time to resent the FBI. But you don't know him like I do. He wants to return the stolen items to their rightful owners. He wants to atone for what he did."

Trip shook his head. "I realize you haven't had contact with him in fifteen years, but people don't change that much."

"Yes, they do. There are actual studies."

"Like we've both pointed out, he's your father. You can't help but see his actions through a filter of emotion, but you can't ignore reality, Norah. Your father is running a con."

"I'm not ignoring reality. I don't believe it."

"Then I guess I'll have to convince you."

She thought about that for a minute. "How?"

"Simple," Trip said, amazed. Not many people were able to face life, especially the unpleasant parts, without flinching. Norah met life head-on, dared it to kick her in the teeth. The problem was, sometimes life wore steel-toed boots. "Puff wasn't involved in the actual robbery. It only took us a day to get to the lighthouse. He had three days before he was caught."

"But why would he leave a trail of breadcrumbs for himself?"

"There's only one way to find out." He glanced at the note from the clue bag, still lying on Norah's side of the table.

She opened it, read it, then held it out.

Trip took the note from her, more interested in its content than its style. "*From water to land, ice to sand, tropical, arboreal and seasonal at hand,*" he read out loud. "*Endangered and rare, common and spare, north of the border, your destination's there.*"

He met Norah's eyes. "The Detroit Zoo."

"Should you be jumping like that with a leg wound?"

"*Water, land, arboreal,*" he repeated from the clue, "you've got habitats. *Endangered, rare, common,* you've got plants and animals. Has to be a zoo. North of the border. What else could Lucius mean but Detroit?"

"It's not my father's handwriting, and it's definitely not something Lucius would write. He has a contempt for rhymes. He says it's like putting the imagination in prison. Unless it's an Irish poet, then he tolerates it."

"This"—he picked up the elephant and the note—"has Lucius written all over it. The bits of treasure, the possibility there's a fifth man, the scavenger hunt aspect to keep it entertaining. It's just enough to whet your appetite and suck you in. You know you're being conned, but he makes it impossible to walk away."

"I don't think I'm being conned," she reminded him.

"It would be helpful if you kept an open mind." Not to mention losing the attitude. "We know Lucius left the other conspirators for three days; we know the loot wasn't at the hideout where they were killed and he was arrested. The assumption has always been that Lucius took the loot and hid it somewhere. You want me to prove I'm right? I say we follow the breadcrumbs and see where they lead us. If we don't find the main cache in three days we go see your father again."

"But what is he getting out of it? What's the point of all this?"

Trip shrugged. "He strikes me as a man with a sense of humor."

"He has plans for the loot. We aren't going to find the big payday this way."

"Maybe not, but we'll recover some of the stolen goods."

"And your job is to recover everything."

"We can call him if it will make you feel better. Maybe he'll tell you what this is about."

"Not over the phone." Norah smiled. "But he'd get a kick out of it, and I hear laughter is the best medicine."

chapter 15

THE SKY WAS A PUFFY MASS OF CLOUDS WHEN they left the motel room the next morning, the air was so crisp it nearly crackled, and the Harley was gone. What surprised Norah the most was that she didn't even blink, just looked at the silver car in the space where the Harley had been parked and thought, Oh good, heat. Not being curled around Trip was a plus, too, considering the state of their relationship, which was, not to put too fine a point on it, nonexistent, except where the robbery was concerned. Which was exactly as it should be, she reminded herself, and let it go . . . Okay, what she actually did was suppress it, but it amounted to the same thing with the caveat that there'd be a reckoning later. But Trip would be gone by then, so he wouldn't have to pay for her lack of perspective, and she'd be able to handle it without him around to pity her. Pity would make it so much worse.

When they got to the car, she held her hand out for the keys. Trip gave them to her without resistance, which was kind of disappointing since she'd had all her arguments lined up, and now she wouldn't get to demonstrate how firmly grounded she was in the case, and that she hadn't spent a miserable night pretending to sleep while she was really concentrating on staying on her side of the bed so she didn't inadvertently brush his wound and cause him more pain.

"You'd think the FBI could do better," she said as she climbed into the driver's seat of the late model silver sedan. "I'm going to have to memorize the license plate if we park it anywhere more crowded than this."

"Not being noticed is the point here," Trip said from the passenger seat, "and anyway, it's what's under the hood that counts."

She nodded, ejecting the image of those heart-studded boxers from her brain, then giving her nerve endings a stern talking-to. *Those boxers are a slippery slope*, she told them, one that would start with mind-blowing pleasure and end up dropping her right into the emotional muddle she'd just worked her way out of. Trip was not part of the ADVENTURE anymore, at least not in that way.

She started up the sedan and directed it out of the parking space at the back of the motel lot toward the road at the front, the driveway taking her past the office. The manager came racing out, a small, round woman in her fifties, who might have been moderately pretty without the panic on her face.

Norah jammed on the brakes, Trip rolled down the passenger window, and the manager hurried around to his side of the car.

"How was your stay?" she said, definitely not what

they'd been expecting. Arson, violence, even potential murder, but a status report with that expression?

Trip put his hand over the manager's, and looked deep into her eyes. "Talk to Kizi lately?" he asked her, and when her mouth dropped open, he turned to Norah. "Go," he said, which was all the impetus she needed. She pulled up to the road, and he said, "Right," before she could even look both ways or remark that there was a lot of traffic for such a small town.

Right took her in the opposite direction from most of the traffic, at first, anyway, since at least four vehicles made U-turns and came after them. Norah stomped on the gas pedal, the car leapt ahead, the engine roaring. "You weren't kidding," she said, easing off.

"We're up against people who know this area like the back of their hand," he said, apparently a bad news first kind of guy. "We're going to need all the speed we can get, but at least the roads are two-lane. That'll work in our favor."

"You think Kizi called the manager."

"I think somebody instilled the fear of whatever gods the Ottawa pray to in her."

"Some sort of nature religion, maybe an Earth Mother type of belief system."

"Yeah, that's the important thing here."

"I'm trying to be calm," she snapped at him.

"Calm is good," Trip said, no doubt flashing back to her climbing out of the driver's seat last time they were in a fix like this, which had been bad enough in her Escape but would be impossible in the sedan. Not to mention his wounded leg would present a problem. "We weren't on the news last night," he continued, keeping his voice to a quiet, even level.

"You're not talking to a mental patient."

"Are you sure?"

"I've spent the last few days with you," Norah shot back, which, as far as she was concerned, explained her slipping hold on sanity. "Can we get back to the confirmed lunatics?"

"Those guys knew they winged me, and we weren't going far," he said, sounding disgruntled now. "They probably reached out to everyone they know, and it spread from there."

"Seven degrees of separation?"

"Let's hope not. That would mean Hollie and those guys who followed us in Chicago know where we are."

It wasn't a stretch to think Hollie might know, considering she was probably still in the state. "Maybe I should worry about these guys first," she said, watching them in the rearview mirror, a caravan of trucks, cars, and SUVs, none of them new, all of them wobbling in and out of the line, jockeying for position. Then most of them peeled off, leaving three vehicles behind the sedan.

"Want some more bad news?" she said to Trip. "They seem to be communicating with each other."

"There's a shocker." He twisted around and looked out the back window. "They're going for a squeeze maneuver. One of them will stay behind us, one of them will get in front, and the third will come up alongside us in the other lane and force us off the road."

"I wouldn't enjoy that."

"Definitely not since I doubt they'd be as focused on me this time."

"You think they'll hold a grudge?"

"They seem like the type."

"What if I keep them from getting in front of me?"

"That's the defensive way to handle this situation."

"And defensive isn't going to be enough," Norah

said, not that the grimness in his voice was her first clue. Hearing the part about the grudge had pretty much put her on the offensive.

"We'll have to take them out, then get to the highway as fast as possible," Trip said. "Before somebody else finds us."

"Do you know where the highway is?"

"GPS," he said, pulling out his phone. "Not that we can miss I-75 since it runs right down the middle of the state. But it would be nice to come across it on a road where there's a ramp. Once we're on the highway they'll have no way of knowing where we are."

"So, violence." She glanced over at him. "Got any suggestions?"

"Don't worry about denting the car."

She snorted softly, smiling despite herself. "Something more specific might be helpful."

"Just keep driving, it'll come to you."

Great. For days he's been dictating to me. Now, when I want him to tell me what to do he clams up. And asking again would make her look needy and pathetic, not to mention there was her pride, which he'd stirred up by making sure she knew he was there for the FBI, but not for her and her father. So, what the hell, if he was willing to put his fate in her hands, then damn the torpedoes, full speed ahead.

They'd left the town behind, the road curving through farmland and woods. The vehicle immediately behind her, a pickup truck that sounded like a ninety-year-old chain smoker with pneumonia, nosed out into the next lane. She swerved, keeping the sedan in front of the truck, one eye on the rearview mirror, the other on the tight curve coming up ahead. The truck was in and out of the oncoming traffic lane, and the driver was getting good and angry.

They hit the curve, both vehicles slowing drastically. Norah kept to the right lane, the guy in the truck taking it as an opportunity to get around her. And oncoming traffic wasn't cooperating, which was to say there wasn't any. Damn, Norah thought, punching it as they came out of the turn, then shrieking when her windshield filled with horse and buggy, equipped with one of those triangular warning signs.

"Amish," Trip yelled, bracing himself in the passenger seat because the road was bounded by deep ditches, with marshland on one side and heavy forest on the other. The buggy didn't have anywhere to go, and neither did she, coming up fast on the buggy. And then it got worse.

A semi appeared down the road. Somebody wasn't going to be happy in a minute. Norah decided it wouldn't be her. She floored it, the sedan rocketing forward, giving her just enough room to slip in front of the pickup, the car giving a little shimmy when their bumpers brushed.

The pickup driver found himself next to the buggy, staring at the word MACK in capital letters and made the only maneuver he could, cranking the wheel hard to the left and going airborne into the swamp. Norah just caught the splash before she buzzed around the buggy and whipped back into the right lane.

"One down," she said to Trip.

"That was luck."

"What have you got against luck?"

"Nothing, but there are two more guys back there who are already on the phone getting reinforcements. And after your little demonstration, there'll be more than three of them. Picking them off one at a time isn't going to cut it."

So what do you suggest? She didn't waste time asking the question, though. The other two vehicles, a low-riding car and an SUV, were around the buggy and coming up behind her. And she could only think of one maneuver that might work. It might kill them, too, but it was all she had.

She poured on the gas, the sedan's engine roaring as they sped down the long straightaway in front of them, with another sharp curve ahead. She hit the edge of the curve with a quarter or third of a mile between the sedan and the other two vehicles, stopping so fast the sedan shuddered as the tires lost traction, the back end sliding and the tires smoking as she forced the car into a tight U-turn.

"What are you doing?" Trip said, one hand on the dash, eyes on the two vehicles barreling down on them.

"You wanted a master stroke," she said, accelerating to a modest speed and keeping the car dead center on the white line.

"Back off, Norah, this is a suicide mission."

"They don't want us dead, remember?"

"Unless it's us or them."

Norah kept going, filled with a recklessness that was part adventure and more hurt than she cared to admit—the pain she'd suppressed last night—figuring she'd deal with it later. *Later*, apparently, was now, and while she had no intention of dying, or even being hurt, it gave her a bit of a kick to give Trip some of his own medicine. Payback? Sure, and it was absolutely insane. But it was a lot of fun, too.

She pressed harder on the gas pedal, aiming straight for the last two chase vehicles, accelerating as they raced toward each other, no hesitation, no second-guessing, her hands firm on the wheel. When she was close enough to see their faces through their windshields, when Trip shouted, "Noraaaaaah," and the other drivers were yelling, too, she swerved sharply toward the SUV, which was slightly ahead.

The SUV driver took evasive action out of pure reflex, cutting the wheel sharply to the left, which sent him hurtling over the ditch and into the woods beyond. Norah was already cutting the wheel hard toward the car, that driver going airborne like the first, his yell trailing off behind him like he'd fallen over a cliff instead of making a short trip into a shallow marsh.

Norah slammed on the brakes, turned around, and drove back the way they'd come, slowly, checking both vehicles as she passed by them.

"They could have guns," Trip said, his voice an octave higher than usual.

"They weren't even out of their vehicles yet, and I wanted to make sure they were okay."

"What the hell were you thinking?"

Norah shrugged and kept driving, keeping the car to the speed limit. "It always works on TV."

"TV? *TV*? Jesus Norah, you almost killed us with a TV stunt?"

"I didn't almost kill us," she shot back, more than a little irritated. Being on familiar ground again, at least intellectually, helped her keep her cool. "I challenged drivers who were probably men and likely bullies. Aggression in bullies is used to cover up a lack of self-esteem, often with a host of underlying fears and phobias."

"Bullies don't always back down when you confront them."

"That's true, but the confrontation took them out of their behavioral comfort zone, and when I introduced unexpectedness—I swerved, in other words—they were confused and frightened enough to flinch."

"And if one of them had been a psycho with a death wish?"

She shook her head. "Those guys are usually loners."

Trip sat back, clearly steaming. "You're getting a kick out of this, aren't you?"

"Absolutely."

"A thousand things could have gone wrong."

"And nothing did, so why are you tearing me apart?" She already knew the answer—she'd taken his role in the operation and left him to sit back and be rescued.

Trip huffed out a breath and flopped back in his seat, proving her point. He didn't sulk for long. "I didn't think the second guy was going to take the bait," he said, glancing over at her with a grudging little smile that warmed as he talked. "He stuck with you for a second."

Long enough for her to start thinking of alternatives, but what she said was, "I never doubted he'd lose," which curiously enough was the absolute truth.

"And that's why he did," Trip said. "Half of any success is believing you can pull it off."

Norah looked over at him. "You know, you're a pretty good natural psychoanalyst."

Trip scowled at her. "There's no reason to get insulting."

chapter
16

THE DETROIT ZOO ACTUALLY OCCUPIED A COR-
ner of Royal Oak, a bit to the west of the city and right
on the service drive for I-696. And just in case the road
signs, and the long brick wall with DETROIT ZOO in big
white letters didn't announce their arrival, a water
tower decorated with animal silhouettes and blazoned
with the name of the place loomed at the entrance.

The zoo was open til five, which gave them a couple of hours, but Trip wasn't at full speed and neither,
frankly, was Norah. All she could think about was
sleep—a halfway decent meal and then sleep, ten solid
hours if she could get it.

Trip directed her to an honest-to-god hotel with room
service and everything, and since she was so recognizable, he made all the arrangements. She kissed her good
night's sleep good-bye before she walked into the room
and saw there was only one bed.

"Wishful thinking?" she said, dropping her small overnight bag on the desk.

"A man by himself doesn't ask for a room with two beds."

"Trust me, they've seen weirder things here."

"Best not to draw attention if we don't have to."

Norah picked up her bag. "I'm getting my own room."

"We've been through this already," Trip said, sounding exhausted.

"I don't think the guys who invaded my house and chased us out of Chicago are going to stumble across us here."

"Maybe not, but people who don't have our best interest in mind keep finding us, and I'm in no shape to kick down doors if you need to be saved."

"Then I won't scream for help."

He smiled slightly. "You're not really a screamer anyway."

Norah rolled her eyes. "I'm taking a shower, and checking out the tub. Maybe it's big enough to sleep in."

Trip just grinned at her, so she took a long, hot shower, washing her clothes out when she was done. She would have stayed in the bathroom for the rest of the night, but her empty stomach was talking louder than the muddle of what she felt about Trip. So she cinched the belt of the hotel robe tight and opened the door, her courage faltering a little when she saw Trip's eyes darken as he realized she wasn't wearing anything under that single thin layer of terrycloth. Not exactly a scenario designed to help her self-control, but she kept her gaze off him, and that did the trick. Until he spoke.

"I ordered dinner," he said in a nighttime deejay kind of voice that made her want to laugh, or at least giggle hysterically.

"Thanks," she said instead, dropping into the chair

at the desk and taking out some notes she'd brought along in the hope she'd have time to work on her book.

"Okay, then," Trip said, "I'm going to take a shower before it comes."

"Sure," Norah said, then streaked to her feet but only making it halfway across the room before Trip came back out of the bathroom holding a scrap of black lace—not a thong, but not far from it even if it did cover the top half of her butt cheeks.

"The shirt is bad enough," he said, "but these?"

"It was a gift store, in case you didn't get that from the boxers and the *I'm Too Sexy* T-shirt, which was the only one they had in medium. And apparently the place was frequented by strippers, because that lace is scratchy, and after wearing those things for a couple of hours stripping wasn't completely out of the question. I was seriously considering going commando—"

Trip sounded like he was strangling.

Norah realized she was rambling, and her verbal territory was only making matters worse. She eased over and took the panties from him, stuffing them in the pocket of her robe.

He just stood there, staring down at her.

"Shower," she said, "cold."

"There's not enough cold water in the state, and this is the Great Lake State, so that's saying something."

She turned him around and shoved him into the bathroom, closing the door behind him and not saying a word, especially since her response would not run to the verbal. Her response would be to tear the door open and join him in the shower because he was right, there wasn't enough cold water in the world to counter the heat moving through her. He certainly wasn't helping matters, looking at her like that. How much did she think she could take? She wondered, getting angry, which was hardly helpful. Anger was a hot emotion, and it could turn so easily . . .

She spun away from the bathroom door before she talked herself into trouble. When Trip came out, she was back at the desk with her notes, the television on low, pretending to work. She looked up, though, she couldn't help herself, catching Trip's gaze in the mirror. He didn't say anything, but there was so much tension in the room she could have knit a sweater out of it, so much untapped angst that when someone knocked on the door she jumped.

"Room service," Trip said, and even though she'd passed the point where she could imagine putting anything in her stomach, at least it provided a distraction. And then the distraction took on epic proportions.

"Hollie," she muttered when Trip opened the door, and she saw the tabloid wannabe standing in the hallway, "nauseating in an entirely different manner."

"Isn't this cozy?" Hollie smirked, surveying the room, one bed, the two of them in hotel robes, and coming to the obvious conclusion.

Norah bit back a denial. She'd only be playing Hollie's game. "How did you find us?"

"Puh-leeze, what kind of investigative reporter would I be if I couldn't eavesdrop on a few backwoods treasure hunters?"

"Now you're an investigative reporter? I thought you were making a documentary."

"That was before you ditched me. As you can see, it was just a waste of time."

"You're right," Trip said, in an about-face that left Norah and Hollie gaping at him. "There's no point in fighting the inevitable. You've got a room in the hotel, right?"

"Yes," Hollie said.

"How about we let you know when we're taking off in the morning. You can tag along."

"I can tag along? Me?"

"Sure," Trip said, "Lurch, too."

"Who's Lurch?"

"That homeless guy who carries your camera around. You can even let him turn it on tomorrow."

Hollie narrowed her eyes at him, then looked at Norah. Norah did a hands up, no idea what he was up to. "What's the catch?"

"No catch," Trip assured her, "just be ready to go first thing in the morning."

"You'll forgive me if I have Loomis—Lurch," she said when he looked confused, "sleep outside your door."

"I won't take offense if he does."

"Okay, see you in the morning."

Norah waited until the door closed. "What was that all about?"

"Just having a little fun."

"Then you're not letting Hollie follow us tomorrow."

"I thought about it."

She crossed her arms, waiting for an explanation.

"Don't you want to know why she's so fanatical about this?" Trip said.

"Why didn't you just ask her? I mean, she would have lied, but—"

"She would have known we were looking at her as more than an irritant, and if she has something to hide she'll be a lot more vigilant. And don't give me that crap about being a closet psychologist. I happen to have a lot of experience with the criminal mind. It comes with the profession."

"Sure, whatever you say." There was another knock. "That's probably room service," she said, "maybe you'd like to ask Hollie to join us for dinner."

"What the hell, there's another robe in there."

Trip went to the door and let in the waiter, and while he was tipping the man Norah looked under the covers. "Oysters, strawberries, chocolate cake. You've got to be kidding." She picked up the phone, but he went back to the door and pulled in another room service cart.

"So what was the point of that, and I don't mean the obvious one."

"Just pointing out the elephant in the room."

"You must be talking about your ego."

"You know what I'm talking about."

Norah held her ground, but her appetite was gone. "I just don't think we should be sleeping together."

"After I made it clear that my goal is the loot, you mean. Would you rather I lie to you?"

"No."

"And you aren't the type of woman who lies to herself."

"No, but—"

"And then there's this." He backed her against the wall and kissed her. She was lost the second his lips touched hers. There was only Trip, pushing her robe open, then moving into her, pressing her against the wall, his hands hot on her skin everywhere, making her forget her reservations, grateful she was a means to an end. Use me, she thought, moaning a little and moving against his hands, not looking forward to the day when he'd leave but deciding to make the most of the time between now and then. Mostly now, she amended, grabbing the wrist attached to the hand wandering in the vicinity of her waist and tugging upward, Trip obliging her by cupping her breast and rubbing his thumb over the nipple, and when his mouth replaced his hand, she arched, banging her head on the wall and not caring because it felt so good, the way pleasure speared down and exploded in her belly.

Trip straightened, tugging on her arms, but her knees
had gone weak and the rest of her just wanted his mouth
and his hands on her again, wanted him inside her—

"Bed," he strangled out.

"Floor," she said, trying to pull him down.

"Too hard," he said, and she laughed. "That's my
point."

"The floor, too, and I'm not up to carrying you, so—"

"Right, bullet wound," she said, suddenly able to walk,
hell, she would have run if it had been more than a few
feet, shoving Trip down on the bed when they got there,
and straddling him.

"Hold that thought," he said, shoving her off and hobbling into the bathroom, reappearing with his jeans in
one hand, fumbling out the wallet with the other and
holding up the little foil packet he took out of it like a
trophy.

Norah definitely felt like cheering when he flopped
down on his back and pulled her astride him again. He put
his clever mouth on her breast, slipped his fingers down
her stomach, then inside her, the lovely haze of pleasure
narrowing, building as his hand disappeared so she could
take him in, a long, slow slide intended to drive him
crazy, but nearly pushing her over the edge, too.

His hands moved to her hips, but she pulled them
away, twining her fingers with his, keeping control. She
set a pace that was slow and delicious, shuddering as
he moved with her, loving the way his body felt under
her hands and mouth, all that strength surging up as
she pressed down and they both came apart, her heart
pounding as she collapsed beside him, every nerve ending humming with pleasure and filled with so much
peace she never wanted to move again.

And then her stomach growled.

"I don't think you should have any oysters or chocolate," Trip said, sounding worn-out but in a good way. "I'm pretty sure I couldn't handle you on aphrodisiacs."

"There's really no such thing, anyway. It's all in the mind."

"Then I'm doing something wrong."

Norah laughed a little. "Trust me, you did everything right."

"Actually, you did everything right."

"It was definitely a team effort."

"*Team*. There's a word I haven't heard from you in a while."

It was a word she'd never heard from him. He'd trotted out the concept before, but only when it suited his agenda and always with the firm understanding that he would lead and she was expected to follow.

Norah sighed, rolling onto her side, away from him. She felt Trip curl around her, and it made her eyes well up because she knew it wasn't real.

"I shouldn't have said that."

"You're trying not to lie to me, remember?" And she was trying not to lie to herself, either.

"Norah?"

She rolled back over, went into his arms, letting her actions speak for her, now and in the future. They'd be a team, and he'd be the leader. She'd enjoy the fringe benefits, too, with no expectations and no regrets. But she'd take a lesson from him and keep her own goals firmly in mind.

chapter 17

"WOW, THAT'S TOO BAD," TRIP SAID, SHAKING his head over the sad state of Hollie's tires. They were standing in the hotel parking lot, Hollie, Lurch, Norah, and himself, getting ready to hit the road, except Hollie's BMW wasn't roadworthy.

"Don't stand there acting all innocent," Hollie snapped at him. "I know you did it."

"I'm wounded."

"Ahhhh." Hollie whipped around, stomped to the edge of the lot and kicked the bushes planted there. For a full minute. "Fine," she said when she'd stomped back, looking like an outraged Barbie doll, "go off to the zoo without me. Yeah," she smirked, "I know where you're going, and I'll be right behind you."

"Don't miss the penguins," Trip said, "I hear it's a real kick to watch those little guys swim around in circles and never get anywhere."

Lurch actually cracked a smile.

"And where the hell were you?" Hollie yelled at him.

"Sleeping right outside our door, exactly where you left him," Trip said. "You know, Hollie, I don't think you're paying him enough to sleep on the floor. You're lucky nobody called hotel security and had him thrown in jail."

Hollie pulled out her phone, glaring at Trip while she dialed information and asked for the nearest rental car place.

"This is fun and everything," Norah said to Trip, "but, you know, places to go."

"Right. I'm driving."

Norah climbed into the passenger seat without argument. "If you can handle vandalism," she said, "I guess you're well enough to get behind the wheel. Not to mention I'd like to avoid a repeat of yesterday."

"Not up for another episode of vehicular assault?"

"I'm not up for any kind of assault."

"Too bad, I had plans for tonight," Trip said, getting a kick out of the way she blushed.

"What I'd like to know is how you pulled that off," Norah said, tipping her head toward Hollie and her flat tires.

Trip started up the sedan. "You slept like a rock last night."

"Apparently so did Lurch."

"That's what I paid him for."

Norah burst out laughing, looking more relaxed than he'd ever seen her. "If I didn't think his mercenary heart might come in handy, I'd love to tell Hollie."

"She'd probably ask for a cut."

Trip pulled into the Detroit Zoo entrance, parking in the structure because the lot that fronted the street was too exposed, and there weren't enough vehicles to hide their sedan.

As they crossed the drive from the structure to the entrance, Trip reached over and folded her hand into his.

She tensed, her gaze zipping to his face.

"We're not wearing wedding rings," he said. "It should look like we're dating, and people who are dating hold hands."

"Marital status has no bearing on hand holding. It's the state of the relationship that matters, the closeness and personality of the participants—if they're comfortable with their partner and with public displays of affection, that sort of thing."

"Oh. Are you sure?"

Norah took one look at the grin on his face and smiled a little herself. "Want to see my diploma?"

"No, but I'd like to read your book. Starting with chapter four."

Norah winced slightly. Her hand flexed in his, but she didn't let go. It was all for show anyway, so chapter four and holding hands meant nothing, right? "Why would anyone care if we're dating or married?"

"Because if we're not married and we're not dating, what are we doing here together?"

"Maybe we're scientists."

Trip shook his head. "Scientists would have made an appointment to study or observe or whatever scientific thing they were here to do."

"I still don't get why it matters."

"People notice stuff like that, not always consciously, but they notice."

"And you don't want to be noticed."

"Do you?"

"Not if I'm doing something illegal."

"Don't think of it as illegal, think of it as reclaiming stolen property."

"I'm pretty sure the officials and the police would consider it illegal—that's if they didn't throw me in jail until I tell them where the rest of the loot is."

Trip grinned. "You didn't use to be so cynical."

"And then I met you." But Norah was smiling, too. Better yet, she'd relaxed again—at least her hand wasn't clamped around his hard enough to cut off circulation any more. "We have a date with an elephant," she said, taking the map the cashier had given them. She stopped inside the entrance, spreading the map on top of a handy garbage receptacle.

Trip looked over her shoulder, both of them searching for the elephant enclosure. Both of them came up empty.

"No elephants," Norah said. "Where did the elephants go?"

"Let me check the Internet," Trip said, taking out his phone.

Norah walked over to the gift shop and went inside. She was back out within two minutes, flipping through a thin booklet. "It says in here they determined that the amenities and the climate here were not good for pachyderms," she said, hurrying toward a long pavilion off to her left. "The elephants were sent to California where the weather is always warm and they have an actual herd."

"Hooray for the elephants," Trip said, following her into a switchback line-up system that was completely empty.

Norah walked the lines, back and forth. Trip hopped the low barriers and met her at the front just as an old-fashioned steam engine pulling a line of passenger cars was arriving.

"That's the difference between you and me," she said, sliding into the closest car with bench seats and open sides. "Shortcuts."

Trip hopped in after her. "We both arrive at the same destination. I just get there faster."

"Ever heard the saying, 'It's not the destination, it's the journey'?" she said—a little self-righteously, in his opinion.

"That's practically an FBI motto. This operation happens to be a race, but a lot of ops are undercover, and an agent who doesn't pay attention to where he is and what he's doing every minute won't make it to the destination. It's the so-called normal people who miss out on the important things because they're focused on getting a bigger house or that fat promotion with the corner office."

"Or tenure?"

Trip didn't say anything, the train's whistle covering his lack of inspiration, because his first impulse was to deny it, but a denial would ring false, and Norah would notice false.

"Everyday people have to pay mortgages and buy groceries and put their kids through college," she said as the train shuddered out of the station, picking up speed until it was moving at a snail's pace, suitable for toddlers and grandparents. "They don't have the luxury of thinking only of themselves."

Trip found himself speechless again, no train whistle to cover it this time, which was all right since this time he was reviewing his own life and coming up lacking.

"I'm sorry," Norah said. "We should be focusing on the clue."

And he shouldn't need her to remind him of that. "So the elephants have gone to Disneyland," he said, "what about their enclosure? What happened there?"

"A pair of white rhinos have taken up residence. The girl in the gift shop says they're very happy there."

Trip crossed his arms, giving her a half smile, impressed. "Did you get their names, too?"

"Tamba and Jasiri, but I don't think calling them by name is going to make them any friendlier."

"The elephants wouldn't have been a picnic, either."

"So how are we going to get in?" Norah wanted to know.

"We'll figure it out when we get there."

The train took its sweet time, but it was faster than walking, especially with a bullet wound that was admittedly minor but still hurt like hell with every step he took. The sky was a uniform, gunmetal gray, the air warmer than it had been, but Trip slung an arm around Norah's shoulder, liking the way she settled against him. The train dropped them at the far northwest corner of the zoo, only a deserted café between the station and the enclosure now occupied by the rhinos.

"Now what?" Norah said when they were standing at the wall in front of the deep concrete moat where the rhinos lived. They were nowhere to be seen, probably inside the soaring concrete bunker that had once housed the elephants. "The moat and pool were altered in the makeover, but the brochure doesn't say anything about the building."

"If they'd found something during the renovation, it would have been in the papers, which means it would be on the Internet."

"It stands to reason there's nothing hidden inside the enclosure."

"I agree, not only because it would be idiotic to get inside a cage with elephants, but because nothing about this has been difficult."

"So we're looking for someplace well hidden but not inaccessible."

Trip worked his way around the outside enclosure until he came upon the public entrance. Inside was a fairly large room with lighted panels around the outside, referencing various aspects of rhino zoology, from natural habitat to the preservation efforts of places like the Detroit Zoo. The other side of the room was lined with glass panels that overlooked the rhinos' indoor enclosure, where Tamba and Jasiri grazed on a pile of greenery being tossed to them by a man wearing a zoo uniform and a bored expression.

"Feeding time," Trip said.

"We'll have to wait," Norah said.

"Can't. Hollie knows we're here, and we didn't slow her down for long. She won't have any trouble finding us here, either. All she'll have to do is ask around."

"So we're on a deadline. What do you suggest?"

At the end of the room was a door, labeled off-limits to any but zoo staff. Not to mention it was locked. Trip lifted the cover of a small box at the right side of the door. "Keypad, and the door's probably equipped with a silent alarm. We'll have to charm ourselves in, the same way Puff must have done."

"*If* he hid the clue."

Trip beat a fist on the door. The guy on rhino feeding duty looked up, frowned, and shook his head. Trip banged some more. Tamba and Jasiri didn't appreciate it. Neither did their caretaker.

"Shit," Trip said, "he's going for his radio."

"Let me." Norah stepped up to the glass and drew a big question mark on it with her finger, then put her hands together like she was praying, an innocent expression on her face.

The caretaker hesitated, then put down his rake and came to the door, opening it enough so they could see that the name patch on his shirt read BOSCO, but not so wide that he couldn't slam it shut in a split second.

"What can I do for you?" he asked, his eyes on Norah.

Trip nudged her forward.

She stepped back. "I, uh, was wondering what their names are?"

He scowled at her for a second, said, "Read the walls, lady," then slammed the door shut.

Norah rounded on Trip. "What was that?"

"You got him to come to the door. I assumed you had a plan."

"My plan was getting him to open the door. You were supposed to do the rest."

"He was ogling you. I figured you'd have better luck getting us in. You know all the tricks, or did you make them up for that book you wrote?"

"Of course not. Those interactions are fact."

"And you grew up with one of the greatest con men of all time. Some of it had to have rubbed off on you."

That, Norah thought, was exactly the problem. She loved her father, but she didn't want to be like him. She'd seen the hurt he'd caused her mother, and while she would hardly inflict a lifetime of pain on the man inside the rhino building by coercing him into letting them inside, that sort of behavior led to a slope she didn't want to slip onto.

"C'mon," Trip wheedled, "where's the girl who ran three guys off the road yesterday? What happened to your sense of adventure?"

"Conning me into conning him? Weak, Jones." But she squared her shoulders and rose to the challenge. Slapping Trip across the face was just gravy.

"Hey," he shouted, loud enough to carry through

the door, even if Norah hadn't made sure they were in front of the glass.

She reared back again, Trip catching her by the wrist just as the door flew open.

"Ouch," she whimpered, twisting to make it look like he was applying pressure. "You're hurting me."

He let her go, and she stumbled back, right into Bosco. Bosco caught her, then swept her behind him, shifting the rake he held and stepping forward. Trip put his hands up to ward Bosco off, stepping back. He turned on his heel and started to walk away, looking over his shoulder for a long moment. The threat she saw there probably wasn't all for show, but either way it did the trick.

"Thank you," she said to Bosco, not having to work too hard to make her voice breathy because it had just sunk in that she'd slapped Trip across the face. Hard. At the time it had seemed like a good idea. Now it felt more like suicide. It probably would be if they left without something to show for all their trouble.

"Is there someone I can call for you?" Bosco wanted to know.

"No. If I could just sit down for a minute." She looked around. "There are no seats out here," she said, which she'd already known.

"I'm not supposed to," Bosco said. "There's a café just up the way." And he started to lead her that way.

Her legs gave out, and she leaned into Bosco, who staggered back a step or two. "Jeez, lady," he said, "at least make an effort. You weigh a ton. If you pass out there's no way I'm picking you up."

So much for chivalry, Norah thought, wondering where the hell Trip was as she stumbled toward the door, getting there just as Bosco slumped against her, nearly dragging her to the floor. Then his weight disappeared and Trip was there, easing Bosco down.

"What took you so long?"

"I was enjoying the show, Meryl," Trip said. "Or maybe I should call you Powderpuff. You're definitely a chip off the old con man."

"Great, thanks. You didn't hurt Bosco, did you?"

"You slapped me across the face," Trip reminded her. "You're not worried about me."

"You signed up for this, he didn't. And it was your idea to con him."

"Feeling guilty?"

"Maybe a little," she said, which perked her right up. Her father never felt guilty. He always said it was a waste of—

"Guilt's a waste of time," Trip said, dragging Bosco through the employee door and propping him up against the wall.

Norah shook off the flashback to her childhood, this time with Trip's face in place of her father's as he pontificated on his every-man-for-himself philosophy of life. Trip had a moral core her father would not only have found amusing but useful. Sure, Trip tended to compromise his ethics, but he was doing it for what he saw as a greater purpose. And he was usually dealing with criminals—not that that made it all right, but for a lot of people, including Trip, conning a criminal was justifiable behavior.

"Norah," Trip called out, "you going to help me look?"

"What if someone comes along?" she said, taking the opposite side of the small area where the zoo personnel cared for the rhinos. "Shouldn't one of us keep watch?"

"Tourists will think we work here. There shouldn't

be any other zoo employees along, unless one of them
tries to call our buddy, here, and doesn't get an answer."

"You could fake it."

"That only works in the movies. More likely the person on the other end will ask a question I can't answer,
and then this whole place will be on red alert. We're only
getting one shot at this, and we both need to search."

She agreed, not that it did them much good. The area
wasn't much more than a staging place for food and
bedding material. There weren't many hiding places, at
least not ones that would have gone unnoticed by the
zoo employees for fifteen years.

"Now what?" Norah said when they came up empty.

They both looked around, Trip's face eventually turning up to the ceiling, high above their heads.

"There's no place to hide anything up there."

"Not inside."

Norah followed him out the employee door and the
public door, where he stopped, hands on his hips, staring at the roof.

"You think it's on top? In the rain and snow and
birds' nests? For fifteen years?"

"There has to be an access ladder," was Trip's response, and he started off to look for one.

The outside enclosure was surrounded by hulking
formations made of concrete molded to look like rock.
Those escarpments curved around the building on one
side. Norah followed Trip to the point where the fake
rock and concrete bunker met, and there, tucked in a
narrow niche, was an iron ladder. Trip had already
climbed about a third of the way up.

Norah took a deep breath and put her foot on the
lowest rung. She was no fan of heights, but she followed him, staying on the ladder with just her head and
shoulders over the rooftop. And it was a big rooftop,

covered with rocks and dirt and decades of bird droppings.

Trip walked a pattern, back and forth, kicking through the debris, every once in a while bending to pick something up to give it a closer study. "Eureka," he said the third time, returning to Norah's perch to show her a package, bigger and heavier than the one they'd discovered at the lighthouse, wrapped in heavy plastic and sealed with duct tape.

She held out her hand, but he wiped it off and stuffed it into his own pocket. "We have company," he said, barely waiting for her to start back down the ladder before he climbed on.

"Hollie?" she asked him, scrambling down as fast as she could.

"She isn't alone, either," he said by way of confirmation. "There are a couple of other guys following her. Either our friends from up north, or the goons from Chicago."

And either way it was bad news for them.

chapter
18

"WHY DIDN'T WE JUST STAY UP THERE?" NORAH
asked when they got to the bottom of the ladder.

"Because they'd find us. Even down here we don't
have anywhere to go." The rhino building backed up to
the very edge of the zoo property. Only one pathway
led to the door. Looking inside was a no-brainer, but if
they were thorough they'd find the ladder as well. And
then they'd be trapped on a building tall enough to
house elephants with nowhere to run and no way down
except gravity. "They look like the kind of guys who
know what they're doing."

"Oh. How many are there?"

"Enough," Trip said, because there were three including Lurch and excluding Hollie, and with a bad leg
he didn't figure he could take on any more than that. In
fact, he was counting on Lurch doing his usual dull-as-

a-post routine and hanging back until the other two did Hollie's dirty work.

"Is there anything I can do?"

He handed her the clue, which was larger and heavier than the last one and would only slow him down. "Hide this somewhere."

She looked at it for a second, then lifted her shirt and stuffed it a couple inches down her jeans, tucking her shirt overtop of it. "What else?"

"You get to deal with Hollie if it becomes necessary."

"Really?" Some of the grimness faded from her eyes. She flexed her fingers and rotated her wrists, then curled her hands into fists and held them up. "Ready."

Trip rolled his eyes. "Listen, Rocky, you have the next clue. It's your job to make sure Hollie and her crew don't get their hands on it."

"And the best way of ensuring that is to incapacitate Hollie, right?"

Trip shook his head, latched onto one fist, and pulled her down to the far corner of the building. There was a slight protruding edge, not quite wide enough to hide them but probably ample to give them the advantage of surprise.

Hollie didn't exactly try to camouflage their arrival. Neither did the muscle brigade.

"Where'd she hire those guys?" Norah whispered. "Thugs R Us?"

Trip smiled briefly. "I'll take out the first guy who comes around that corner," he said softly. "You keep Hollie out of my way."

"With pleasure."

His back was to Norah, but he could tell she was smiling, evilly. He probably should have been more concerned; dead bodies were so messy. But he had enough to handle, so Hollie was on her own.

The first goon appeared, Trip stepped out, swept his feet out from under him, and punched him once in the face, turning as the next guy came at him. He tried to step forward, but the first guy grabbed his right ankle, leaving him to hop on his bad leg. The second guy moved in, both of them stopping as a rabid shriek split the silence. They all turned in time to see Norah hurtle herself away from the building and kick the guy on the ground in the side until he let go of Trip's leg.

Trip never took his eyes off the second guy, ducking the punch thrown at him and dropping a couple of shots into his attacker's kidneys, then a stiff uppercut to the jaw as he tucked over the pain in his midsection. He went down, but not out. Trip took a second to look around, racing over to where Lurch was pulling Norah off Hollie, or trying to since both Norah's hands were full of blond hair, and she wasn't letting go.

Trip waded into the melee, planted a hand in Hollie's face, and shoved her onto her butt. Hollie screeched, holding her head, which was minus a blond wig. Trip didn't have time to appreciate the sight, already heading for Norah. But she had the situation well in hand, going completely limp and catching Lurch by surprise. As his grip loosened and she slid down his body, Norah elbowed Lurch in the nuts. Lurch jackknifed and fell over on his side, groaning and retching. Norah ended up on her butt on the ground, next to Hollie and facing her.

Hollie seized the opportunity, getting one hand on Norah's throat. Norah broke her grip, lifted both feet, and kicked out at Hollie, who jerked out of the way, but not far enough. Norah caught her in a glancing blow, sufficient force behind it to have the breath whooshing from Hollie's lungs. She slumped onto her side, wheezing.

Trip turned around to check on the other two attackers, both on their feet but hanging back.

"You didn't tell us we were going to get attacked by a lunatic," one of them said to Hollie.

She waved them off, taking a minute before she said, "I didn't know," still wheezing as she sat up.

One of the guys took the hand she held out and pulled her upright. She snatched her wig from Norah on the way to her feet, plastering it on her head and fussing with it for a second. It looked halfway decent by the time she was done. She had her breath and her color back, too. Her expression was still homicidal. "I only wanted to talk to you," she snapped.

"Right," Norah said, letting Trip pull her to her feet. "What are the steroid twins here for?"

"They were here to discourage you from running away, that's all."

"You should have brought more than two," Norah said.

"I should have brought tranquilizer guns." But Hollie had calmed down a little. "I noticed you limping this morning," she said to Trip. "I thought a little muscle would get you to stick around and talk. And by the way, I'd really like to know how you got hurt. Were you shot? A gunshot would really give my film an edge of excitement."

"It's time to give up the documentary cover story," Trip said. "You've missed too much to be hanging around for that reason."

"I can fill in."

"Why are you really here?" Trip said, his gaze level on hers.

Hollie lowered her eyes. For a second Trip thought she might cave, but she lifted her gaze to his again and said, "I'm here to document the search for the Gold Coast Robbery loot. You found something, didn't you?"

"Lurch isn't even carrying a camera anymore," Norah put in, but Trip figured the only way to get the truth from Hollie—short of beating it out of her—was to wait her out.

"You," he said to Hollie's hirelings, "take off before I call the police."

"You attacked us."

"Just go," Hollie said.

"And you and your cameraman," Trip said, flicking a glance at Lurch, not moaning anymore but still curled into a fetal position on the ground, his hands between his legs. He didn't really know what to say about the pair of them. "I'm at a loss."

"I'm not," Norah said, still spoiling for a fight. "I'm fed up. I didn't want to do your show in the first place, where, I might point out, you were combative from the start." She stopped ranting, her eyes narrowing on Hollie's face. "Why is that? Why did you start off being argumentative?"

Hollie tried to walk away.

Norah stepped in front of her. "You disliked me even before we met? Why?"

"You're being paranoid."

Norah shifted in front of her once more. "C'mon, Hollie, you tried to make a fool of me on national television, and when that didn't work you went on cable news and tried it again."

"I was just doing my job."

"Hah. You put your career on the line, and you love your career. Why would you risk so much unless you love something or someone . . ." Norah sucked in a breath, comprehension dawning. "It has to be Raymond. I knew he was up to something, or someone, more accurately."

"Now you're just being ridiculous."

"Am I really?" Norah pulled out her cell phone. "How about we call him, right now, you and me—"

Hollie reached out and snapped the cell phone closed, which made Norah smirk.

"I'm being ridiculous, huh?"

"All right, all right." Hollie held up her hands in the vain hope it would make Norah shut up. Then she talked some more, which worked much better, not to mention it was pretty enlightening. "I met Raymond at a symposium on the relevance of high school in a culture that demands at least a Bachelor's Degree to get a halfway decent job."

"That sounds like Raymond."

"We had lunch a couple of times, then dinner, then . . . you know, and he was just about to dump you, but then your stupid book became a big deal, and he said it would reflect on the college if your boyfriend broke up with you just as the book hit the bestseller lists."

"But I broke up with him."

"Exactly, but he still wouldn't take our relationship public. Then he had the nerve to suggest I interview you on my show."

"I thought it was Myra's idea."

"Myra," she snorted. She was pacing now, arms crossed, talking to herself more than them. "Myra called, but I would have turned her down if Raymond hadn't made such a big deal out of it. He wanted me to plug the college, too, but the bit about giving you good publicity, that's what put me on edge."

Trip rolled his eyes. "Pushed you over, more like."

Hollie spun around, went toe-to-toe with him, one

sarcastic comment away from homicide. "Laugh it up, chapter four."

"What the hell is in chapter four?"

"Hey, you really did read my book," Norah said to Hollie, not even sparing him a glance, let alone answering his question.

"Guilty." Hollie blew out a breath. "It wasn't very helpful."

"You were filtering it through your negative feelings toward me."

"Chapter four?" Trip prompted.

Both women ignored him, Hollie pulling Norah a few steps away, asking her what she could do to get Raymond to take her seriously.

He didn't hear Norah's response, probably some psychologist mumbo jumbo about how men weren't in touch with their true feelings. She was probably right about that, but he didn't give a damn. The only thing he wanted to get in touch with was her book, and not because everyone they ran across, including complete strangers, thought he was the epitome of chapter four. Because Norah never disagreed with them.

"AND ON A PERSONAL NOTE," NORAH SAID TO Hollie, "the only way I ever found to make Raymond more attentive was when I was halfway out of the relationship. Then he tried to keep me in."

Hollie rolled her eyes. "That was because of your book—Oh, sorry, I didn't mean that the way it sounded."

"I know," Norah said. She'd been talking to Hollie long enough to worm her way around most of the woman's anger, all of which was Raymond Kline–inspired and completely misplaced. "But it wasn't all about my book." She looked over to where Trip was scowling and fidgeting, antsy to be on his way. "Men like to pursue, it's hardwired into their DNA."

"So I should let him pursue? What if he doesn't?"

"Then he's not really interested and you're better off without him."

Hollie's face fell. "It doesn't feel that way."

"I understand, but not everyone we fall in love with is right for us. Women are particularly good at making some man the center of their life and ignoring anything that points to him only sticking around because it's convenient, and the first time someone *better*"—she used air quotes—"comes along he'll be gone. There are signs, Hollie, and one of them is when you have to play games to keep him interested."

"But your book—"

"Says the same thing. There are actions you can take to get a man who's already interested to ask you out, or to make a stale relationship fresh again. And if he has one foot out the door, there are steps you can take to decide if he's moved on or just getting restless.

"But you have to be able to tell the difference, and you have to let him go if that's the right course of action."

"You make it sound so easy."

Norah's eyes shifted to Trip again. "Trust me, I know it's frightening and agonizing to make these kinds of choices when your heart is involved. But holding on to someone who doesn't want to be held is only going to hurt more in the long run."

Hollie crossed her arms, not completely ready to accept that one yet.

"And you really ought to think about why you're following us," Norah added, glancing at Trip again, practically vibrating with impatience now. "Is it about me or the story?"

"Oh, it's about the story," Hollie said, no doubt, no hesitation, "especially now that you've cleared my mind about Raymond."

"Great." Norah blew out a sigh. "Let's keep that between us, okay?"

Trip came to join them. "If the bitch session is over—" They both turned on him, and he clamped his mouth shut over the rest of that crankiness. "Unfortunate turn of phrase," he said. "Can we go now?"

"Are you good?" Norah asked Hollie.

"Let me put it this way," Trip put in, not giving Hollie the floor, "we leave now or I unleash Lurch on you."

Sure enough, Lurch was a few feet behind Trip, sending Norah dirty looks. She dropped her eyes to his crotch and he half hunched.

"Damn it, Norah"—Trip took her by the elbow and pulled her away from Hollie, lowering his voice—"don't you have any sense of urgency?"

"Of course I do. I just don't like to be threatened."

He grinned. "I wouldn't really have set him loose."

"I know." She headed off toward the train station, Lurch and Hollie following along behind.

"Fuck," he said, "the least you could have done with all that jawing is talk her down from stalker mode."

"I tried. She's persistent."

"Great, let's all have tea and finger sandwiches to celebrate."

"More like cosmos at a club opening. Don't you watch *Sex and the City*?"

"No heterosexual male watches *Sex and the City*— at least not with the volume up."

They arrived at the station, and since the wait was about fifteen minutes Norah went back to the cafeteria for takeout and soft drinks. Hollie tagged along.

When the train came they all hopped on board, Norah

and Trip in front, eating pretzels and slurping Coke, Hollie and Lurch a few seats behind them—far enough that Lurch couldn't wrap his hands around Norah's neck. They all trooped through the exit, and crossed the street to the parking structure. Hollie's rental car, a white Ford Focus, was parked right next to Trip's silver sedan. The sedan's tires were flat as pancakes.

"Wow, that's too bad," Hollie said, grinning from ear to ear.

Trip opened the trunk of his car, pulled out the tire iron, and lifted it above the rear window of Hollie's rental.

"Hey," she screeched, yelling, "do something" at Lurch.

Lurch shrugged his shoulders, which technically followed Hollie's instructions, but didn't go very far toward stopping Trip, who held out his free hand and said, "Keys," the tire iron still poised to strike.

"No way."

"Hand them over or you can pony up for a new window on this car, and then I'm going to hotwire it, so you'll be buying a new steering column, too."

Hollie opened her purse, but she pulled out her cell phone. "I'm calling the police."

"Go ahead," Trip said. "Call the local news while you're at it. Let's tell everyone you're following us around while we search for fifty million dollars in stolen goods. I always wanted to be the grand marshal of my own private parade."

Hollie's face turned red, a vein in her forehead throbbing. She glared at Lurch, who did a great job of standing in place and ignoring her. "Fine," she finally huffed out, handing Trip the keys to the Focus.

Trip beeped it open and got in. Norah sent Hollie an apologetic look and got in, too, or tried to. She had to take the package out from under her shirt before she could bend in the middle.

"Don't tell me you're buying that pathetic act she's putting on."

"Not entirely, but I can tell you she knows enough about Raymond for me to believe she was involved with him. And it answers a lot of questions, like why she was angry with me from the start, and why she's following us around now. She thinks she's helping Raymond get the loot for the college."

Trip started the car and pulled away, Hollie giving Lurch an earful. "Did she say that?"

"No, but all he had to do was mention it to her. When he wants something he'll use whatever leverage he can get. Manipulation is the least of what he'd do."

Trip glanced over at her, one eyebrow lifted above a slight smile. "Being passive aggressive, are we?"

"You're not manipulative. You came right out and told me you were after the loot and everything else took a backseat to finding it. And I don't do passive-aggressive. I do the regular kind of aggressive."

"Yeah," Trip said, grinning full-out, "I've noticed."

chapter 19

THE CLUE THEY'D RETRIEVED AT THE DETROIT Zoo had been packaged for the long haul, wrapped in heavy plastic and completely sealed with duct tape, then wrapped and sealed again, packaged to keep the contents safe through Michigan's extremes of weather. It took Norah the better part of fifty miles and Trip's pocketknife to work her way into the package. He wasn't happy about the wait. "You're not very long on patience today," she said to him.

He stopped drumming his fingers on the steering wheel. "Just anxious to know what's in there."

Norah reached in and pulled out a small book, setting it on the dash. Then, remembering the contents of the last packet, she held the bottom of her T-shirt out with one hand and dumped the rest of the contents into it. "Hmmmm."

"That doesn't sound promising."

"Actually it is. The book," she said, retrieving it from the dashboard. The title and name of the author were on the cover, along with a small gold rectangle showing a man sitting on what looked like bales of cotton overlooking a river, with a steamship in the background. "It's a copy of *Life on the Mississippi* by Mark Twain. The copyright is 1883, which probably means it's a first edition.

"There's also an ancient photo of a Conestoga wagon, a small bronze statue of"—she brought it close so she could read the tiny lettering on the base—"Lewis and Clark, and a string of pearls." She rubbed them on her teeth. "Real pearls."

"What does the clue say?"

"No poetry," Norah said, upending the package then peering inside when nothing fell out. "In fact, there's nothing written of any kind, except the book." She sifted through the pages, careful of its age and fragility. "No writing in the margin, no letters circled to spell out code words, no notes stuck between the pages."

"Okay, the gems in the first packet didn't have anything to do with the Detroit Zoo. They were likely there as an incentive to keep on the trail. Which means we can probably ignore the pearls. That leaves the Mississippi River and Mark Twain, a Conestoga wagon, and a bronze of Lewis and Clark."

"St. Louis?" Norah said.

"Why St. Louis?"

"It just sounds right," Norah said. "Mark Twain was born in Hannibal, Missouri, which is on the Mississippi River."

"Maybe we should be going there."

"It doesn't fit with the rest of the items. St. Louis is on the Mississippi, too, and one of its nicknames is the Gateway to the West."

"The wagon. What does the statue of Lewis and Clark mean?"

"I'm not sure, but I would hazard a guess that they went through the area on their way to the Pacific. Give me your cell."

Trip glanced over at her.

"I'm not going to read your contact list or listen to your messages."

He dug it out of his back pocket and handed it over.

Norah stared it for a second, at a loss. "How do you get onto the Internet?"

Trip took it back, punched a couple of buttons, and held it out. Norah typed in "Lewis and Clark + St. Louis," sifting through the first few entries. "They spent the winter of 1803–1804 near St. Louis preparing for their expedition," she said after a couple minutes. "More importantly there's a life-sized statue—oh, never mind, it was dedicated in 2006. But there's a Museum of Westward Expansion. It would fit with all the clues."

Trip didn't say anything, just followed the signs for I-94.

"Do you want me to punch St. Louis into the GPS?"

Trip still didn't say anything.

Norah twisted around and looked over her shoulder because he seemed angry, and since she hadn't done anything—lately—somebody else must be responsible for his snit. "Is Hollie following us again?"

"No." He scowled at the road some more.

"What the heck is wrong with you?"

"We're being conned."

It was Norah's turn to be at a loss for words. She wanted to disagree with Trip, even though she was tired of arguing about her father's motivation. The problem was, she did believe Lucius would use her to give the FBI its comeuppance. But she also believed him when he said he wanted to get the loot back in the hands of those it rightfully belonged to. "We decided to follow the breadcrumbs, remember?"

"Yeah."

"It was actually your call."

He shot her a look. "It doesn't feel right anymore."

That comment struck her as strange, coming from Trip, but after mulling it for a minute Norah decided she was filtering it through her feelings, not to mention a healthy amount of wishful thinking, when all Trip referred to was the case. Trip always thought about the case first. And it was okay, as long as she remembered that. "What doesn't feel right about going to St. Louis?"

He looked over at her again, the crankiness on his face replaced by mild surprise. "No comment about my feelings?"

"You don't like being psychoanalyzed."

"You're catching on."

"You have no idea." She was getting an education in all sorts of ways.

Trip chose to leave well enough alone. "It's been three days since we left Chicago," he said, "the amount of time Puff had between the robbery and his arrest."

Again she let it go. "We got stuck at the lighthouse overnight," she reminded him, "and then there's all the time we wasted with Hollie and the other lunatic treasure hunters. Even if you insist on Lucius being the perpetrator of this scavenger hunt, he could have fit in at least one more city, and St. Louis is only three hundred miles from Chicago."

"Yeah," Trip said, but Norah was done with the guessing game.

"How about you fill me in on your thought process, and spare me the twenty questions routine."

"I'm not really sure myself why I'm having second thoughts."

"Gut feeling?"

"I trust my gut. It's kind of a job requirement."

Norah didn't have any response for that.

"And it's not like we can't come back and pick up this leg of the search where we left off," Trip finished.

"So why did we take the detour to begin with?"

"It made sense at the time. The lighthouse could have been the hiding place for the entire cache of stolen loot. When we found the clue instead, the Detroit Zoo was a confirmation that we were on a treadmill. Going to St. Louis feels like chasing wild geese."

"You think there will be another clue there."

"I don't think we'll find the main cache under a loose floorboard in the Lewis and Clark museum. It's too public, for one thing."

"If you believe Lucius is behind it, then you have to believe he could have charmed his way in, just like he did at the bank."

"What would be the point?"

He had her there, and the more she thought about it, the less sense it made. If the scavenger hunt was intended to keep them busy and out of Chicago, that meant her father had lied to her. She wasn't prepared to go there.

"I'm sorry, Norah," Trip said, too observant, as always.

She looked out the window, throat tight, willing herself not to tear up. "It's not important," she said.

"Yes, it is."

"It's not important to you." Except in how it affected his mission. "You don't know for a fact Lucius is behind this."

"It's the only logical conclusion."

"He's my father. I don't have to be logical."

"So your vote is for St. Louis."

"Does it matter?" she asked him, knowing she was being defensive and not caring.

Trip started to respond, holding his hand out instead when his cell phone rang.

Norah handed it over, not liking the half of the conversation she could hear.

"How?" he said, biting off the word, his expression hardening, then, "the man was on his deathbed the last time we saw him," which Norah took to mean her father, a fact Trip confirmed, snapping the phone closed and dropping it on the console between them. "Apparently Puff wasn't as bad off as he led everyone to believe," he said.

Norah smiled, she couldn't help it.

"I realize it's good news on a personal front, but it also means he conned us, just like we figured."

"Like you figured. I'm still not convinced."

Trip shook his head, but he also grinned, reluctantly. "I guess you have to admire the man's style."

"That," Norah said, "is why he gets away with it."

Trip met her eyes, still smiling, but with conviction. "Not this time."

NORAH WOKE UP AN UNDETERMINED AMOUNT OF time later, her cheek creased by the seat belt and a crick in her neck. She blinked a couple of times, then stretched, rubbing at her neck and trying to get her bearings. She was in the car, traveling on I-94 on the outskirts of Chicago, according to the billboards. And then it all flooded back, the zoo, Hollie, St. Louis. And Trip.

She looked over at him, driving with one hand flopped

over the steering wheel, his face, strong and handsome in profile, his lean body loose, all of him still as a statue, like a blank canvas for her to paint her memories onto. She closed her eyes and could feel his skin under her hands, the ripple of muscle, the heat and strength of him, just the thought enough to have her stretching again as the need moved through her, and not just her body. Her heart flopped in her chest, and she jolted a little, thinking, of course, *I'm in love with him*. Looking back she could recognize the stages, interest, attraction, infatuation, attachment. Love.

It was a little lowering to realize that, despite all her study on the subject, she hadn't recognized anything past attraction. Writing about feelings and experiencing them were so . . . there was no comparison, and she held on to that for a second because she'd never been in love before. Maybe she'd had a crush or two, but she'd never felt this overwhelming rush of emotion— which was too pale a word, but it was the only one she had for a feeling that seemed to blossom and grow until her toes curled and her scalp tingled. A feeling that filled her and warmed her, and scared her to death at the same time because it could take her over, make her do things and want things that went beyond rational, that were bad for her or foolish. What kind of stupid was she, Norah asked herself, to fall in love with Trip Jones?

The answer was, the worst kind, the love-is-blind kind of stupid, the kind that wanted to think with her heart, see the world through rose-colored glasses, believe he would change for her. Fortunately, she had a brain, not to mention a hell of a memory and a past that included just the kind of man she'd been foolish enough to fall in love with. She didn't have to compound one folly with another. Being in love was one thing; making life-altering decisions because of it would be the real mistake.

"You finally awake?"

Letting Trip find out would be an even bigger one. Sex was sex, especially to men. If Trip knew she'd fallen in love with him, he'd feel a need to establish some distance between them. She couldn't protect her father, let alone herself, unless she was kept in the loop. Then there was the part where she didn't want to give up one moment with him. He'd leave, and she'd be devastated, but it didn't have to happen any sooner because of something she couldn't help and neither of them wanted. Foolish, she knew, but that was love.

She took a deep breath and opened her eyes, pretending for all she was worth that nothing had changed. "You want me to drive?"

"No," he said, voice deep and quiet. And cool. "Thanks anyway."

His gratitude, coming, as it did, as an afterthought, spoke volumes. She'd made the same offer just after Trip had tossed down his verbal gauntlet. He'd turned her down then, too, probably figuring she'd get behind the wheel and point the car anyplace but Chicago. He was wrong. Not that she hadn't considered it, but she needed to find her father and make sure he was all right.

Trip had already switched back to FBI agent mode. The wall was up, and she would be wise to stay on her side of it.

"We don't have to be enemies, Trip," she said. "I want to believe in my father, but that doesn't mean I don't understand who he is."

"I get that, and at some point you're going to have to make a choice. It's inevitable, Norah."

"And you think by pulling away you're going to make that choice easier for me?"

"Aren't I?"

"You're seeing it as a choice between you and my father. Isn't it really a choice between right and wrong?"

"Who's right and who's wrong is open to interpretation, to your view of the circumstances and your ability to rationalize. And don't tell me feelings won't come into play, Norah. He's your dad, and I'm ... not prepared to use our personal relationship to sway you."

That sounded honorable, but Trip wasn't only thinking of her. He wasn't in their "relationship" for the long haul. Using her feelings to gain her cooperation would be the same as setting a trap for himself, because, being an honorable man, he'd feel obligated to her. Obligation was worse, in her opinion, than pity.

They didn't have far to go, for which Norah was thankful since she spent the miles in a fog of misery and self-castigation. And then they pulled in front of her house. She took one look at the front porch, and a particularly nasty curse word sprang to her lips but remained mercifully unsaid. The hits just kept coming, was her next thought, as she opened the car door and climbed out. "Did you try knocking?"

Lucius jerked upright and spun around, looking guilty just because he was trying so hard to look innocent. Norah had known this moment would come, but on the heels of her emotional upheaval, the last thing she needed was to be faced with her father.

"Norah, darling," he said expansively, arms wide as he limped his way down the walk to wrap her in a hug.

"Lucius." She hugged him back, but she kept her eyes on Trip, walking past them to climb the porch steps.

"Not Dad anymore?"

Norah let that be a rhetorical question because she couldn't explain to her father that calling him Dad felt like taking sides. At least she worried it would sound that way to Trip. Thankfully, Lucius let it go, too, keeping his arms around her shoulders even after he turned to face Trip, returning from the front porch with his hands full.

"Disposable cell phone," Trip said, holding it up for Norah's benefit, "and a set of tools suitable for disabling an alarm system and picking a lock. That alarm system is state-of-the-art."

"I reached out to a friend who was going to talk me through it."

"Why didn't you call Norah to meet you here and let you in?"

"Well, now—"

"Because you knew we were on a wild-goose chase," Trip answered for him. "Which you sent us on."

Norah felt her father lean on her a little more, and even though she factored in the likelihood he was playing her, she said, "Why don't we go inside and hash this out where we can all be comfortable?"

Trip's jaw tightened, and he sent her a long, speaking look before he turned and led the way up the walk. When he punched the code into the keypad by the door, he didn't bother to hide it from Lucius.

Norah helped her father inside, steering him into the parlor. He lowered into an overstuffed chair, giving Norah a flashback to her childhood, to the memory of him, twenty-five years younger, sitting in that exact same chair.

"You're a lifesaver, darlin'," he said with a heavy sigh.

Trip snorted. "You wouldn't need saving if you'd stayed in the safe house where you were sent to recuperate."

"Kind of obvious," Norah said, "and hardly helpful."

"And you're already defending him."

"Because you're attacking him."

Trip looked at Lucius, who smiled benignly while Trip's jaw began to flex. "Where were the agents assigned to you while you were crawling out of your bed?"

"They really should have been more observant," Lucius said, "considering the onerous responsibilities they carry."

Trip swore, pulling out his cell phone and dialing a number as he walked away so he wouldn't be overheard.

"Aye, call your handler," Lucius called out to him. "Heaven forbid you make any autonomous decisions."

Trip glared at him. Norah took it as a sign of his self-control that he didn't pull out his gun.

"Do you have to make everything as difficult as possible?" she said to her father.

"I was merely entertaining myself," he grumbled. "I spent fifteen years at the beck and call of lazy, pusillanimous federal employees."

"And you were getting a little payback. I get it. But Trip is neither lazy nor cowardly."

Lucius sent her a sidelong, measuring look.

Norah popped up an eyebrow and stared back. "If you want to talk about motivations, let's discuss what you're doing here."

"Where else did you expect me to go?" Lucius blustered.

"I expected you to stay in custody," Trip said as he rejoined them.

"I've served my debt to society."

"You have seventeen more days, by my calculation."

"'Twas your kind that let me out."

"Into protective custody," Trip reminded him. "In effect, you escaped from jail."

Lucius sat back, and although Norah had decided to

stay neutral, it killed her to see the pain on her father's face.

"I'll go upstairs and rest, shall I?" he said. "Before you have my old carcass hauled back to prison. You'll call me for supper, will you, darlin'?" he said to Norah.

"Of course, Dad." She helped him to his feet, but he waved her off at the foot of the stairs, stopping for a moment before he started up.

"The master bedroom is still the same?"

"Yes, but it's my room now." And she wasn't about to be chased out of her own bed again, not even by familial duty. "You can use the spare room, Lucius. First on the right."

He put his hand on the newel post and his foot on the first riser, then turned back to give her a slight, wistful smile. "Seeing your mother's things . . . I miss her."

"She didn't change anything after—after the divorce. And I haven't changed anything since she died, except the bed because, well, you can imagine why."

"Maybe I could take a look later on."

"Of course," Norah said, watching him climb the stairs slowly. Once he'd safely navigated the turn into the spare room she returned to the parlor and dropped into a chair, shaking her head.

"Trying to take it all in?" Trip asked her.

"It's been a hell of a day."

"You ain't seen nothing yet."

She looked over at him, lounging against the mantelpiece.

"It won't be long until Hollie finds out Lucius is here and broadcasts it to the world."

"Great, we'll be right back where we started."

"Not if we can get Lucius to tell us where the loot is first."

And he was looking at her like she could pull off that miracle. "What makes you think he'll tell me the truth?"

"You're his daughter. If anyone can con him you can."

chapter 20

"WILL THIS DAY NEVER END?" NORAH SAID, peering through the leaded glass window in her front door.

Trip looked over her shoulder, then stepped around her and opened the door. "Come on in," he said to Raymond Kline and Myra Newcastle. "The more the merrier."

Norah ignored Raymond as he passed her by, then she bumped cheeks with Myra when the taller woman bent to greet her.

"Raymond said he was coming by," Myra said, "so I decided to tag along with him. I hope you don't mind."

"It's nice to see *you*," Norah said pointedly.

Raymond refused to get the message. "Hello, Norah," he said, stepping forward to kiss her cheek like Myra had done.

Norah ducked away. "What are you doing here, Raymond?" she said, then had a brain wave and pulled open the front door again. Sure enough, Hollie's BMW was parked at the curb across the street.

Norah went to the top of the porch steps, out of the shadow of the house where Hollie would be able to see her, and beckoned. Nothing happened for a second or two, then the driver's door opened and Hollie stepped out. She stood there a moment, long enough for Norah to imagine her heaving a sigh, then she started across the street.

"Lurch is going to sit in the car?" Norah asked when Hollie was at the foot of the steps.

"Lurch is no longer in my employ."

"Good for you. Isn't it a relief to stop pretending?"

Hollie followed Norah inside and traded a look with Raymond Kline. "Can I get back to you on that?" she said when he looked away, clearly not happy to see her.

Norah hooked her by the arm and towed her into the parlor, where Trip, Myra, and Lucius, apparently having come back downstairs when he heard the ruckus, were all arrayed. Raymond and his skunky expression trailed along behind them. "Now, where should we start?" Norah said, beginning to enjoy herself.

Raymond dropped into an armchair. "This isn't one of your group sessions," he snarled at her.

Norah looked around the room, crowded with an aging con man, a college dean with fidelity issues, a vindictive ex-morning show hostess, a college administrator turned literary agent, and a G-man with ulterior motives. "If there was ever a group that needed psychoanalysis, this is it."

"'It takes one to know one,'" Trip said, and although his smile meant that he was kidding, Norah said, "I'm as screwed up as the next person."

Trip was lounging against the mantel, and he looked really good, which Raymond hadn't missed, especially when Norah went to stand beside him.

"So Raymond," she said, making no effort to placate his temper, "what brings you to this neighborhood?" He tried to answer, but she cut him off. "I mean, it's not prestigious, it's not up-and-coming, it's just a middle-class Irish neighborhood where families have owned their homes for generations and everyone is living their quiet lives, raising little nuns and altar boys, and *aspiration* is a four-letter word."

"Now, Norah, I never—"

"I'm sorry, isn't that what you said when you were trying to convince me I needed to sell this house and move to a better address?"

"Blackguard," Lucius spat, sitting forward so fast Raymond pressed back in his seat.

"You stay out of this," Norah said to her father.

"But it's our family home, darlin'—"

"Zip it," Norah said, pointing a finger at him. "Unless you're ready to explain a few things."

Lucius zipped it.

His interjection, however, had given Raymond time to regain his composure. "I may have said those things, but I'm certain my sentiments didn't carry the negative spin you placed on them."

"So you were just kidding?"

"Of course."

"Bullshit."

Raymond got to his feet.

Norah stepped forward. "I'm not going to smile and keep the peace while you rewrite history. And speaking of history, let's talk about your relationship with Hollie."

"*What*? How—Who—" Raymond sputtered, his eyes

shifting between her and Hollie, who was also on her feet, looking every bit as rattled. "It was meaningless," he said, the fallback position of cheaters everywhere. Except they didn't usually say it in front of the "other woman."

"Bastard," Hollie snapped at him.

"What the hell is this, Norah?" Trip said, shoving away from the mantel.

"Getting the truth."

"Really? It sounds like you're still angry over this jackass breaking up with you."

"Which means I still have feelings for him? I never loved him, but I am stinging over the affair. No one likes to be made a fool of."

"Ditto," Hollie said.

"I'm sorry," Norah said immediately. "I'm not trying to hurt you, Hollie—"

"But you wanted me to see what a heel he is."

"Something like that," Norah said.

"And you're not the one who hurt me."

"No, you did that to yourself."

"Hey. And ouch. And why?"

"You can be a doormat or a force to be reckoned with. You chose to sneak around and be the other woman instead of insisting he treat you like you were important to him."

"I was on TV," Hollie said, completely missing the point. "I was important."

"Not where it really mattered. If more women demanded their men be honorable, men would have no choice."

"What are you looking at me for?" Trip wanted to know.

"We're talking about me here," Hollie said, saving Norah the task of coming up with an answer, which was good since her mind had gone blank. There were a lot of things she needed to say to Trip, but this wasn't the time or place.

"The point is, Hollie, he didn't want to be with me, so here's the real question, Raymond. Why did you string me along for so long? I tried to break up with you several times but you wouldn't let me, and you clearly weren't interested in having a real relationship with me since we haven't had sex in . . . a really long time," she finished, shooting Trip a look, "so there was another reason you clung to me like poison ivy. Especially since you clearly preferred Hollie. Although, I have to wonder why you took up with her since you didn't go public with the relationship even after we were through."

Raymond collapsed back into the armchair, scowling over at Myra. "Anything you want to call me?"

"Let's see, *blackguard*, *bastard*, *jackass*," she ticked off on her fingers. "Norah didn't actually call you anything derogatory, but the tone of her voice pretty much said it all, so I'm good."

"But I'm still waiting for an explanation," Norah said. "And if your answer is anything but you were after the loot, don't bother opening your mouth."

"I never made any secret of wanting the loot," Raymond said. "For the college, of course."

"And you were willing to use me to get it."

Raymond dusted a speck of imaginary lint from his sleeve. "I suppose that's one way to look at it."

"What other way is there? I was up front about my father before you hired me. And you wormed your way into my life, kept me close, hoping to get your hands on the loot."

"There's a wealth of information in there to be studied," Raymond said, and for the first time since she'd met him, she saw a fire in his eyes. It wasn't all about the money, either, which made the route he'd taken even sadder.

"You should have told me the truth."

"I tried to broach the subject several times, and you shot me down."

"So when you couldn't get what you wanted from me, you went to Hollie. What did you think my being interviewed on her show was going to get you?"

"I believed reminding the public your father was due to be released from prison would bring outside pressure to bear."

"And I'd have no one else to turn to but you."

Raymond lifted his chin. "You're not exactly the belle of the ball, Norah."

Norah didn't feel as much as a twinge over that observation. It was true, after all; she didn't have many friends. But only because she preferred to keep to herself.

"I tried to stay in your life."

"How selfless of you, Raymond, seeing as I'm so unpleasant to be around."

"Now, Norah, I didn't mean you're unpleasant. Just . . ."

"Cold? Closed off?"

"You have trust issues."

"I wonder why that is?" she said, meeting his eyes long enough to get her message across before she turned to her father, the other inspiration for that particular facet of her damaged psyche. She might have added Trip to her list, but he'd only lied to her in the beginning. Since Hollie's stage he'd been careful to be truthful. As much as he could be, considering his employers.

"I'm sorry you got dragged into this, Hollie," Norah finally said.

"I didn't exactly get dragged."

All eyes shifted to Hollie.

Hollie turned red. "I . . ." She lifted her chin. "I was curious. And jealous, I admit it. Raymond had explained to me why he was so interested in you, and he told me you changed the subject every time he tried to bring it up."

"And you wanted to give me what Norah wouldn't," Raymond said, not unkindly. His ego was definitely getting a boost, especially when Hollie nodded miserably.

"But you didn't want me to turn to Raymond," Norah said.

"I knew you wouldn't"—Hollie gestured to Trip—"not after he showed up."

"So why did you go on the biggest cable news program in the country and make sure everyone knew about my connection to the robbery?"

She shrugged, as if it went without saying. "My producers refused to allow me to talk about it. They would have cut me off if I'd asked you about the robbery. But Raymond wanted the loot, so I took the story elsewhere."

"Hell of a way of getting your boyfriend what he wanted," Trip put in, "letting every kook and treasure hunter in the country know about the loot."

"I thought having other pursuers would hide me. I knew it was a risk making it into a race, but I was determined to win it. I guess I didn't think that through very well."

"You weren't thinking at all," Norah said, "you were feeling. And being manipulated."

"It's your fault, Norah," Raymond snapped at her. "You could have been reasonable."

"You could have been a human being, Raymond."

Lucius made a particularly derogatory noise.

Raymond stood, straightening his impeccable suit

jacket and squaring his jaw, all wounded dignity. "I would have expected you to keep the school at the fore-front of your thoughts, Norah. I see now I was mistaken." He headed for the door. "You might want to consider the ramifications of your present course. If the board got wind of this—"

"If the board gets wind of this, they're going to hear both sides of the story. I wonder which one of us has more to lose?"

Raymond shook his head sadly. "You've turned out to be quite a disappointment, Norah."

"Happy to be of service."

He stood there for a few seconds, waiting, Norah assumed, for her to come to her senses.

"You can see yourself out," she said.

Hollie scuttled after him, shooting them an apologetic look before she hit the door on Raymond's heels.

"Doormat all the way," Myra said.

"Isn't he your ride?" Norah said.

"I'll call a cab."

"While we're waiting, perhaps you could introduce me to your friend," Lucius said, twinkling at Myra.

"Myra Newcastle, Lucius MacArthur, my father. Myra's my agent; Dad, leave her alone."

"But darlin' I've been in jail for fifteen years."

"First, *ewww*, second Myra's too smart to take up with a fast-talker like you. Go find someone else."

"Is that an order?"

"*Ewww* again, and you're not leaving this house until we can figure out"—she glanced at Myra—"everything."

"That's my cue to leave," Myra said good-naturedly.

"Sit tight for a minute, Myra." Norah stepped into the hall, beckoning to Trip, who joined her, leaving Myra and Lucius in the parlor, making small talk in hushed voices.

"Can we tell her?"

"No."

"Once Raymond gets his mind made up he doesn't change it. There's no way he'll give up. Myra could keep an eye on him."

"She destroyed her usefulness there."

Norah sighed. "You're right."

When they went back into the parlor, Lucius and Myra, who'd moved to the end of the sofa nearest his chair, sprang apart. Norah sent her father a quelling look. He put on an innocent face.

"I really do have to go," Myra said. "I'm meeting my son for dinner."

Norah walked her to the door, coming back to see Trip and her father giving each other the evil eye. "Oh, come on. Can you two try to get along? You have more in common than you think."

"We don't trust each other, we have that in common."

"None of us trust Raymond and Hollie. Why don't we talk about that?"

Trip clammed up, which ticked her off. "What's with the silent treatment? Why didn't you ask Raymond and Hollie anything?"

"Like what?"

"Like did they hire those guys who chased us out of Chicago a few days ago?"

Trip shrugged. "They would have lied."

Norah blew out a breath and dropped onto the antique horsehair sofa. "So what do we do now?"

Trip looked at Lucius again. "It would be nice if we could go get the loot."

"Well, now, I'd love to oblige you, boyo, but I can't."

"Of course not."

"Why can't you?" Norah asked him.

"Because I don't know where the loot is."

* * *

"WHY DON'T YOU KNOW WHERE THE LOOT IS?"
Trip asked Puff after a sketchy moment where he had
to fight off the mental picture of his hands around the
man's throat.

"I'm not the one who hid it," Puff said.

"You must have some idea where it is, Dad," Norah
said, not sounding too happy with him, either, but still
buying his crap hook, line, and sinker.

Lucius leaned forward, wincing a bit, but looking avid.
"What did you find at the lighthouse?"

Trip refused to take the bait, seething because he believed Lucius knew exactly what they'd found. Norah
gave her father the highlights—the PG ones.

Lucius went into grifter mode, smiling and shaking
his head like he just couldn't believe it. "Helen Aber-
crombie."

"The bank teller you conned into getting your friends
into the bank?"

"Face like a mud fence," Lucius said, "but a very ac-
commodating personality, if you take my meaning. She
handled the scavenger hunt for me."

"You didn't do her any favors."

"That, boy, is a matter of opinion."

"Or in your case, ego."

"I don't recall hearing any complaints."

"Let me be the first," Norah said. "Can we discuss the
robbery without all the reminiscing?"

"Now what fun would that be?"

"Oh, so much more for me."

"So you were telling us how you trusted Ms. Aber-
crombie with fifty million dollars worth of stolen goods."

"We had no choice," Lucius insisted. "Helen forgot to
tell us about one of the silent alarms, Noel Black tripped
it, and the cops were on their tails. It was only a matter of

time before they ratted me out. Helen was my only option."

"Not buying it," Trip said. But it was just plausible enough.

"The clues contained bits and pieces of the loot. Norah said so. If you'd bothered to follow the trail to the end, you'd have found the main hoard, I'm sure of it."

"Why don't we just ask Helen?" Norah said.

"Because she's dead," Trip said. "The only way to prove Puff wrong is to head back out and pick up where we left off. All of us."

Lucius sank back against the sofa. "I'm not up to a road trip just now. In fact I'm all done in for today. I'll just go up. If you're done with me." He struggled upright, Norah jumping to her feet to help him up the stairs.

She came back down a couple minutes later. "My dad is settled into the guest room closest to the stairs. You can use the other one—the one I slept in when you were here before."

Trip let that go. That didn't mean he agreed with her, but he wasn't willing to make a big deal of it until he saw how the rest of their conversation went. "You know he's not telling the truth," he said. "Hell, he's rewriting history as he goes along."

Norah sank onto the sofa. "I don't know what to believe anymore."

"Norah—"

"He said pretty much the same about you, Trip, and you've admitted that finding the loot is your top priority, so what am I supposed to do?"

"At least I've been truthful."

"And he's my father."

"Exactly. You know what he's capable of."

"I knew what he was capable of fifteen years ago.

Now he's just a sick old man." She held up a hand. "I know you're angry."

"Not at you."

"A little at me."

He huffed out a laugh. "Yeah, a little at you."

She pushed off the couch and crossed the room, resting a hand lightly on his chest as she stretched up to kiss him, softly, just her lips touching his, all it took for his irritation to disappear.

"Thank you," she said, stepping back.

And he let her.

chapter
21

PUFF WAS RESTING IN ONE OF THE SPARE BED-
rooms. Norah was showering in the bath she'd had
added to the master bedroom. Trip prowled the house,
pissed off and feeling trapped. He didn't know what to
do about the loot, and he didn't know what to do about
Norah.

He'd wanted to take that kiss deeper, but there was
an invisible line he had to honor, even though Puff
wouldn't hesitate to use her feelings to his advantage—

"Hey."

Norah's shout had Trip racing up the stairs in time
to see her father pulling the master bedroom door shut.

He jumped about a mile when he saw Trip at the head
of the stairs. "Jesus, Mary, and Joseph, boy, what are you
doing skulking about the place like a sneak thief?"

"Funny, I was just about to ask you that."

"I only wanted a quick peek." He sighed eloquently. "I've fond memories of that room."

"Do you?"

"Believe it or not, I love my daughter, and I loved her mother."

"Let's get something straight. I don't believe a word that comes out of your mouth."

Some of the affability and false, to Trip's view, sentimentality fell away from Lucius's mask. "Since we're talking plain, I don't much care for the way you're treating my girl."

"I'm treating your *girl* just the way she wants to be treated. We both know she wouldn't accept anything less."

"Don't count your chickens, son. When push comes to shove, Norah will side with family."

"And you're the only family she has?" Trip shook his head. "Family is important to her, but honesty is even more important. She'll do what's right."

"Because you're romancing her? I see the way she looks at you." Puff's eyes narrowed. "And you're not just playing a game, are you boy?"

"I've been completely honest with Norah about my motivations. Can you say the same?"

"Of course not, but I will say my Norah is no fool. She knows I want the loot, and she knows why."

"Right, because you're feeling regret in your old age, and you want to atone for your sins by returning the items to their rightful owners."

"I'm not saying there wouldn't be something in it for me, but at least I'm trying to do what's right. You can't say the same about the FBI. It's an organization that puts a con man like me to shame, the way it uses people and exploits weaknesses. And I wonder now,

how many secrets are there to be exploited in a cache
of loot that includes safe-deposit box contents from
some of the wealthiest and most influential men in
Chicago?"

"This city has always been a power source, and the
Bureau wants to tap in," Trip said with a shrug, not
about to get drawn into a philosophical argument about
who was right and who was wrong.

"So why don't we work together?" Lucius said. "Once
we find the loot, you can trundle back to Washington
with the papers and your people can ferret out all the
juicy tidbits and wreak havoc with them. None of us
will get what we want unless we stop this pussyfooting
around and work together."

Trip snorted. "Did you miss the part about me not
trusting you?"

Lucius grinned, a seemingly guileless smile so like
Norah's it caught Trip off guard, until he remembered
that Norah's *was* guileless. Puff's was just another con.

Norah pulled open the bedroom door, jerking back
when she saw them standing there. "What's going on?"

"Just having a conversation," Trip said.

"About you," Lucius added.

Norah rolled her eyes. "Whatever's going on, leave me
out of it. I can take care of myself."

"Of course you can, darlin'," Puff said, kissing her
on the cheek.

Trip could only stand there and watch. Even if he
let Puff goad him into a competition for Norah's affec-
tions, a public display in front of her father would only
make her uncomfortable.

"I'm feeling peckish," Puff said, laying a hand on
his stomach.

"Well I'm starving," Norah said.

"What do you say we go whip up some scrambled

eggs and toast, like we used to do when you were a little girl. Remember?"

Norah smiled, a little sadly. "Whenever you were home Mama would sleep in on Saturday morning, and you'd make me breakfast."

"Aye, she had a way of knowing when to leave us to our own shenanigans, didn't she?" Puff said in his best Irish brogue.

Norah's eyes were misty. Trip was rolling his.

They started off, but Norah stopped at the head of the stairs and looked back at Trip. "Are you coming?"

"Of course," Lucius said expansively, "you're welcome to join us."

"You two go ahead and have your memories. I'll grab something later." He went into the spare room where Norah had slept before and plopped down on the bed, lifting his right butt cheek to pull the package Law had taken delivery on, about the size and shape of a book, from beneath it. He tossed it onto the dresser, then decided to take a shower because what he wanted to do was lie down, and if he did that he wouldn't get back up for eight or ten hours, and he was serious about keeping Puff in his sights.

He hadn't counted on Norah.

Lucius was working hard to ingratiate himself, and Norah was eating it up. But Trip couldn't work up a good case of resentment any more than he could spare much concern over Puff's antics.

Trip's mind was filled with Norah, animated, laughing, her eyes shining, taking her from cool and attractive to warm and pretty, someone he could imagine across the dinnertable, walking with through the park, in his bed . . .

Whoa. He took a huge mental step back. Sex was an acceptable reaction, as long as it didn't distract him from

the op. It was the other stuff that posed a problem, especially that one about walking through the park, since in
his imagination they were holding hands. He didn't do
that stuff, the holding hands, the sending flowers, the
deep and meaningful conversations, the cuddling after
sex. Happily ever after was for other people. Handy, since
Norah made it clear she understood that about him.

So why did her pragmatism irritate him?

WHEN HER BEDROOM DOOR OPENED AROUND
midnight, Norah played dead. It wasn't Lucius, since
he'd left only moments before after keeping her up for
two hours, reminiscing from the armchair in what had
once been her mother's room, but was now hers. And
it couldn't be another intruder sneaking into her room,
since unauthorized presences were announced by what
sounded like World War II air raid sirens loud enough
to wake the entire populace of England, Wales, Scot-
land, *and* Ireland. That left Trip.

Trip had been bursting to get her alone all evening,
but not in a good way.

"Norah?" he said in a whisper, not touching her,
which meant he already knew she was awake. And then
he said four words that no woman ever wanted to hear
from a man. "We need to talk."

"Will you marry me?" were words women wanted to hear from men. "I'll do the dishes" was good and
"Did you lose weight?" was always a winner. "We need
to talk" was conversational purgatory for women. Men
were not verbal creatures. When a man wanted to talk
there was bad news coming. If they'd been any other
couple she'd be steeling herself for the we-can-still-
be-friends discussion. Since they weren't together in the
usual sense of together, there wasn't a breakup in the

offing. Then again, if he couldn't relax and trust her, there might be.

He sat down on the edge of the bed and put his hand on her hip. "Are you asleep?" he asked her, which she'd always thought was a ridiculous question.

"If I was asleep I couldn't tell you I was asleep."

"You could keep pretending and not answer me."

"Go away, I'm tired."

"You slept in the car, why are you so cranky?"

She sat up. "Are you serious?"

"It's the middle of the night. I've had about three hours of sleep in the last two days, so yeah, I'm serious."

"You're the one who wants to talk."

"I think we need to."

"No, we really don't." She knew what he wanted to say, and she was tired of talking about the loot, tired of thinking about it. Tired of thinking period.

She rose to her knees and kissed him, and it was hard and a little angry. She just wanted to let go, get out of her head with all the craziness running around there and forget, for a little while, that she was being torn in two directions by two men with two different agendas, both of which she could further. And both of whom she loved.

If Trip was going to use her, she should at least get to decide the manner, and while she knew that wasn't rational, right here, right now, she was going to have her way. With him.

Not that he was objecting. He was all heat and hardness, meeting her kiss, his tongue sweeping into her mouth as he worked his hands up under her sleep shirt and stripped her panties down to her knees. Norah laughed breathlessly as she fell onto her butt so he could take them off completely, her breath shuddering back in as Trip pressed her into the feather bed on top of her mattress.

She reached for him but he held her off, bending to kiss her again, just his mouth on hers, a deep kiss that ended with him catching her bottom lip between his teeth. She shuddered, tried to pull him on top of her again, needing more contact, needing him in her, filling the emptiness. And not just in a physical sense.

Having her father back in her life should have been a happy event, but in all her daydreams of this moment she'd never imagined the possibility he'd lie to her, use her. Even if it was for altruistic reasons. She needed peace, just a few moments of peace. But Trip refused to oblige her, holding her off while he removed her shirt and his boxers, staking her hands by her head when she reached for him again. He laid his mouth on hers, sliding it down her neck and the slope of her breast to take one nipple into his mouth, drawing hard. Every muscle and nerve ending pulsing as he slid his fingers into her at the same time.

And then he was gone again. Just that one amazing crescendo of pleasure and Trip was back to foreplay.

"Please," she said, suddenly hating foreplay. She wanted to be exhausted. She wanted a nice sweaty wrestling match ending with the mother of all orgasms. And if that didn't do it, they'd go for it again. Trip could handle it. He'd need a few minutes in between, but he could definitely handle it. That thought was all the foreplay she needed.

"What's going on with you?" he said, lifting his head to peer into her face in the darkness when what he was doing to her didn't get a reaction. "You're all tensed up."

"No talking," she said, shoving him over and pouncing on top of him. "No talking, no thinking, and no foreplay."

"Every man's fantasy," he said, groaning as she took

him in, hot and hard, filling her body and fuzzing her mind.

His hands were strong at her hips, his body surging up as she pressed down, his face tight as they took each other. She came in a rush that started low in her belly and spread outward until her whole body throbbed with it, and she moaned and wrapped her arms around herself as she sank down beside him, body and mind in a pleasant haze until he said, "Not so fast," and loomed over her, and she realized he hadn't gone with her, that the tight expression on his face had been him holding back.

"I don't know what's going on with you," he said, his voice low and soft in the darkness, "and it's not like I object to being used like this, but—"

"You're talking again," Norah said.

"And there's going to be more foreplay, so brace yourself."

Brace yourself must have meant emotionally because Trip twined his fingers with hers and kissed her again, another long slow kiss that was more than his mouth on hers, it was him cherishing her. She was acting a little crazy, and it must have thrown him, but any other man would have gone with it, especially since he was getting what he wanted.

Trip kissed her and waited for her to kiss him back. And she gave herself to him again, this time whole-heartedly. What else could she do when he was being so patient and . . . She wouldn't call it loving, but it seemed as if he cared for her beyond her usefulness to his job.

So she let go of everything but him, put herself into the moment, feeling the pleasure blossom low again as his mouth moved to her breasts, as his hands skimmed down her ribs, as he slipped into her again and every cell in her body came alive. Her skin tingled, her breath sighed out, and she began to move with him, the climax stealing up on her slowly this time, washing over her in gentler waves that were no less amazing, with her heart adding more weight to the moment than any physical sensation could have, and Trip joining her this time when she went over the edge.

Trip flopped to one side and she groaned, missing the weight of his body on hers. It made her feel safe and comforted, pushing away the unreality of the whole situation that had made her feel like she was having a really long out-of-body experience. She definitely knew she was in her body right now, especially when he gathered her close, his front to her back, and pulled the covers over them.

His breathing slowed as he settled against her, and Norah fell asleep with his arms wrapped around her and troubles of the morning far away.

chapter 22

TRIP WAS SLEEPING THE KIND OF SLEEP THAT A man with his job rarely got, deep, dreamless, blissful. Norah was warm against him, the house was secure—

And the alarm was going off. He whipped out of bed, Norah right behind him, just as the bedroom door began to swing open.

Trip grabbed the doorknob and jerked, getting a glimpse of a tall man in a Robin mask, stumbling off balance before he let go of the doorknob on the other side, caught his footing, and turned to run.

"Stay here," Trip ordered Norah. "I mean it. And no weapons."

He set off after the Boy Wonder, who knocked Lucius down as he stepped out of the spare room at the top of the stairway and fell right into Trip's path. Trip was running full-out, so he couldn't hurtle over the old con man without momentum taking him into the open stairwell, and he couldn't stop, so he threw himself sideways into the wall, twisting so he didn't fall on top of Norah's father and crush him to death. It would have solved a big problem, but he'd probably never find the loot without Lucius. Norah would be pretty upset, too.

He went down in a tangle, popped back up to his feet, and raced down the stairs two at a time to find himself at the open doorway, watching the same kid in the same Robin mask race down the sidewalk, appearing under the streetlights and disappearing in the gloom between. He wasn't running very fast. Trip figured he could catch him and get some answers.

If he wasn't naked.

And if Norah wasn't upstairs keeping an eye on her old man, who would walk all over her without a second thought or a hint of guilt.

He shut the door and reset the alarm before he headed upstairs. Sure enough, Puff was sitting in the easy chair in the master bedroom, trying to get Norah to pour him a shot of whiskey.

"I don't keep alcohol up here, Lucius," she was saying.

"Just nip downstairs and get me some," Lucius said with a little laugh.

"Trip told me to stay put."

Lucius made a rude noise. "You'll be taking orders from him now?"

"No," Trip said as he stepped into the room. "She knows the value of teamwork, and her part of the deal in cases like this is to stay out of my way so I don't have to worry about her getting hurt."

"What are you doing here?" Lucius demanded, shifting around to glare at him. "Why didn't you go after that bastard?"

Trip looked down, figuring the reason was obvious.

"Some FBI agent you are," Lucius grumbled, his brogue getting thicker with agitation. "Someone breaks in here, intent on doing mischief, and you were busy taking advantage of the situation instead of doing your job. Or is your intimacy with my daughter intended to imply some sort of commitment that will continue after you've gotten what you want?"

Trip crossed the room and retrieved his boxers, stepping into them.

"Well? You're not going to answer my question?"

"No," Norah said, "he's not. I'm over thirty, Lucius, I'm not your little girl anymore. I never really was."

"Of course you were—"

"Listen to me," she said, crossing the room to kneel by his chair. "I've been on my own since Mama died when I was eighteen. I kept this house, and got myself through college, and dated and worked and survived."

"The world is a cold, hard place, darlin', and people are almost always wearing a mask."

"Do you think I don't know that? Even if I hadn't been making my own way for all of my adult life, I'm a psychologist. Understanding what twists people is my job."

"But darlin'—"

"I know what I'm doing, Daddy." She got to her feet and went to hold the door for him. "Sometimes I wish I didn't."

Lucius pushed himself out of the chair, walking stiffly to the door. He stopped in front of Norah. He didn't speak, but his hurt and upset were clear on his face.

"You should trust me," she said softly.

"Should I?"

"Yes." But she knew he couldn't. Trip could see it on her face; it was breaking her heart.

And there was nothing Trip could do to make it easier for her. Just like there would be nothing he could do to spare her when he walked away.

NORAH RATTLED AROUND THE HOUSE THE NEXT morning, doing chores to keep her hands busy, if not her mind. Then there was the part where the house was dirty and laundry needed to be done. She went into the spare room Trip had used briefly and straightened the bed, then she plopped down on it because the room smelled like Trip and she couldn't shut him out. She could have left the room, but she liked the way Trip smelled. And she had to admit she was weak where he was concerned. Last night had proven that.

She'd wanted a bout of fast, hot, sweaty sex. Mind-numbing sex. Trip had apparently heard that the brain was a sexual organ, because he'd taken his time. Which was what had confused her so much that she'd decided not to think about him at all, she recalled. But avoidance never solved anything.

That's what she'd been trying to do last night, avoid reality, avoid her feelings. Trip had been insistent on slowing things down, making it emotional as well as physical, and there was only one motivation she could think of—and it was the other reason she'd avoided memories of the night before. Trip didn't love her. Once the loot was found, he wouldn't stick around. And yet she refused to believe he'd played on her emotions last night to make sure she stayed on his side rather than her father's.

There was no doubt they were both jockeying for her support, but Trip wouldn't use her. Not in that way.

And yet . . . She caught sight of the package she'd received a week ago when Law had been there installing her alarm system. It sat on the dresser where Trip must have put it, about the size and shape of a hardcover book, and all but flashing the word *distraction*.

Norah picked up the package and shook it. It wasn't heavy enough, and it didn't have the solid feel of a book, but it didn't make any noise, either. It was taped up like Fort Knox, which was good since it appeared to have some miles on it. Her address was on a label that looked like it had been typed on an actual typewriter rather than a laser printer.

Taped up like Fort Knox . . . She flashed back to the package she and Trip had retrieved from the zoo, her mind buzzing a little, denial warring with dawning reality.

She took the package into her bathroom and attacked it with her fingernail scissors, managing to cut down the short end even with her hands shaking. When it was open she took it to her bed and upended it. Nothing came out, so she reached inside and pulled out a wad of tissue paper, wrapped around one of those vacuum seal plastic bags people used to preserve steaks on TV.

Except there wasn't steak inside the bag. There was jewelry. A lot of jewelry. Norah turned it over in her hands for a minute, replaying the conversation they'd had less than twenty-four hours ago. Lucius had assured her his reasons for wanting the loot were altruistic. His body language had sent a different message, but she'd chosen to believe his words. Now, finally, her brain had to wrap itself around the truth.

Trip was right. But he didn't know the half of it.

"Norah?"

She lifted her head, looked toward her bedroom door.

"Norah, darlin', are you in there?"

"I'm . . ." She took a deep breath and lifted her chin, her voice stronger this time, loud enough to carry through the closed door. "I'm busy, Lucius. I'll talk to you later."

There was silence, but she knew he was still standing there. Finally he said, "All right," the floor creaking as he walked away.

Trip wouldn't be far behind. He'd been shadowing Lucius all day, and he'd keep on shadowing, convinced it was the only way to find the loot. Well, she thought with a soft puff of laughter, she'd have to tell him about the package at some point. After she'd had time to digest it herself.

Surprisingly enough she wasn't aching from her father's betrayal. It hurt, sure, but she'd expected it on some level. What she had to get over was betraying him back. He deserved it, no doubt about that, but she hated that it was necessary.

She put the jewelry and the tissue back in the package, and stuffed it under her pillow. No point in hiding it since she'd only have to dig it back out to show Trip. Once she found him.

She left her bedroom, closing and locking the door behind her and not feeling a bit guilty about it. She ran into Lucius first, sitting in the parlor facing out the doorway where he could see the stairs. He lowered the paper he'd been reading and smiled at her.

"Are you looking for Trip?"

"As a matter of fact, I am."

"He went out, darlin'."

Norah didn't buy it. He'd said it in an even, believable tone, but there was no way Trip would leave the house without letting her know.

"He said he was just going to the market a couple of blocks over," Lucius said. "You can probably catch him if you hurry. He hasn't been gone two minutes. Probably hasn't made it to the end of the block yet." And he shook the paper out and lifted it in front of his face.

Norah frowned at it, pretty sure he was grinning behind it. But she didn't waste any time, going to the front door and punching the alarm code in. She went all the way out to the sidewalk and looked in the direction Trip would have gone if he'd walked to the market. Nothing.

She turned to go back in the house to look for him, but somebody tossed a smelly blanket over her head. She felt a hard shoulder in the pit of her stomach and she was hauled off the ground, kicking and screaming—or trying to—which did her no good. She was carried a short distance and dumped back on her feet, but before she could get rid of the blanket her hands were wrenched behind her back and tied.

Norah twisted around and kicked out with her foot.

"Ouch, sonuvabitch."

Norah went still. "Bill Simonds?"

The blanket was whipped off her head, and there was her next-door neighbor. They were in his gloomy, ramshackle house. She knew that because she could see her neighbors' houses, just a little off-kilter from the view out her own parlor windows. What was even more shocking was the second man in the room. Or maybe she should have said kid. "Bobby Newcastle?"

He ducked his head, not meeting her eyes. "Hi, Professor MacArthur."

She shot a glance at Bill, then stepped closer to Bobby. "You have to let me go, Bobby. My dad's going to be really worried about me."

"No, he's not," Bobby said. "Who do you think told us to kidnap you?"

Okay, Norah thought, stumbling over to the nearest chair and dropping bonelessly into it. Now she felt betrayed.

TRIP HAD BEEN AVOIDING NORAH ALL MORNING, knowing she'd be reading into his behavior last night— probably correctly. He wasn't really prepared to look her in the eyes and see her drawing conclusions about his feelings. Especially since he wasn't sure what they were. There was just something wrong with her figuring it out before he did.

They needed to talk about the loot, though. Lucius was playing a waiting game, knowing the FBI wouldn't strand an agent there forever in the hopes the loot would turn up. Trip wasn't about to go back to Washington a failure. That left him with two choices, head to St. Louis and follow the rest of the clues, or find a way to get the truth out of Puff MacArthur. Trip preferred option number two, since he still felt that St. Louis was a wild-goose chase. And since Puff would die before he told Trip anything, option number two required Norah.

Now all he had to do was convince her. She wasn't upstairs, though. Her bedroom door was locked, and when he knocked all he got was silence, the empty kind of silence. He searched the rest of the house, including the basement, but he couldn't find her anywhere.

And his gut was talking big-time.

"Where's Norah?" he asked Lucius as he came into the parlor.

"She went to the market a couple of blocks over," he said, not even lifting his head from the paper. "We're out of eggs if you've a mind to go after her and add it to the list."

"I'm not really a fan of eggs," Trip said, taking a seat where he could see the front door. He got to his feet almost immediately. He should have given it a half hour; it was perfectly plausible that Norah had gone to the store, but his gut was screaming at him now. He couldn't believe Lucius would do anything to harm Norah, but given a choice between instinct and history, hell, given a choice between anything and his gut, he'd go with his gut.

And, he added, giving it almost as much weight, he trusted Norah. "She would have told me if she was going out," he said.

"Think you've got her under your thumb, eh?" Lucius said.

"Norah isn't under anyone's thumb. You might know that if you'd been around her for more than five minutes of the last fifteen years. She won't be used."

Lucius got to his feet. "Not by the likes of you."

"She's not exactly toeing the line for you, is she?" Trip said, his voice purposely taunting. "You want me gone, but she's sticking up for me."

"She'll come around."

"Will she? As long as I'm in the picture you can hang it up, Puff."

"Back off, boy," Lucius growled.

But Trip wasn't biting this time. This time he was running the show. "You've waited fifteen years to get your hands on all that money and power." Trip took another step closer, backing Lucius into the chair then resting his hands on the arms and leaning right down into Lucius's face. "You'll have to keep on waiting as long as Norah wants me around, and that pisses you off, doesn't it, Puff?"

Lucius's hands were white-knuckled on the chair arms, and Trip knew he was getting to him.

"Millions of dollars so close you can smell it," Trip said, "but you can't touch it. Diamonds and gold and best of all secrets, all those juicy secrets, and you can't cash in. I'm standing in your way, a big federal road block that isn't going anywhere because your daughter, Lucius MacArthur's daughter, is thinking with her glands—"

"I get it. That's why—" Lucius clamped a hand over his mouth.

"That's why what?"

Lucius relaxed, working to look bored, which was how Trip knew he had him. "Where is she?"

"I won't tell you, and you can't touch me. If you do anything Norah will have your balls when she gets back."

"I don't have to lay a hand on you." But he was relieved at what Lucius had revealed. Norah was coming back, which meant she hadn't gone far. "You just admitted to kidnapping. You're going back to jail."

Lucius snorted. "My girl won't stand for that. She won't let you prosecute me."

"It's not up to her."

"Why don't we see what she has to say about it? I imagine she'll tell you she was out running errands or out with another man. That suit from her college, maybe."

"I guess that depends on how long she's gone. And what happens to her while she's with whoever you hired to take her."

Puff went white, then red. "I wouldn't harm a hair on her head."

Trip believed that, at least; he couldn't do otherwise. So he took a mental step back and refocused his energy into productive thought instead of blind rage. Lucius wouldn't harm Norah. And she didn't know where the loot was, which meant there was another reason he wanted her out of the house.

Think, he told himself, pacing away from Puff. The bedroom door was locked. Why would she lock it? She didn't want to keep him out, that much was clear from last night. And thinking about last night had the panic rising again. He shoved it down. If she didn't want to keep him out, it must be her father she'd locked out, her father who'd been trying to worm his way into that room since the second they got back. Hell, he'd probably orchestrated the whole damn thing.

"You set this all up," he said to Lucius.

"I don't know what you're talking about."

"The beating, the safe house. You weren't hurt as much as you pretended to be. The second I brought Norah to Marion you started planning your escape." A miscalculation Trip would have to live with. "Once you slipped out of the safe house you came straight here, knowing this is the first place we'd look. Except we were conveniently tied up three states away, along with all the treasure hunters, because they followed me and Norah out of the city and left the playing field clear for you."

"Do you hear yourself boy? I'm even impressed with the man who could think that far ahead, and keep the FBI and half the country occupied while I slip in here and grab the loot, which we both know isn't here."

It sounded far-fetched, even to Trip, but Lucius was probably the best grifter to walk the face of the earth. His only mistake was reaching too high for the brass ring, and even that he'd managed to work to his favor. In fact, the whole thing made sense in a twisted sort of way.

"There's something in this house you want bad enough to risk alienating your own daughter."

"Alienating, bah," Lucius sneered, but there was a thread of doubt in his voice.

"It's a big risk," Trip pushed. "If you can't get me out of the house—and you can't—you'll have to leave her where she is, and I'm willing to bet the whole fifty million and my job that Norah isn't there willingly. The longer she's subjected to whatever—or should I say whoever—you got to grab her, the angrier she's going to become. That'll work against you, Puff, and you're going to need her to deal with me, so time is on my side." And he sat down, arms crossed, willing to put his money where his mouth was.

Lucius picked up his paper, calling Trip's bluff.

But Trip wasn't done yet. "There's one other thing you haven't considered," he said. "The man, or men," he qualified because he couldn't imagine one man being able to handle a pissed off Norah, "who has her. What are they going to do when they don't get the word to let her go in the next couple of hours?"

Puff's hands fisted around the edge of the paper.

"It's your game, Puff."

"You're on the court, too, boyo."

"Me? What can I do?"

"You can go look for her. Be a cop. Ask the neighbors if they saw anything."

Trip got up and peered out the window at the deserted street. "Seems to me this is the kind of place where everyone has an honest job to go to, and those who don't mind their own business." He turned around. "It's the kind of place someone would count on being able to abduct a woman in broad daylight and get away with it."

Puff sighed. "You're a hard, cold man, Jones. I

wonder what Norah will make of you when she finds out."

"Why don't we ask her?"

"Is that a challenge, boy?"

"You bet your ass, old man."

chapter
23

"I DON'T BELIEVE YOU," NORAH SAID. "MY FA-ther wouldn't have me kidnapped. He knows I have no idea where the loot is. Raymond and Hollie are behind this." She knew she was grasping at straws, but she'd close her hands over thin air and defy gravity if it meant she didn't have to believe her own father, the father she'd loved and missed for fifteen long years of felony conviction, would do this to her.

"Who?" Bobby asked.

"Raymond Kline," Norah said. "I told you to go talk to him because you're failing your classes." Still no glimmer of recognition in Bobby's eyes. "He's the dean of the Midwest School of Psychology, the college you attend. Remember?"

"Oh, that dude. Never met him in my life."

"But . . . your mother works with him. She's an advisor at the college."

"Not for long. Once we get our hands on that fifty mil, we're never gonna hafta work again. Except you," he said to Bill Simonds. "You're just the hired help."

"Not as long as I got her," Bill said, hooking a thumb in her direction.

"Wait a minute," Norah said.

Bill shot her the proverbial look that could kill, but he settled for being rude. "Shut up."

"I'll deal with you later," she said, turning back to Bobby. "What does Myra have to do with any of this?"

"Um . . . I'm not supposed to talk about that."

Crap. Norah let her shoulders slump. *Another betrayal.* She'd been hoping Bobby's presence was just a coincidence, that Raymond had blackmailed him into kidnapping her in return for not flunking out. That hope flew out the window.

She wanted to grab him by the neck and shake the truth out of him, but she needed to get out of there first and worry about the details later. Or let Trip worry about them. The details were his department, although there was going to be hell to pay when she got face-to-face with Myra.

"Bobby, you have to let me go."

"Can't. But I'm just supposed to keep you here for a little while. D—Lucius is going to call and tell me when it's okay to release you."

"Not if I have anything to say about it," Bill put in.

"We're just renting your house," Bobby said. "You aren't even supposed to be here."

"*Surprise*, genius, you're not the only one with a plan. Shit, you're not even paying me enough to deal with her."

Norah rolled her eyes. "Like you're such a picnic," she said.

Both men turned to stare at her.

"Explain away," she said. "I can't wait to hear how you're going to justify kidnapping. Consider it practice for your criminal trial."

She could see Bill struggling, and for a minute she feared she'd pushed him too far. In the end, though, he was so proud of himself he couldn't resist showering her with his brilliance. Then there was the part where he figured she wouldn't be around later to make trouble for him. It was now that mattered, though, and the best way to find an opening was to distract him. And what better distraction could there be than to let him pump himself up on ego?

"It was me following you," he began. "I made a deal with a loan shark. Yeah, I can see you think I'm nuts, but look at this place."

Norah didn't waste her time. Where her house was all polished woodwork and bright charm, his was dingy and depressing.

"This house has been in my family just as long as yours has been in your family," Bill was saying, "but I ain't no fancy college professor making six figures."

The truth was she probably made less than he did. She'd just been left in a better position financially because her mother had taken out mortgage insurance, and left her enough to make sure the taxes were paid until she could finish college and start bringing in a decent income. And saying that would only piss him off more. She wanted Bill to relax, not give him a reason to take his anger out on her.

"I was one of the guys in the car that buzzed you after your talk-show gig, and I was working with them on the way out of Chicago. If not for that bitch, Hollie, we'd have had you but I gotta thank her, too, since her interference kept them from going all *Godfather* on me. As it is, they made it clear I put you into their hands this time or they break my—"

"Here's a preview," Norah said, jumping to her feet and kicking him in the kneecap. He went down like a redwood, howling and holding his leg. Bobby froze, his eyes shifting between her and Bill, not sure what to do, but since Bill was already hobbling to his feet, she barged into Bobby and bolted for the door, hearing the air whoosh out of Bill's lungs as the kid fell on top of him. She glanced over her shoulder and saw Bill kick Bobby aside and lunge to his feet, a pistol in his hand.

Norah was at the front door, but her hands were tied behind her. Bill's first shot splintered the woodwork beside her head. She had no choice but to turn around, fumbling for the doorknob behind her then struggling to turn it as Bill brought his gun to bear on her legs, taking his time so he could wring as much satisfaction as possible out of wounding her.

She abandoned the doorknob, deciding to race down the hall when Bobby dove for Bill, shoving him off balance just as the door burst open and sent her sprawling. She twisted—it was that or do a face-plant into the worn wooden floor. She landed on her side, saw her father on the stoop and her heart fell. Until she saw Trip behind him. Armed. And his gun was bigger than Bill's.

Trip shoved by her father and headed for Bill, no hesitation, no concern for his own safety. Norah took one look at his expression and knew without looking that Bill had surrendered. And probably wet himself.

And then Trip looked at her and she felt the blood drain out of her face, too. "I was abducted," she said in her own defense. "Why are you mad at me?"

"I let you out of my sight for five minutes and you do something stupid."

"Stupid?" she said, her voice rising into a shriek. "Are you kidding me? What did I do that was stupid?"

"You went outside."

"How was I supposed to know someone was going to kidnap me?"

"Because someone has been trying to kidnap you from day one."

"Yeah, well, where were you?"

"Busy listening to the Lord of the Lies dance around the truth. Why aren't you yelling at him for having you kidnapped?"

She shot her father a look. He scrambled over to help her up. "Let me explain, darlin'," he whispered behind her back under the guise of untying her hands.

Norah ignored him. "I am angry," she snapped at Trip, "but I understand why he did what he did."

"For the money."

"And you chose your job over me."

"Do you hear yourself? You're not making any sense."

"I don't have to make sense. I didn't ask for any of this."

"If it wasn't for your old man robbing a bank, neither of us would be here."

"And that would make you happy, wouldn't it?"

Trip held her gaze for a second or two, the air all but crackling between them before he turned away to deal with Bill, tying his hands with a curtain cord so old the drapes it held back fell to the floor in a cloud of dust. But the curtain cord held. Then he looked at Bobby.

"Don't hurt the boy," Lucius said, abandoning her to head for Trip.

Norah was still bound, but the ties were loose enough for her to wiggle one hand free. She rubbed her wrists absently, watching from the entryway as Lucius ranged himself next to the kid, the two of them squaring off against Trip in the stream of afternoon sunlight pouring in through the filthy, curtainless front window. They were talking loud, arguing. The words failed to make an impression on Norah because pieces of the puzzle were falling into place, and not just about the loot.

Lucius looked over at her, their eyes met, and he went sheet white.

"Time for explanations," she said, even though she had a pretty good idea what was going on, if not the exact details.

"Let me deal with these two," Trip said, meaning, of course, Bill and Bobby.

"Do whatever you want with him," Norah said, pointing to Bill, "but the kid is coming with us."

Trip frowned at her, but he checked the ties on Bill's wrists then shoved him into the hall closet and braced a chair under the knob. Bill didn't object. Bill was probably thinking about the potential wear and tear on his kneecaps.

Trip caught Bobby Newcastle by the back of the shirt and quick-stepped him to Norah's house, and by the time they got there, he'd called his handler and arranged for Bill to be taken into federal custody.

"Talk," Trip said as soon as Norah's front door closed behind them all.

The silence was deafening.

"Who are you?" Trip said, pointing at the kid.

Bobby tried to sidle back into the shadows. Norah was behind him, so she shoved him back into the light.

"Take a closer look at him," she said to Trip.

He did, his frown of confusion fading away as his gaze switched between Bobby's face, Lucius's face, and hers.

"Well, I'll be a sonuvabitch," he said, his gaze finally landing on Norah. "That answers a question or two."

"Yeah, like why my mother finally divorced him after staying married to a man who'd proved himself untrustworthy for so many years."

"That's uncharitable, darlin'."

"Don't play the guilt card with me, Lucius. Not when you've got enough hanging over your head to keep the Vatican in business for the next decade."

Lucius opened his mouth, but she shot him down again, not in the mood for his games. "Tell me what Myra has to do with this," she said, needing the explanation, but needing the time more, to decide how she was going to handle the situation.

"Wait," Trip said, "why do you think your agent is involved?"

Norah gestured to the kid, still standing partly in front of her quaking in his shoes. "Meet Bobby Newcastle, Myra's son and, apparently, my half brother."

"And Puff's co-conspirator, I take it."

"He's the one who grabbed me," Norah said to Trip by way of confirmation, "after my—*our* father sent me outside looking for you."

"Kidnapping isn't his only skill," Trip said.

Norah shot Bobby a sidelong look. "Robin, I presume?"

He gave her a wobbly half smile and edged away from her.

"You're scaring the boy," Lucius said.

"He won't know fear until he spends a night in a cell with a lifer named Bruiser who thinks orange is his color."

Bobby let out a little squeak and dropped toward the nearest chair. He missed, thunking onto the floor. He stayed there.

"What I'd like to know is where's Batman?" Trip

said, adding, "The guy who tried to run us over outside the TV studio," when they all looked confused.

Norah filled him in on Bill's exploits. "And since Bill's going into custody, and he's a big, fat coward, I imagine he'll rat out the loan shark first chance he gets. Your friends will pick the guy up, and we won't have to worry about him."

"Maybe that problem is solved," Trip said, turning to Lucius, "but there'll just be someone else coming after you if we don't find the loot."

Lucius wasn't talking.

Bobby was too scared of everyone to talk, not to mention he probably didn't know anything. Puppets weren't known for their brain power.

Trip looked at Norah and crossed his arms.

She did a hands up. "I don't know where the loot is hidden."

They all turned to Lucius again. Lucius looked like the next ice age would come sooner than any information from him.

"Let me start the ball rolling," Trip said, filling Norah in on the conclusions he'd already drawn, about Lucius overplaying the severity of his injuries so he could slip out of the safe house.

Norah just sat there as he talked, reeling at the idea that her father had taken one look at her, after fifteen years, and out of all the reactions he might have had, he'd chosen to see an opportunity. It hurt, so much she was beyond tears, beyond anything but frozen, emotionless shock. And then she caught Trip's eyes on her. Her father was watching her, too, the two of them standing on opposite sides of her chair, shooting glances at one another over her head when they weren't staring at her. Shock, it turned out, wasn't the only thing she felt.

It wasn't even the strongest. But her anger was just as cold and emotionless, at least outwardly.

"Puff has been trying to get us out of the house since day one," Trip finished.

"Because the key, maybe literally, is here," Norah finished. "I already came to the same conclusion." And her bet would be the master bedroom since her father had spent so much time trying to get in there, and not just since they'd gotten home. "You sent Bobby here to try to steal whatever is hidden in the house. And when he failed you sent us on a wild-goose chase so you could escape the safe house and break in here while we were occupied three states away. And when *that* didn't work you had Bobby break in again, expecting Trip to chase him and me to be easily manipulated. Which was bound to fail, since I'm your daughter, but wasn't a total loss because you discovered that Trip and I were involved. So you had me kidnapped, figuring Trip would go after me and you'd be left alone to retrieve your clue or key, whatever is in this house that you're so desperate to get your hands on."

"First that fed figures it out," Lucius grumbled, "now you." He sat in his favorite armchair, looking crestfallen. "I'm losing my edge."

Norah would have laughed if the situation hadn't been so heartbreaking. "It's just that we know we're being conned, so we're looking for it."

"Then what do you need me for?"

"To fill in the blanks," Trip said. "Start from the beginning."

"The robbery." Lucius smiled a little, smugly, thrilled to let them in on the brilliance of his game now that they'd already figured out most of it. "I won't bore you with the planning of it, or the execution, as I'm sure you already know those details.

"It was child's play to get my so-called partners to pass off the loot to me. In case they got caught, I reasoned. I'd be safe since I wasn't actually there when the crime took place. There'd be no witnesses who could identify me, and the teller who'd let us into the bank couldn't rat me out without getting some federal heat for herself.

"But I miscalculated with the cops. Or maybe I should say we set our sights too high. We chose a bank in the high-rent district, patronized by the rich, so there'd be lots of expensive baubles and unreported goodies in the safe-deposit boxes. We didn't count on there being secrets in there, but the rich are also the powerful and the well-connected, and the secrets they stashed away had the entire Chicago PD mobilizing, not to mention the state police and the feds. We had no hope of escaping with that loot, especially after Noel Black and the Hanes brothers proved themselves to be morons."

"Money does that to people," Norah observed.

"Money is just a way to keep track," Lucius said. "Those boys were so stupid they all wound up dead, and they got me arrested. Myra was the only one I could trust."

Trip said what Norah was still too raw to put into words. "Because you were having an affair with her."

"Had." Lucius looked over at his son. Bobby pushed himself up from the floor and went to stand behind his father's chair. "That episode was over."

"Then it was because of Bobby."

"Aye." He passed a hand over his face. "I still feel the fool for what I did, Norah, hurting your mother, hurting you, although you didn't know about it yet. But your ma, bless her beautiful heart, decided we shouldn't tell you. She didn't see why I should lose you, too."

"And you would have," Norah said. "I'd have taken

her side." And although a part of her understood that knowing of Lucius's infidelity then would have taken the confusion out of that time of her life, it probably would have destroyed her relationship with her father. She wasn't too happy about it now, but she wasn't under the same illusions about his character as she'd been in her childhood. In fact, she was banking on it.

"You were barely eighteen at the time of the robbery, and your mother was ill. I didn't want to burden you," Lucius continued, getting back to his narrative, "so when Myra came to see me in jail, I came up with this . . ."

"Scheme," Norah supplied.

"Myra had hopes," Lucius said, seeming a little embarrassed.

For the life of her Norah couldn't understand why he should give a damn about playing her when he'd broken her mother's heart and used both his own children. "So you strung her along, made noises about being a family," she said, her voice sharp with hurt and anger, sharp enough that Lucius narrowed his eyes on her face. She drew in a breath and got her temper under control, schooling her expression and modulating her voice. She even managed to sound almost admiring when she said, "You got her to leave the clues, not the teller."

"And when you were out on bail, awaiting trial," Trip said, picking up the thread of the scam, "you hid the main cache of loot. Why didn't you just run?"

"He thought he could talk his way out of it," Norah said. "And then he got fifteen years."

"Who's tellin' this?" Lucius snapped, his accent thickening with his anger. "I figured I'd be out sooner, but those bloody federal agents kept after me for the loot." His gaze jumped to Trip. "And when I wouldn't tell the blackguards, they blocked my parole."

"I'm surprised they let you out now," Norah said. "No one knew where you were."

"My boy knew."

"He was only three when you went to jail," Norah said.

Trip only leaned back against the mantel, not surprised at all. "I was wondering how you got in touch with Myra and the kid when you were allowed no visitors, sent no mail, and made no phone calls."

"No access to the outside world," Lucius sneered. "It was absurdly simple to get information in and out of that place."

"You bribed another inmate?"

"That's thinking small, Norah darlin'."

"A guard," Trip said. "Maybe more than one. And then he had himself beaten up, knowing the FBI would move him to a safe house."

"And you sent us on a wild-goose chase to keep us busy and out of your hair," Norah finished, having no trouble when she understood that, having created the opportunity to contact someone, Lucius hadn't chosen her. Yet again. There'd been so much pain already, this new injury barely made a ripple.

"Did you find lovely things?" Lucius asked her.

"Yes," she said, not just talking about the items from the robbery.

"Then it was worth the trip."

Her father would probably never know how much. She couldn't help but look at Trip, meeting his gaze and knowing he was reliving those moments, too. But not for the same reason. "And it gave you a chance to slip the guards."

"Guards, hah. *Babysitters* more like. A little blood and bruising, a bit of limping, and a groan now and again," he shrugged, "it doesn't take much to fool men so unimaginative that they all wear the same suits and stupid sunglasses.

"The thing is," he continued, "being there provided me a perfect alibi. I contacted the boy, here, figuring to send him in to get the key, but when he told me about the new security system, I knew I had to come myself, and then I couldn't get in, even with instruction, because you let this—"

"FBI agent."

"—install that bloody alarm system. Jesus, Mary, and Joseph, Norah, why would you be letting him talk you into that contraption?"

"Because someone"—she looked at Bobby—"broke in here. And since he did it on your instructions, you have no room to complain."

"Never stopped me before."

"Why didn't you just come to me?"

"Because he"—Lucius pointed to Trip—"was already here. I never doubted the feds would use you, Norah, but I didn't count on you cooperating with them."

"That's the problem with the Long Con," Trip said. "Since the key to the loot is hidden here, it all hinged on Norah, and she wasn't under your thumb."

"And you think she's under yours?"

"I don't think she's under anyone's," Trip said.

But they were both expecting her to make a choice, the two of them staring at her, Lucius trying to hide his hope, Trip apparently not feeling any. Trip looked downright confident, in fact, arms crossed across his chest, a slight, expectant smile on his face. She could almost see the beginnings of his smug grin when she announced to her father that she had to do what was right, be a law-abiding citizen. Side with the man she loved.

His certainty, his smug belief that her choice wasn't

between right and wrong but between her father and her lover, made it easier, just slightly, for her to cross the room until she was standing beside Lucius's chair.

And then she looked into Trip's eyes.

chapter
24

"NORAH?" TRIP SAID.

"It has to be this way, Trip."

"You're choosing him? You're choosing him and the money?"

His words, the ease with which he'd reduced her to a mercenary after everything they'd been through, cut her heart in two. She'd asked for it, but still it tore her apart.

She didn't let it show, reaching down and slipping her hand into her father's and squeezing it, just for a moment, before she let go again. She couldn't afford to let him know she was shaking.

"You know he's lying to you," Trip said.

"I know he's lying to you."

"He had you kidnapped."

"He had his reasons."

"Yeah, fifty million of them, and they're all more important to him than you are."

Norah didn't say anything.

He crossed the room and took her by the upper arms, jerking her up to her toes. "He's using you."

She shook him off. "He's my father."

Trip let her go and backed off, his face going expressionless. Except his eyes. His eyes were hot and intense, boring into hers with the kind of silent condemnation that brought the blood to her cheeks. And the iron to her spine.

"I'm sorry," she said, stepping forward, almost against him, hating the relief she saw in his eyes before she took his phone and he understood that she hadn't come to her senses. It wasn't a momentary confusion on her part. She really had chosen a con artist and an inept burglar over him. "This is the way it has to be, Trip. They're my family, and I haven't had that in a really long time."

He caught her by the wrist, a muscle in his jaw working. "Just give me two minutes," he said, his gaze shifting to Lucius, then back. "Alone."

She could see it in his face, the struggle between what he might have wanted, without the job, and what he had to do because of it. And then he blew out a breath and she knew he was seeing her side of it. It was about the robbery for him. It was about closing his case.

It was about family for her, and he couldn't— *wouldn't* put himself in her life. Not in that capacity.

She put her hand over his, her heart aching, her throat so tight she had to swallow before words would come out, and then all she could manage was, "No."

If she let him get her alone, it wouldn't matter whether she changed sides or not. Lucius would always wonder what Trip had said to her out of his earshot, and what she'd said to Trip. And no matter how much fast-talking she did, her father would never trust her. And she needed him to trust her. She was turning her back on the only man she'd ever loved, breaking her own heart. It had to count for something.

She curled her fingers around Trip's and pulled her wrist free, very gently. He didn't try to stop her this time, but the way he was looking at her . . .

She flipped the phone open, blinking a couple of times before she could see the buttons well enough to even speed dial.

"Whaddya want, Jones?" his handler growled by way of greeting.

"Mr. Kova . . ."

There was silence. She could almost see the man sitting back in his chair and taking stock. "Mike."

"Mike," she repeated. "Call off your man or you'll never see the loot."

"I take it this means Jones isn't toes up."

"No, he's fine." *Angry, but fine.*

"Okay, then I assume you know where the loot is."

"If I even think the FBI is around, I'll toss it into Lake Michigan."

"You do that and—"

"What?" She turned away from Trip, away from her father. The rest of her life hinged on this phone call and she needed to concentrate. "What will you do? My dad has served his time, and the insurance companies have paid off on the claimed items."

"How about obstruction of justice? How about possession of stolen goods? How about just pissing me off? I can make you disappear with a snap of my fingers."

"With a documentary filmmaker watching my every

move? Not to mention the university, my neighbors, my agent, and all the people who read my book and will wonder where I've gone."

"Do you think that would stop the FBI?"

"Lake Michigan," she said.

He went silent again, assessing the conviction in her voice. He must have decided there was enough because he said, "You send Jones away and who'll have your back?"

She huffed out a slight laugh. "You and I both know that's not why you sent Trip here."

"It was a fringe benefit."

"True." She had to give him that.

"What I said still goes. How are you going to keep breathing when the treasure hunters come after you?"

She turned to meet her father's eyes. "We're not keeping it. Lucius wants to give it all back."

"What will that get you?"

"Nothing, but at least the rightful owners will have their family heirlooms, and hopefully some closure."

All she got was silence, the confused, pissed off kind, then Mike said, "Give the phone to Jones."

Norah handed it over. He took it and turned away from her, but she didn't need to see his face to know Mike was ordering him back to Washington.

He snapped the phone closed and spun around to confront her. "You got your way, professor."

"You're just angry because she won't be your lapdog," Lucius said.

Trip looked at Lucius, just looked at him, and he took a step back.

Norah went over to stand with him, curling her hand into the crook of his arm.

"Is that how you feel?" Trip asked her.

"Did you really believe she'd side with someone like you over her own family?" Lucius said, emboldened by Norah's support.

Trip kept his eyes on her, waiting for an answer.

Giving him one was the hardest thing she'd ever had to do. "I told you how I feel," she said in a voice that barely shook, "you just don't want to hear it."

He crossed his arms, not missing the fact that Bobby had come to stand behind his father and sister, the three of them forming a unit. And he was the enemy.

"Well," he said, "you've turned out to be your father's daughter."

"I was all along," Norah said, watching him go colder and so angry, angrier than she'd ever seen him before.

"So I'm getting sent away because I told you the truth, and you're sticking with a man who lied and mistreated you? Hell, he had a whole other family, Norah."

"And I'm not happy that he didn't tell me, but we keep coming back to the same thing."

"Family," Trip said.

"They're not perfect but they're mine."

"And I will never be."

"No," she said, "you never will be. You were honest about that, too."

"Then there's nothing left to say." He turned on his heel and walked out of the room.

And Norah watched him go, let him go, because she had to. Even though it hurt like hell.

"GOOD THING HE DIDN'T HAVE A GUN," LUCIUS said after Trip had retrieved his things from upstairs and walked out the front door, closing it so quietly after himself Norah could still hear the click echoing in the depths of her empty heart.

"He had a gun," she said. He just hadn't needed it. He had other weapons at his disposal, and he'd pulled them all out. Better he'd used a real gun, she thought. Then she'd be dead instead of just wishing she were.

Lucius would figure that out. He was studying her, and he was shrewd when it came to reading people. It was what made him such an extraordinary grifter. She had an advantage, though, a built-in smoke screen. He wanted to believe her. Just like she'd wanted to believe him.

"A man doesn't get that angry without being there," he said, "heart and soul."

Just the thought of Trip's heart was enough to have her eyes welling. "He was angry because he didn't close his case," she said, and made herself buy it, or at least consider the possibility. "I'm nothing more than a tool to him. I knew that going in."

"And you played him."

"He played himself," she said.

"The best marks always do."

Lucius levered himself up from his chair and hugged her. Norah closed her eyes and let the grief out, just for one second, putting it away before her father stepped back. Trip was the past; time to get the treasure disposed of and move on with her life.

"I knew you'd come around," Lucius said when he'd stepped back.

"Start talking," she said, "and it better be the truth, because I can still change my mind."

"You'd give in to that government stooge?"

"No, but I'd kick you out for conning me."

He closed down, eyes shuttered, face expressionless, and she knew she was walking a fine line. If he decided to cut her out, it meant she hurt Trip, and herself, for nothing. But then, she recalled as her father glanced toward the stairway, what he wanted was in the house. Her house. And he needed her to get it.

It allowed her to relax a little, and to remember something he'd once told her. The bigger the reward, the bigger the risk, and you had to face it like you'd already won. Any hesitation and you were lost. But she had to be herself, too, or he'd wonder at the sudden change.

"Well? I'm waiting."

"For what, darlin'?"

"For the rest of the story. For you to tell me what's hidden in this house."

Lucius seated himself again, taking his time to get comfortable. Then he looked up at her, his expression innocent. "I don't know where it is."

"You have got to be kidding me."

Lucius sighed, acting completely put-upon.

Norah paced across the room trying to get a handle on her anger. It came back with her, had her looming over her father, shaking a finger in his face. "You lied to me about everything, you cost me my job, you had me kidnapped, you made me piss off the FBI, which could land me in jail, and you think you're going to sit there and con me?"

"No need to shout, darlin'," Lucius said. "And watch your language."

"I'll use whatever language I want. And cut the *darlin'* crap."

"What do you want from me?" Lucius shot back. "I'm an old dog."

"Well, here's a new trick for you. It's called the truth."

Lucius shot to his feet, all pretense at infirmity abandoned. "Where's the fun in that?"

"I'm your daughter. You're not supposed to lie to me."

Lucius shook his head. "It had to be done because of Jones."

"No, it didn't. You could have told me the truth and trusted me to decide what do with it. I quit my job because of you and all this"—she gestured around her—"isn't free. So I'll say it again, start talking."

Lucius drew in a breath and let it out slowly, never taking his eyes from hers. "I knew the feds would be coming after me when my sentence was almost over," he finally said. "They'd been at me on and off over the fifteen years, holding out freedom as the price of honesty."

"Bastards," Norah said, and meant it. Lucius was a criminal, but he was also her father, and while the FBI was only using the tools at hand, she hated that they'd tortured him like that.

"As my release date got closer, I knew they'd step up the pressure."

"So you used the scavenger hunt."

"I didn't want to, dar—Norah, but I had no choice." He held up a hand. "I know, I could have told you the truth, but you have to understand, I hadn't talked to you in fifteen years, and I didn't know what those people had told you."

"The truth," she said simply. It was all they'd needed. "But the truth is rarely black and white."

Her father smiled hugely. "Now that's my girl talking."

"I'd prefer to do some more listening."

Lucius twisted around to look at Bobby, still standing behind him. He hadn't made a peep since he'd taken up his post at Lucius's back, but he'd taken in every word.

"Son, could you give us some privacy?"

"But—"

"Robert."

"Wait," Norah said to Bobby.

He turned back at the door to the parlor. He wasn't meeting her eyes.

"I wish I'd known," she said. "I could have helped you in school."

"I won't be needing school," he said. "That was just a . . ." He looked at his father.

"Cover story," Lucius supplied.

"Cover story," he repeated. "We're going to be rich . . . aren't we?"

"Of course, son," Lucius said. "Run along. I'll call you when it's time."

Bobby smiled and left without a backward glance.

"He's not the sharpest tool in the shed, but he's a good boy," Lucius said.

Norah nodded, thinking *tool* was a pretty apt description. But then, in her father's world everyone was a tool. And once a tool's usefulness had been exhausted, it was discarded.

The FBI worked the same way. Both of them claimed to be doing the right thing. Both of them had ulterior motives that weren't so pure.

Norah just wanted to get her life back. Even if she had to spend it alone.

"It's just you and me, Dad," she said, choosing the familiar term of address deliberately. "Tell me the rest."

Lucius went to the small dry bar and poured a shot of Jameson's into a crystal tumbler. He slammed it back, then poured two fingers more and went back to his chair. He started to talk, without any prodding this time, unless she counted the whiskey he sipped to loosen his tongue as he revealed the final points of his plan, which was ingenious, actually, so ingenious she didn't have any trouble being impressed, and letting him see it.

When he was finished, she said, "You know that's not going to work anymore. Trip is gone but the FBI will be watching both of us. We're going to need another plan."

"And you're going to tell me I should allow you to make the decisions."

"You've been out of circulation for fifteen years. Is there any other choice?"

Lucius tossed back the rest of his whiskey. "No," he said. But he didn't like it.

Neither did Norah, but she couldn't turn back now.

chapter
25

NORAH SPENT THE NIGHT ON HER LAPTOP. SHE
opened a brand-new e-mail address in her father's name
and set about making arrangements for the rest of the loot.
It was pathetically easy. She felt like hell the entire time,
and not just because she didn't sleep. Because she was
going to be alone, again. She'd been alone for fifteen
years, no family, no partner of significance, since Raymond Kline had been little more than occasional company for dinner. Being alone hadn't really been so bad.
Problem was, now she knew what she'd been missing.

It wasn't as if she hadn't known what she was doing,
she reminded herself as she punched the alarm code into
the keypad by her front door and let herself out. She
closed the door silently behind herself and turned, stopping in her tracks to stare at the person standing on the
sidewalk outside her wrought iron fence.

She stood there a second, caught between what waited

for her at the curb and what she'd left inside. It didn't take much thinking to convince her that going forward was still the right course.

She went down the steps and along the paved walkway, stopping inside her front gate where she still felt safe. She wasn't completely stupid.

"Myra," she said, looking up and down the street, empty and dark except for the streetlights. The night was clear, but the stars couldn't penetrate Chicago's ambient haze of light, even at four a.m. "Is Bobby with you?"

"No," Myra said, wringing her hands. "He's home, sleeping. He believes Lucius, but I know better. You and I know better, Norah."

"Lucius is a con artist."

"*Yes*. He lies for a living."

"You lied, Myra. To my mother."

"I didn't even know your mother."

"You knew Lucius was married."

Norah hadn't been sure until that moment, but when Myra looked away, she knew she was right. "You lied to me. You've been lying since the day we met."

"No, I—"

"Either tell me the truth or save your breath."

Myra curled her hands around the wrought iron gate bars. "I met your father—"

"The last couple of years are all I want to hear about," Norah said, resisting the urge to vomit. "I'll assume you convinced me to write a book so you could insinuate yourself into my life, hoping to have an inside track on the loot."

"Well . . . yes. Lucius still had a couple of years in prison when I came to work at the college."

"On purpose. So you could meet me."

"Yes."

"Why didn't you just get Bobby to find out where the loot was?"

"I had no idea he was in contact with Lucius," Myra said, "and I never expected your book to take off like it did."

"That's flattering."

"Really, Norah, you're not exactly ... You teach psychology, and the biggest challenge your students face is staying awake in your lectures."

Norah felt her face flush, but she had to admit it was true. Facing a classroom full of staring faces made her feel like she had to deliver information without any embellishment or humor. Writing was a whole other feeling. She wrote as if she were talking to a friend, sharing personal experiences and laughing over them. "Glad to surprise you," was all she said.

Myra chuckled softly. "It was quite a surprise, too. And inconvenient, to say the least."

"The publicity. It wasn't my favorite part of the writing experience," Norah said. Not to mention it had caused her trouble, being recognized when she and Trip had been trying to stay under the radar while they followed Myra's clues. And then there was Hollie Roget, although she'd have been a nuisance in any case, since she wanted Raymond Kline, for reasons that still escaped Norah. But at least Hollie had been honest, mostly, about her feelings.

"I never expected to like you so much, either," Myra said. "I didn't think we'd become friends—"

"We were never friends, Myra. You don't know what that means."

"You haven't been in love, Norah, really in love. Not like that."

Norah didn't reply. She didn't even want to think

about how wrong that statement was. Then again, even though she loved Trip desperately, she couldn't do desperate things to keep him. It would change who she was, and she liked who she was, despite everything she'd been through in the last few days.

"We can get the loot together, just you and I," Myra was saying. "We'll split it fifty-fifty."

"What about Bobby? My brother."

"Bobby is my son. My responsibility."

"What if I said my father is mine?"

"Then I'd call you a fool."

Norah snorted out a laugh. "You'd have been right about that until yesterday." She tried to push through the gate.

Myra held her off. "Norah, please. We can—"

"Get out of my way, Myra."

She held on a second or two longer, then let go of the bars, backing off slowly.

"And don't even think about following me."

"I could go inside and wake your father."

"You don't even have to go inside, Myra, just touch the front door and the alarm will go off. But it won't do either of you any good. It's too late for you to stop me now."

"You can still change your mind. If anyone can talk you out of going, it's Lucius."

"If that were true, I'd be in my bed sleeping." She hiked her laptop case and purse up on her shoulder and pushed through the gate.

She didn't look back. Myra would take whatever action she had to take, just like Norah was doing what she had to do. And just like her father would do when he found out that she'd double-crossed him.

* * *

BY MIDNIGHT, TRIP WAS BREAKING INTO THE MU-
seum of Westward Expansion in St. Louis. The Gateway Arch soared overhead, its stainless steel surface
shining dully in the city lights. The Mississippi River
flowed just yards away, but Trip didn't hear the gentle
lapping of the current against the St. Louis levee. He
was completely focused on the task at hand, he tried to
tell himself, not thinking about anything, or anyone,
else. Especially Norah.

He'd only stayed at her house long enough to gather
his things together, along with the last clue from the
Detroit Zoo. Norah hadn't even looked at him when he
went out the front door. She hadn't watched him out
the window. He knew, he'd checked. And he was
ashamed of himself for it. Now.

At first the shame had just made him angrier. It was
about three hundred miles from Chicago to St. Louis,
and it had taken Trip that long to cool down and think
rationally . . . Okay, somewhat rationally. He wasn't
seeing the world through a red haze any more, or resisting the urge to drive his car into the other drivers
whose only crime was being on the same road as him.
He didn't want to go back and yell at Lucius, either; he
intended to tie up this loose end then head back to Chicago to close his case.

And he would be going back. As soon as he could
look at Norah MacArthur without the urge to wrap his
hands around her neck.

The alarm system presented little problem for him.
The museum didn't hold items of great value, no jewels or priceless works of art. Some of the items on exhibit, Indian peace medals struck in silver, cowboy
paraphernalia, even some of the items carried by set-
tlers heading west in Conestoga wagons, would fetch

decent prices from collectors, but only for their historical value. The most precious contents of the museum were probably unknown even to its curators. That was *if* Puff had sent Myra there fifteen years earlier. Trip figured he had a fifty-fifty chance of finding something from the Gold Coast Robbery hidden there.

He took his time in the museum, not bothering with a map, just covering the semicircular space methodically. He came across the Lewis and Clark exhibition first, a series of thirty-three murals spread around the outermost wall of the museum. Each mural consisted of a photo of some natural landscape that related to the expedition, with an excerpt from the journals kept by William Clark during their trek, ranging in time from 1804 to 1806.

Trip decided almost immediately that the murals provided no place to hide even a small cache of loot from the robbery. He perused the entire exhibit, though. Better to be thorough.

The museum also boasted a full-size Conestoga wagon. It was the only other potential hiding place, so Trip made his way through the silent, empty museum, ignored the barriers around the wagon, and climbed on board. It took him about an hour to go over it from top to bottom.

He was lying underneath it, searching for likely cracks in the planking, when someone said, "Come out from under the wagon," in a tone that would have had more impact if the voice of the speaker hadn't cracked.

Trip almost grinned as he crawled out and got to his feet, not surprised to be confronted by a museum guard who was little more than a kid. A kid holding him at gunpoint.

"Step away from the exhibit, sir," the kid said, sounding steadier when Trip continued to do as instructed, making his way out of the exhibit with his hands raised about shoulder level.

"I'm not trying to steal anything, honest," he told the kid, stopping about ten feet in front of him.

"Sure, whatever you say, but I have to detain you anyway."

Trip shrugged. "Okay. Do I get a phone call?"

"Keep your hands where I can see them."

"I'm with the FBI, Jerry," Trip said, reading off the kid's name badge. "I'm going to call my handler."

"No, you're not, sir."

Trip lowered his right hand anyway.

Jerry didn't know what to do, faced with an intruder who claimed to be a federal agent—*claimed* being the operative word, and as Trip saw the kid come to that conclusion, that it was easy to make assertions, he said, "Let me get my ID out," and reached for his back pocket as if to retrieve his badge from his wallet.

As soon as Jerry dropped his eyes, Trip struck out with his arm and knocked the gun sideways. It went off, the shot going well wide. By then, Trip had Jerry disarmed. He backed off, eyes wide, arms lifting as Trip's had been.

"Relax, I'm not going to shoot you."

"You're not?"

"I need you to call the head guy, get him down here."

"The curator? What for . . . Shit," Jerry said, his eyes focused about ten feet to Trip's left. "Dude, I shot a hole in the wagon. Schiffer's gonna be pissed."

Trip blew out a breath, laughing a little. "Tell everyone it was damaged in an Indian attack."

"You think that will fly?"

"I'd believe it, and it's better than reporting your gun went off when you were trying to shoot a federal agent."

"But, like, you broke in here." Jerry started walking, heading toward the offices. "How was I supposed to know you were a fed?"

"Nobody would have cared once they took my ID off my cold, lifeless body."

Jerry's steps faltered, his face going white. "I was just doing my job, man."

"Sure, whatever you say. Could you call Schiffer, get him down here?"

Jerry took out his phone, dialed a number, but he was shaking his head. "Schiffer isn't going to like this."

Too bad, Trip thought, sitting where Jerry indicated. In less than sixty minutes, Jared Schiffer arrived, looking like he'd just gotten out of bed and severely pissed, just as Jerry had predicted.

"What the hell is going on?" he demanded, his gaze going from Jerry, who sidled back against the wall, to Trip, who stayed in his seat.

Trip did, however, hold out his cell. "My handler wants to talk to you."

Schiffer narrowed his eyes, glared at Trip a few seconds, then took the phone. Trip had to give the man credit; he didn't let Mike Kovaleski intimidate him.

"What I want to know," Schiffer said after he'd listened a half a minute or so, "is why this couldn't have been handled during the hours of normal operation, or, at the very least, without your man breaking in."

Trip could hear Mike yelling at the curator. He couldn't make out the words, but Schiffer could, which was all that mattered. He said, "You have rounds" to Jerry, then handed Trip his phone back and said, "Follow me."

"What did you yell at him?" Trip said into the phone, getting to his feet and following Schiffer through the door he unlocked.

"The usual threats," Mike said in his usual tone of voice, which sounded like he was chewing gravel. "I assume you're closing in on the loot."

"I'm following a lead," he said shortly, his eyes on Schiffer, who was listening unashamedly. "I'll call you in a day or two, give you a progress report." Once he found out what Norah and Lucius were up to.

"Glad to hear there's progress," Mike said. "There is progress, right?"

"Gotta go," Trip said, and hung up, but not before he heard Mike bellow out a laugh. It didn't mean he wouldn't be expecting a break in the case sometime soon. Mike might appreciate quick wits, but he also expected quick results.

"Your handler said you would fill me in," Schiffer said as he settled behind his desk, gesturing to a chair in front of it.

"No, he didn't."

Schiffer sighed. "You dragged me out of bed, and I'm not even getting an explanation?"

Trip glanced around the office, which was immaculate. The desk was completely barren except for a blotter. There was no dust, and the carpet bore vacuum marks. Having the FBI drop in was probably the most exciting thing that had happened to Jared Schiffer in his entire life. Too bad Trip couldn't tell him why he was there; having a part, even peripherally, in the Gold Coast Robbery would have given the man conversational fodder for the rest of his life. Then again, depending on the answer to his next question, Trip might have no choice but to clue Schiffer in.

"I need to know if you've ever found anything hidden in the museum, specifically the Lewis and Clark exhibit or the Conestoga wagon."

The curator stared at him for a couple of seconds,

then took out a set of keys and unlocked his bottom right file drawer. He pulled out a manila folder and placed it on his otherwise empty desktop, maneuvering it just so on the pristine blotter.

"We were checking the Conestoga for dry rot a couple of years ago, and we came across this," he finally said. He flipped open the file and removed a note covered in plastic, sliding it across the desk.

Trip reached for it, read the single word, and swore under his breath. If he'd made the choice to come here with Norah, if they'd found this together, she'd have had no choice but to side with him. Although, if he'd come here with Norah, Puff would have had time to break into her house, retrieve whatever he'd hidden, and they'd both be out of luck. Puff and the loot would be long gone.

The saying *Everything happens the way it's supposed to* ran through his mind. He thought that was bullshit. If everything happened the way it was supposed to, he'd have closed his case and he'd be . . . in Washington, without Norah. But at least he'd never have discovered her capacity for betrayal.

He got to his feet, the note, unnoticed, crumpled in his hand.

"Wait," Schiffer said, jumping out of his chair. "At least tell me what it means, *Gotcha*."

"It means I was right all along," Trip said. "I just found out too late for it to make a difference."

chapter
26

BY FIVE A.M., TRIP WAS ON THE OUTSKIRTS OF Chicago, calm for real this time. His head was full of questions for Norah, the questions he should have asked her in the first place, instead of losing his temper. But dammit, she'd taken her father's side, after all they'd been through together. Or so he'd believed. Because he'd been filtering everything she said through his emotions.

She'd been counting on that. But she didn't have a clue there was more than anger going on inside him. He could at least be thankful for that. Norah MacArthur had turned out to be a hell of a con artist. Her father's daughter. Trip had been right about that much. He could only imagine what she could have goaded him into doing if she knew . . .

He took a mental step back, putting himself into the operation again. Norah had made her choice, and it

was the right choice, even if it was for the wrong reward. He didn't know what pissed him off more, that
she'd been strong enough to do what they both knew
had to be done, or that he was mooning over a woman
who'd kicked him out of her life. But then . . .

He scrubbed a hand back through his hair, thinking
Fuck it, I'm in love with her. And yeah, that pissed him
off the most. He wasn't giving up his job, and a man in
his position had no business getting involved with anyone
that way. Love was a weakness, he'd always believed.
But he didn't feel weak. Running away was weak.

He pulled up to the curb in front of Norah's house
just as dawn was breaking. He angled out of the black
Mustang GT, made his way to her front door, and
knocked. No answer. He decided to pick the lock, but
when he put his hand on the knob it turned, so he
stepped inside and punched the code into the keypad.

"So you're back."

Trip spun around and there was Lucius, sitting in the
parlor sipping coffee laced, Trip suspected, with the
whiskey sitting in the decanter at his elbow.

"Where's Norah?"

"Gone," Lucius said. "She took off with the key to
the loot."

Trip shook his head a little, then replayed that last
comment. Even when he repeated it, he still didn't
believe it. "She's gone?"

"Aye. Gone. She conned the secret to the loot out of
me and absconded with it. I'd be proud of her if I
didn't feel like such a bloody fool."

Trip sat down on the horsehair sofa, still trying to
wrap his mind around it. "Did she go to the police?"

"Jesus, are you trying to kill me? Isn't it bad enough
that she played me, her own father? Now you're wanting me to think she's gone to the cops, too?"

"Well, where the hell do you think she's gone?"

"Some country that has no extradition agreement with the United States."

"What time did she leave?"

"Middle of the night's as close as I can approximate it."

"And the treasure is . . ."

Lucius sat up, looked over at him for the first time. "There's no way she's gotten the loot yet," he said, not looking all that cheered by the news.

Trip had been so sure he'd misread Norah, that she'd had a good reason for making him leave. Now he found himself having to make a decision between trusting her and working with her father to track her down.

But either way it all circled back to the loot. "So tell me where it is and we'll go get it," he said to Lucius, "hopefully before Norah does."

"That's the problem, boyo, she's got the list."

"List?"

"Aye, list. And the passwords."

Passwords, that didn't sound good. "I don't suppose there's any way you memorized the passwords."

"I knew them fifteen years ago, but now?" He shook his head.

"In that case," Trip said, getting to his feet, "you'll only slow me down."

TRIP'S PHONE RANG WHEN HE WAS SITTING IN AN Internet café, south of Chicago. He'd gone south because, he'd reasoned, going north didn't make any sense, and Norah was a sensible woman. An infuriating woman, but sensible, and north meant she'd be hampered by Lake Michigan and Lake Superior. Unless she was headed for

Canada. Or west. There wasn't a whole lot west, and small towns meant she'd stand out, so he'd ruled out west. Canada, however, had real possibilities. Her passport would be recorded when she crossed the border, but once she was out of the country his resources would be severely limited.

Of course, that only mattered if she had the loot. He was betting she didn't—not yet anyway—and he was betting that wherever Lucius stashed it was south of Chicago. His goal, he thought as he picked up his still-ringing phone, was to find Norah.

"Hello?"

"Trip?"

He froze, even the breath backing up in his lungs, and when he didn't respond she said, "It's Norah."

"I know," he said. Not that her name had been the first thing that popped into his mind. In all fairness nothing had popped into his mind; he'd had to get through the instant rush of emotion first. But the emotion had been anger, and the thoughts that had come along with it hadn't been pretty.

"I'd like to explain—"

"Explain what?"

"I was just at your house, you weren't there."

"I had to leave—"

"After you stole fifty million dollars from your father."

"I didn't—"

"Con the con artist? Sure you did. You conned me, you conned your long-lost brother. You played us all, sweetheart."

"If you would let me finish a sentence—"

"I'll be happy to, but not over the phone."

"Fine, I'll meet you."

"Right," Trip sneered, "I'm going to fall for that."

"Then you pick the time and place," she said, sounding exasperated.

"I plan to. When and where you least expect it."

Norah digested that for a second. "You're going to track me down, put out one of those . . ."

"APBs," Trip supplied. "And no. No APB. This is between you and me. Darlin'."

Norah winced at that. Not the word, the tone. Trip was beyond anger, at least the kind with heat. This anger was cold and hard and unforgiving. That alone would have been enough to make her run like hell, but facing Trip wasn't her only concern. The FBI would never have left her father alone as long as he had the loot. She could get her father out of trouble despite himself, at least where the Gold Coast Robbery was concerned, if she could only handle this the way she'd planned. That hinged on her going in to the FBI willingly, not in handcuffs. Handcuffs seriously compromised her bargaining position.

"Trip, if you'd just listen to me—"

"I will, when we're in the same room and I can see your face."

"Seeing my face didn't make a difference yesterday." And reminding him of that didn't help matters.

"I'm coming for you, professor," Trip said.

"Bring it on."

Trip smiled. It was not a nice smile, which he knew because the kid at the next table took one look at his face, scooped up his laptop, and ran out the door without shutting it down.

"You're on," he said to Norah, "and just to be fair, you should stop using your credit card."

"I already have. I withdrew enough cash for—Good

one. You knew I was smart enough to stay off the grid, and you were hoping to make me reveal something."

Trip clenched his jaw, hard, just for a second. "I hope you have enough, because your credit cards and bank accounts are frozen. And as for staying off the grid, let's not forget you're a bestselling author."

There was a split second of silence, one of those pauses Norah made when she was absorbing the conversation and choosing her words carefully.

"I'm sorry I hurt you," she said.

"Don't be. It was all about the job."

"For you," she said. "This was never a job to me."

NORAH WENT FROM HOTEL TO HOTEL, SOMETIMES twice in one day, thankful at least that Trip wasn't involving the local police. Still, every time she saw a policeman she practically had a heart attack. Even security guards sent her into palpitations. It was a wonder she hadn't been arrested just for looking guilty— not that she looked as guilty as she felt.

She'd turned out to be a better grifter than she'd ever expected, and she wasn't quite sure how she felt about that. Part of her, a small part, was proud, but then there was the part of her that had always feared she had too much of her father in her—the part that had suppressed any spark of originality or adventure and guided her into that medium life that had seemed so safe. Looking back now it just seemed . . . gray. Not that her current situation was all sunshine and roses.

Three days after their dismal phone conversation, she found herself in Atlanta, exhausted out of her mind, pulling into the first hotel she found.

"May I help you?" the young woman at the front desk

asked, her mouth dropping open before Norah could ask for a room. "Oh my gosh, it's you."

"No, it's not," Norah said, closing her eyes and shaking her head over how lame a reaction *that* was. "I'm sorry, Janey," she said, reading the girl's name tag, "I'm really tired. I'd appreciate it if you could give me a room, and . . . keep it to yourself that I'm here?"

"Of course," Janey said, "but could you maybe help me? My boyfriend, Jack, he's been acting really weird lately."

Norah sighed heavily. "Explain *weird*."

"Well, a couple times I walked into the room when he was on the phone, and he cut off the conversation really fast."

"Uh-huh."

"I checked his phone log, and my best friend's phone number was in the outgoing call log."

"Uh-huh."

"And he's keeping secrets from me. Like I saw him looking in my jewelry box, but he wouldn't tell me why."

"You live together, I take it."

"Yes, for about a year now, and we dated for almost two years before that."

"So, you're pretty serious about one another. How's the sex?"

An elderly couple standing a little way down the counter sent Norah a look. She couldn't have cared less. She'd say or do just about anything to get to a bed.

"The sex is amazing," Janey whispered.

"Okay, so I take it you're not in a rut any other way. He's still affectionate, still tells you he loves you?"

Janey nodded.

"Has he ever given you reason to doubt him?"

"Not until lately," Janey said miserably.

"My guess is he's going to propose," Norah said.

"Propose? Seriously?"

"He's talking to your friend because he wants her to help him pick out a ring, and he's probably trying to come up with a unique way to pop the question. That would be why he cuts off phone conversations."

"So I don't overhear his plans. Awwww, what a sweetie."

"Room," Norah said, almost blind with exhaustion. "Secret."

"Sure thing, Doctor MacArthur," Janey chirped, all happy and bursting with love.

"Doctor MacArthur?" the elderly woman said. "Norah MacArthur, the author? Where?"

Norah took the room key and counted out the cash for a night's stay, stuffing the woefully small roll of cash she had left in her purse. Even if she was careful, she wasn't sure she could make it two days on what she had left. But she was sure she couldn't stay in that hotel. Hell, the entire city was out of the question now.

She took the elevator up one floor, then hit the stairs and snuck through the lobby so Janey and company didn't see her leaving. She was almost in tears when she slid behind the wheel of her Escape. It was only a matter of time before someone posted online that she'd been spotted in Atlanta, and not long after that Trip would be hot on her trail. When he got there she'd be gone, and he'd have wasted all that time. Now all she had to do was keep from falling asleep at the wheel. Then again, death sounded so restful.

Two days later she dragged her butt through the door of the latest no-tell motel, this one in a questionable part of Washington, D.C. She went inside, flipped the lights on and shut the door, and dropped her purse and overnight bag on the bed, setting the takeout she'd gotten at the greasy spoon next door on the table.

She was glad to be inside, but she couldn't settle. She was moderately well rested, but she couldn't shake the feeling that Trip was breathing down her neck, which was ridiculous since she'd moved around so much. It was just guilt dogging her heels, she decided, guilt for hurting Trip, guilt for betraying her father. And worry.

For the first time in her life she was flying without a net. No job, no money; well, she had some savings, enough to get her through the next few months. Now she just needed to figure out what she should do with the rest of her life. Turned out teaching wasn't her thing. She liked counseling, though, liked the feeling she was helping people . . . She sighed, dropping onto the lumpy mattress. Truth was, she didn't feel like doing anything at the moment. It was hard to think around the heartache. But after tomorrow she'd be able to move on from that. She looked at the clock next to the bed. Almost midnight. Just twelve more hours—

Someone knocked on her door.

Norah froze, just her eyes shifting in that direction. She didn't even cross the room and look through the peephole, afraid of who she'd see on the other side. Considering the neighborhood she ought to be afraid for her life. What she was worried about was her heart.

"Open up, professor, I know you're in there."

Trip. She closed her eyes, not breathing for a second while she made the mental adjustment from possibility to reality. Reality brought her back around to possibility, as in possibilities for escape, which, she quickly discovered, were nonexistent.

Her room, like all the other rooms, opened directly to the outside along a cement walkway. The bathroom, when she got up to check, had no window at all. In hindsight, not her best choice.

"You have nowhere to go," Trip yelled through the

door, "and the longer you keep me waiting, the unhappier I'm going to get."

She took a few precious seconds to get hold of herself, to start breathing again, before she opened the door. "*Unhappier* is not a word," she said.

"Words are not my weapon, they're yours. And it got my point across." He pushed past her and took a good, long look around. "Not exactly the kind of place you expected to be living with fifty million dollars at your disposal."

Norah shut the door and turned around, staying where she was. "It's not at my disposal."

"Not yet," Trip said.

"Not ever."

"Don't play with me."

"I'm not—" The rest was cut off by a gasp as he crossed the room, took her by the upper arms, and lifted her to her toes.

Trip saw the shock on her face, chased away by fear, and then determination. It pissed him off. He added it to the list, what she'd done a week ago, having to chase her halfway across the country. Losing control of the mission.

Hope. The thing that pissed him off most of all.

There was no rhyme or reason to where Norah went each day. She'd never ditched the Escape—aptly named since there were a million of them on the road, and even with the dents and the undisguised license plate, she'd managed to keep just out of his reach. Of course he hadn't put out an APB on her or her vehicle, and not because he wanted to take her on head-to-head. She was no match for him. He'd kept it between them because he had hope. Hope that she hadn't absconded with the loot.

Trip wasn't used to hope. He dealt with the Criminal Element, and the Criminal Element had only one motive: look out for Number One, which meant he pretty much knew what to expect going in.

Norah had been . . . not just good, perfect. Not so much as a smudge on her record going all the way back to kindergarten. Even now, with proof, he had a hard time believing she'd gone bad. Apparently fifty million dollars could do that to a person, even a perfect one.

"I'm not in the mood for games," he said.

Norah lifted her chin, keeping her gaze level on his. She didn't say a word, or make a peep, but he could see the pain in her eyes. It shamed him.

"Time for that explanation you promised me," he said, letting her go.

She rubbed her arms, looking mutinous. "I changed my mind. You don't deserve one."

"Start talking."

"Or?"

"Or I'll take you in."

"Great, take me in. That's why I'm in Washington anyway."

Trip took a step back, physically and mentally. "What are you up to now?"

"You want me to stop playing games? The games are over." She took a step forward. "You win. Arrest me."

He held his ground, his mind racing a mile a minute, trying to figure out what angle she was playing now.

She held out her wrists and stepped forward, so close her fingers brushed his chest. "Go ahead," she said, "cuff me."

It was the last straw. He put his hands around her wrists, yanked her against him, and kissed her.

And she kissed him back, God help her. She fought his grip, but her mouth was wild on his, and he pulled her hands out from between them, staking her wrists to the door and trapping her body with his while he plundered her mouth. She twisted, fought, protested, and when none of that worked she nipped his bottom lip.

He pulled back, letting her go and covering his mouth with a hand that shook, staring at her and realizing he'd almost crossed a line. "I'm sorry, Norah," he began, the rest of his breath wheezing out when she whipped her shirt off and then her bra, her gaze holding his.

He forgot about being gentle, heat exploding through him again, fueled by anger and a need so overwhelming it stole his breath, his control, everything but the clawing drive to have her. He scooped her up and dropped her on the lumpy bed, stripping her jeans off but ignoring his own clothes because he had to get his hands on her, watch the way her skin flushed and glowed as he touched her, a little roughly but not to punish. Not anymore.

No matter who she might be the rest of the time, at least here she was honest. And amazing, reacting to even the lightest touch of his fingertips. Her hands fisted in the threadbare coverlet, her body bowing as he covered her breasts with his hands, palming her nipples before he took one hard peak into his mouth. She gasped, crying out when he slipped two fingers into her, her breath coming fast and short as she rose to peak, as she went stiff, and he felt her climax rip through her. It was all he could do to keep from taking her, hard and fast, taking his pleasure as she'd taken hers. He didn't want to rush, though he ached from head to toe with the depth of his need. There was no point in returning to reality any sooner than he had to.

He collapsed onto the bed next to Norah, and after a moment or two he felt her touch his cheek, hesitantly. It killed him that she wasn't sure, even here, so he covered her hand with his and turned his lips into the palm of her hand.

"Trip . . ." she whispered.

"What?" he said without opening his eyes.

"Nothing." Even if she'd known what to say and how to say it, he wouldn't have believed her anyway, and if she were foolish enough to bare her heart and he rejected her . . . Well, she'd never get over it.

So she settled for showing him, slipping her hands under his T-shirt and easing it off as he half lifted to help her, then popping the button on his jeans and unzipping them, very slowly, so slowly he cracked one eye open, looking like he was in pain, which made her laugh even though when she got his pants off she could believe he was in pain.

"At least you stopped laughing," he said, his voice low and raspy, but teasing, which almost broke her heart, but then she decided not to think about what would happen after. She intended to make love with him, even if all the love was on her side.

"Definitely not a laughing matter," she said, teasing him back.

"Definitely not," he said, pulling her down beside him.

But Norah was done being passive, not that passive didn't have its benefits—which were still buzzing along her nerve endings—but she wanted to do for Trip what he'd done for her.

She got to her knees, running her nails lightly along his chest, loving the way he groaned, loving how his breath wheezed out when she took him into her hands, loving him, even when he reared up and said, "Now," and took her waist in his hands and pushed her onto her back. She didn't object or take offense. Words were beyond her, too, as he surged into her, hard and fast, and she forgot how to breathe and how to think. Everything was gone but feeling. A dozen different sensations overwhelmed her, the heat of his skin and the feel of muscle sliding under it as she moved her hands to his back, the weight of him bearing her down into the mattress, his fingers moving from her waist to her hips, biting in for a second before he scooped them under her backside and lifted her. He drove into her, deeper this time, so deep she arched, her hands clutching at him and slipping off his sweat-slicked skin as the breath locked into her lungs and there was only the slap of his body against hers, the friction of him stroking in and out, harder and faster as her body coiled tighter and then erupted, another orgasm tearing her into glittering shreds of pure, unbearable pleasure as he buried himself deep and came with a groan that sounded like it was ripped from the soles of his feet.

Norah's hands slid from his back and fell limply to the mattress, the rest of her feeling just as wrung out, weak and weightless and sated, so gloriously sated she barely found the energy to slide up to the pillows when Trip nudged her. She made it, though, forgetting her dinner, forgetting the loot, so exhausted she even let go of the tension between her and Trip.

He didn't. She felt him pick up her wrist and then there was the shock of cold metal, the rasp as he closed the handcuff over her wrist, putting the other one on himself.

She opened her eyes and looked up at him from dry sockets, the pain so deep and intense and hot it seared the tears away before they could form.

"You think I'm going to sneak out in the middle of the night?"

"I think I'm too tired to wake up if you try it."

"After . . ." She shook her head, closed her eyes, not, she realized after all, too destroyed to cry.

The bed dipped next to her as Trip climbed in. He spooned himself behind her, his cuffed hand slipping over her waist to cover her cuffed hand.

She couldn't bear it. The parody of love and trust broke her heart. She pushed away from him, threw off the covers, and tried to search for her clothes. Of course Trip stayed where he was so she came up short.

"Norah?" he said quietly.

She sat on the edge of the bed, shutting her eyes until she could get the pain under control. And the tears. "I'd like to get dressed," she finally said, almost without a hitch.

"Come back to bed. You can get dressed in the morning."

"I need to get dressed now. I can't—" She spied Trip's jeans, one leg over the bottom corner of the bed, and when she stretched until her wrist screamed in pain, she managed to grab them. The key to the cuff was in the pocket.

She unlocked the cuff on his wrist, ignoring the surprise and suspicion on his face. There were bigger issues to dwell on.

"You think I had sex with you so I could escape," she said as she gathered her clothes and stuffed herself into them. "I'm not that pathetic."

"I didn't—"

"And you're not that irresistible. I realize it's been a while, and I'm not—I was never—I'm just a lonely college professor who writes about relationships instead of having them, but I don't use people."

"Contrary to appearances."

"I would have thought you knew me better by now. I was wrong. You're not that smart."

"Norah."

She zipped her jeans, still refusing to look at him.

"Norah." He caught her arm, swung her around to face him. "I didn't sleep with you because I felt sorry for you. I don't think you're lonely and pathetic."

"What *do* you think?" she asked, meeting his eyes for the first time since she'd gotten out of bed.

Trip was the one who looked away. "I don't know what to think."

"Yes, you do. You just refuse to face it." She jammed her feet into her shoes and whipped the blanket off the bed. "That's fine. After tomorrow it will be over for good and you can go your way and I'll go mine."

Trip didn't say anything, not even when she collected a pillow and settled into the single chair by the window, cuffing herself to the ancient radiator on that wall. He looked miserable, but that didn't matter either.

After their visit to the FBI building tomorrow, he'd head out on his next assignment, and she'd go back to Chicago and decide what to do with the rest of her life. Which she'd spend alone, at least until she could get over him. It wasn't going to be easy. Not because of him, she added mutinously, because of her. She didn't fall in love easily. Falling out would be even harder.

On the bright side, it would give her a whole new perspective when she wrote her next book. Like she'd told Hollie Roget on her talk show, success was a wonderful thing, especially when it came to love. But it was failure, and how you dealt with it, that defined your character.

Her character had gotten all the definition it could stand for one lifetime.

chapter 27

WHEN NORAH WOKE UP THE NEXT MORNING
Trip was sitting on the edge of the bed, dressed, holding the package she'd gotten the day they'd met. She
closed her eyes, absorbing a fresh wave of pain, and
when she opened them again, he hadn't moved, but she
felt steadier. And she was sure there was no soft emotion on her face. She'd made that decision last night,
handcuffed to the radiator, reminded of his betrayal
every time she heard the clank of metal and felt the
cuff cut into her wrist.

Trip didn't trust her, so the hell with him. Maybe
she'd gone out of her way to make it appear she'd
played him false, and maybe they'd only known each
other a couple of weeks, and it probably wasn't fair of
her to expect him to know her so well in such a short
period of time. But she did. He was good at reading
people—not just good, incredibly skilled, and he'd spent

that entire two weeks practically in her back pocket. He'd complained, those first couple of days, about how direct she was. He'd commented when she'd proved she could con people. He should have understood her game.

The fact that he was sitting there with a vacuum-sealed bag of stolen jewelry, condemnation on his face, told her he'd let her down. She didn't know why he had such a huge blind spot where she was concerned. She didn't want to know.

She sat up, stiff and sore from sleeping in an awkward position in an uncomfortable chair. Except, she realized when she unthinkingly lifted both hands to rub her neck, the cuffs were gone.

Her gaze cut to Trip's, another automatic reflex she regretted. But she refused to look away.

"I tried to put you in bed, but you wouldn't let me," he said, confirming that he'd taken the cuffs off sometime during the night.

"Am I supposed to thank you?"

He shrugged.

"I see you invaded my privacy, too." She held up a hand before he could respond. "I know, criminals aren't allowed any privacy. I hope that doesn't extend to the bathroom."

She stood, a little unsteadily. Trip got to his feet as well, and moved to block her way.

"There's no window in there, where do you think I'm going?"

"Norah." He blew out a breath, reaching out to brush the hair back from her face.

She stepped back. She couldn't afford to let him touch her, but she kept her gaze level on his.

"Can we talk? There are things I need to say."

"I think we covered everything last night. I won't be long," she added as she slipped by him, but she took her time washing her face and brushing her teeth, making herself as presentable as she could. Just because she was going to jail didn't mean she had to let her appearance go.

It was a thought that made her smile a little, cheering her because it reminded her that she was still really in charge. Trip could handcuff her and drag her into the FBI, but it wouldn't change the outcome. She'd planned it too well, worked out what Lucius would call the long con and executed it to perfection, because Trip was right, she was her father's daughter. But she was also her mother's.

AN HOUR LATER SHE FOUND HERSELF SITTING IN a chair in front of Mike Kovaleski's scarred desk, in his office, deep in the J. Edgar Hoover Building, FBI headquarters, Pennsylvania Avenue, Washington, D.C. Trip lounged against the wall behind her. Mike hadn't said a word since they'd arrived. He just sat there, staring at her with his inscrutable Marine expression under Marine-cut hair going gray. Arms that probably had a Marine tattoo on the biceps were crossed over his wide chest.

"Where's the loot?" he finally said in a voice that sounded like he was chewing rock and definitely brooked no argument.

"First things first," she said, grateful he didn't have a gun since he clearly wasn't used to being disobeyed and he *really* didn't like it.

"I could charge you with obstruction of justice."

"Threats didn't work the last time we spoke. What do you think has changed?"

He shot Trip a look.

Norah resisted the urge to do the same.

"Home turf advantage," Mike said.

Norah rolled her eyes. "You say this isn't a game, and yet you continually use sports metaphors."

"Can the psychoanalysis."

"That was more of a commentary."

"Can that, too."

"Okay, how about this? Do you think I didn't consider the possibility you'd toss me in jail when I made the appointment to meet with you?"

She knew Trip had straightened away from the wall, knew he was staring at the back of her head. If he'd trusted her enough last night to listen she'd have told him about the appointment and none of what he'd put her through would have been necessary. That was what she wanted to say to him.

She ignored him instead, focusing on the man with the power. "When you don't get what you want you throw your weight around like a playground bully."

Mike wanted to make more threats, she could see it. He sat back in his chair, his jaw working as he debated the satisfaction of doing the predictable versus the embarrassment of *being* predictable. "I know you're no dummy if you could get the better of Jones," he finally said, taking what he'd see as the high road. "He's not easy to play."

Norah dropped her gaze to her lap, smiling a little. "He was FBI all the way."

"Christ," Mike said to Trip, "not you, too."

Trip began to pace, not looking at either of them.

Mike heaved a raspy sigh, turning to Norah. "Why don't you tell me what you want?"

"I want this to be over."

"Give us the loot and you get your wish."

"Not so fast."

"You have conditions."

"Wait a minute," Trip said, speaking for the first time since he'd filled Mike in on as much of the con as he knew. "I want to hear the rest of it. Where was the key? What was the key?"

"There was no key," Norah said. "There was a list."

"A list of what?"

"My father hid it in the house," she said, deliberately withholding the answer to Trip's question. "He sent Bobby in twice to find it."

"And both times he failed," Trip said, "so he had you abducted, figuring it would get me out of the house long enough for him to retrieve it."

"But you refused to go," Norah said. "He bet I was more important to you than the mission, and he was wrong."

Trip flicked a glance at Mike. "We know all that."

"There was no way I could find that list on my own, even if I had a decade to search. Lucius knows every nook and cranny of that house. He didn't even show me where it was, he just left the room and came back a few minutes later with it, after he'd visited all three floors of the house."

"And you conned him into giving you the list by making it appear you were throwing your lot in with his," Mike said. "Which Jones didn't figure out."

"I knew something was off," Trip said, "but there were so many cons going on I couldn't sniff it out."

"It's not important," Norah said. "I knew I had to convince my father I'd chosen his side or he'd never give me that list. And there'd be no waiting him out."

"That's a matter of opinion," Mike put in.

"You don't know him like I do," Norah said. "He'd already waited fifteen years. He would have waited as long as he'd needed to, and sooner or later you'd have given up, or looked the wrong way at the right time, and Lucius would be gone. But the treasure hunters wouldn't. They'd never have left me alone.

"At least that's what I thought."

"You misjudged the situation?" Trip asked her, looking cheered by the notion.

Norah got more of a kick out of disappointing him than she should have. "It's more that Lucius made a mistake."

"I did nothing of the sort."

Norah turned around and there, standing in the doorway, was her father. He'd come in while she was busy not noticing Trip. "I see you got the airline ticket and instructions I left for you," she said, happy to have another distraction.

"And you knew I'd be too curious to ignore it."

"I thought you should be here to do the right thing," Norah said. "You wanted the loot returned to its rightful owners."

"And you think they're going to see it done?" he asked, his gaze contemptuous on Trip.

"Would you?"

Lucius opened his mouth and drew in his breath.

"Be very careful," Norah said.

He snapped his mouth shut and plopped into the chair beside hers. "It's a sad day when your own offspring treats you so infamously. I'll be glad to live long enough to see a child of yours become so independent."

Norah smiled softly. "That's one curse I'd be happy to see fulfilled."

Lucius reached over and patted her knee. "You're a good girl, even if you are regrettably honest."

"This is touching and all," Mike grumbled, "but can we get back to the loot?"

"My father—stop me if I'm wrong, Lucius—split the loot into small packages like that one," Norah said, pointing to the package Trip had put on Mike's desk when they first came in. "Then he sent the packages to a bunch of different lawyers with payment and instructions to mail them in fifteen years. One of them came early, the package Law accepted the day he installed the alarm, which is how I put it all together. I didn't know the particulars, but I knew why Lucius was so anxious to get everyone out of the house."

"You could have shared that information with me," Trip put in.

Norah ignored him. So did Lucius, but he made it obvious he was enjoying the way she treated Trip. Norah ignored that, too. She was really tired of being in the middle of both of them.

"I convinced—"

"Conned," Lucius sniped.

"—my father to produce the list of lawyers and the passwords, then I redirected the packages using the code words he set up in case he needed to change the arrangements."

"To?" Mike asked her.

"That's not the point here," Lucius said. "I spent fifteen years in that hell hole of a prison. The insurance companies have paid off on all the claims. The loot should be mine."

"So the mistake you made," Trip said to Lucius, "was sending the packages to Norah's house, assuming you'd be there to collect them and no one would question a bunch of random packages."

"Mistake? I expected you people to make a nuisance of yourselves, but how was I to know you'd take up residence?"

"Somebody's going to tell me where the fucking loot is or the pair of you are going to take up residence in a jail cell."

Norah turned her attention to Mike, not threatened in the least by his bluster. She'd half expected him to arrest her on sight. He hadn't because she had him by the balls, to put it bluntly. And he knew that she knew it.

"The heirloom pieces go back to their rightful owners," she began.

"Technically the insurance companies are the rightful owners, since they paid off on the claims."

"I'm sure you can find a way around that," Norah said.

Mike made a noise in the back of his throat, no words, just an ursine grumble before he nodded once, sharply.

"There'll be a 10 percent finder's fee."

Mike sat forward, looking both outraged and oddly disappointed.

"It goes to my father."

"Nope." Mike sat forward in his chair. "He stole the loot, he hid the loot, he doesn't get a finder's fee for turning the loot in."

"Why would you want to reward him," Trip wanted to know, "especially after the way he treated you?"

"Compensation for spending fifteen years of his life in what amounted to solitary confinement."

"Yeah, because that really worked."

"Just because a government employee took a payoff doesn't mean you didn't try to cut my father off from all outside contact."

Lucius just sat there, looking saintly and wisely keeping his mouth shut. Ten percent, Norah knew he was thinking, was better than nothing.

"Let it go," Mike said to Trip. "You gotta respect her moxie. In her place, I'd do the same."

Trip gave her a long, intense stare, and walked out.

"Don't worry about Jones," Mike told her. "He's just reevaluating. All the good ones do, at some point."

"And when they're done reevaluating?"

"Some stay with the Bureau, although not as agents usually. Some move on."

Norah didn't have the heart to ask which kind of agent Mike thought Trip was. Either way she knew he wouldn't be moving on with her.

"You had to do what you had to do," Mike said to her, "and frankly I'm impressed. Don't ruin it by being maudlin."

"I'm almost never maudlin," she said, "and regrets don't get you anywhere." But she could be sad and still move forward.

"So, I can give you the finder's fee," Mike said to her, "which you deserve anyway since technically it's you turning the loot in."

"And I can do whatever I want with it?"

Mike shrugged. "It's yours. After taxes."

"And you'd be taking care of your old man, now wouldn't you, love," Lucius said.

"Bobby is going to college," she said to her father. "Some of the money is going into investments, and my car is getting fixed."

"You could buy a new one, darlin', any kind you want."

"I just want mine repaired, Dad." She turned back to Mike. "And I want to announce that the loot was found and is in the FBI's hands," she said, sort of holding her breath because she knew she'd get push-back on this point.

Mike didn't disappoint her. "Not gonna happen. Can't afford the publicity. But I'll make sure it leaks out that the loot has been found, somewhere far away from Chicago so the treasure hunters will leave you alone."

Norah took a deep breath and let it out. She checked her watch and knew she was going to make it. She took some folded papers from her purse and pushed them across the desk to Mike. "Sign both copies."

He'd been leaning back in his chair. He jerked forward, grabbing up the papers and paging quickly through. "Are you fucking kidding?"

"You didn't think I was going to take your word, did you?"

"I don't know whether to be pissed off or impressed."

"I know how I feel," Lucius said.

Norah took a pen from the holder on his desk and held it out. "It doesn't matter how you feel. You don't have a choice."

Mike took the pen and signed both copies, keeping one for himself and handing the other back to Norah. "So where is it?"

Norah took the signed agreement and put it back in her purse, then she stood up and opened Mike's office door. She wasn't looking for Trip. It took a couple of minutes, and Mike was getting impatient, before the first courier arrived. She stepped back and ushered him into the office.

"You're shitting me," Mike said. "You had the loot redirected to my office?"

Norah just raised her eyebrows and looked at the box in his hand. And two more couriers showed up in Mike's outer office.

"Package for James Alo—Alo—"

"Aloysius," Mike said.

"Jones," the first courier finished. "That you?"

"No, but I'll sign for it."

"Nope," the courier said, lifting the electronic clipboard out of Mike's reach. "Says here this Jones guy has to sign for it."

"I'm his boss."

"Him or nobody."

Mike picked up the phone, spoke a few short-tempered words into it, scowling at Norah the entire time. Trip returned in less than two minutes. By then there were two more couriers waiting for his John Hancock. He didn't look any more amused than Mike did.

Lucius laughed outright. "You've got to admire the girl's style," he said to Mike.

"Admire, hell, I'd like to offer her a job."

"Over my dead body she works for the feds," Lucius said.

"We can put together a really nice incentive package," Mike said, "even in this economy."

Lucius snorted. "Nothing like government work, eh?"

"I may not know what I'll be doing for the rest of my career," Norah said, getting up and heading for the door, "but there's one thing I do know: I'm not leaving it up to any of you."

chapter 28

"NORAH, DARLIN'."

On the list of people she least wanted to talk to, her father was number two. She stopped anyway. She'd never been one to put off the unpleasant, and in her current frame of mind, she was spoiling for a fight.

Lucius took one look at her expression and smiled grimly. "You're angry," he said. "At him or me?"

"Don't try to make this about anything but you and me," Norah shot back. "Say whatever it is you need to say." *Before Trip comes out that door, and I have to deal with him, too.*

"I just wanted to thank you."

"But . . ." she said, thrown off guard by gratitude when she'd expected guilt.

"Bobby isn't the sharpest tool in the kit," Lucius continued. "He's a nice, steady lad, but he isn't quick-witted like you are.

"You were always my hope, Norah. A parent wants to see themselves in their children, and I see myself in you, and me being the egotistical man I am, that's saying something. What's even more gratifying is seeing you make your own decisions. You've taken the best of me and the best of your mother, and you've become a lovely, independent woman. I'm proud of you."

"And it doesn't hurt that you're getting 10 percent of fifty million dollars. Less the price of Bobby's education, and my automotive repairs."

"Of course, darlin', the least I can do is make sure the boy gets some sort of honest career."

"Seeing as he's not suited to a life of crime."

Lucius smiled, ironic and a little wistful. "That tongue-in-cheek thing you just did there, that's your mother."

Norah swallowed back her tears, not just because she always, always missed her mother, especially now when she was hurting so much over Trip, but because Lucius had really meant it when he thanked her.

She stepped forward and hugged him. "I hope you're going to find something honest to do with yourself," she said when she stepped back. "So I don't have to worry about you."

Lucius patted her cheek. "Again, so like your mother, which is a shame when you have such a talent for my kind of work."

"Not everyone would agree with you."

It hadn't taken the sound of Trip's voice for Norah to know he was standing in Mike's doorway. She'd felt him behind her. Watching.

Norah wasn't going to let him send her running, though. She turned around and met Trip's eyes.

"I'm going to wait for the rest of the couriers," Lucius said. "If I can't have all that lovely loot, at least I can look at it one more time."

Norah nodded as he walked by her, but she kept her eyes on Trip's face. He was still furious.

"If you need me for anything, darlin', I'm staying at the Ritz." Lucius stopped when he got to Trip. "And here, boy," he said, fishing one of the new paperback copies of Norah's book out of the breast pocket of his suit jacket and handing it to Trip. "This is for you."

"I already read it," Trip said, not noticing that Lucius was gone because he never took his eyes off Norah, "at least chapter four."

"And you're angry."

"Not about that. I don't understand why you didn't tell me what you were planning."

"You'd have given it away."

Trip took his time responding, clearly still trying to get a handle on his temper. "I've done a hell of a lot of undercover work, Norah," he finally said.

"Not enough to fool my father. Lucius is the best there is at reading people. You had to be genuinely surprised and angry. I knew you wanted to be the one to find the loot—"

"I was furious, but not because you solved the crime without me. I was pissed because you didn't trust me."

"So was I last night."

"I didn't do anything wrong."

"Neither did I." She turned and walked away.

"Norah."

Her step faltered, but she kept moving, one foot in front of the other, just like she'd been doing for the last few weeks.

Trip followed her into the elevator, pushing the hold button once the doors slid closed. He didn't say anything; she needed to fill the silence so she could bear the heartbreaking distance between them.

"I didn't tell you because I knew you couldn't convince Lucius you weren't just acting. He's a better con artist than both of us put together."

"We could have found the list."

She shook her head. "I lived in that house my entire life. There's not a corner of it I didn't clean or paint or polish in the last fifteen years, and I never found it. And Lucius was never going to trust me after he saw us together that night. In order to convince him that I would take his side over yours I needed a grand gesture—especially after he had me kidnapped, and not just because he knew I had reason to be angry with him, because it meant he was running out of patience.

"Sooner or later he'd have gone for that list, Trip, and after all those years in jail, do you think he'd have settled for more tricks? The next stunt he pulled to get us out of the house would have been aimed at you, and it wouldn't have been harmless."

"So you did it to protect me."

"And myself." It had hurt like hell to make him go, but in the long run it was easier than watching him walk away, knowing he'd made the choice to leave her behind.

Trip snorted. "You know, that's a failing of yours. You can read people, and not because you're a psychologist, because your old man is right, you inherited that natural talent from him. But you don't allow for the possibility that you might be wrong."

"Why am I wrong?"

"For one thing, your father isn't better than you."

"That wasn't a fair test. He loves me, so he wasn't seeing things clearly."

"Neither was I."

Norah went still, something blossoming inside her, something she knew was hope, bolstering the love so it spread, warming her from head to toe. "You were angry because you thought I was betraying you."

"I was angry because you were betraying me, but I've been double-crossed before. In fact I've always seen it coming, or at least been prepared for the possibility so when it happened I wasn't caught off guard. But I was with you. I saw that moment through a haze of emotion, just like your father, and pain, and hell, it was worse than being shot, and let me tell you, discovering I was in love with a con artist wasn't exactly the high point of that day. Although I didn't really accept it then. It took me a couple of days to figure it out. You could have saved me that, Norah, but you were afraid to tell me you're in love with me."

She was listening, listening and trying to make sense of the matter-of-fact, emotionless way he'd said he loved her, and how he'd flung out her feelings like an accusation.

And suddenly she was angry, too, but her anger was hot, burning behind her eyes and tightening her throat, so hot and hurtful she lifted a hand to rub her aching chest.

"Would you have believed me?" she managed to get out. "If I'd told you I loved you, that sending you away was the only way to convince my father I'd chosen his side, what would you have done? You'd have handcuffed me to that radiator last night, that's what you'd have done."

"I handcuffed you to myself."

"What's the difference?"

"I wanted you in my arms, even thinking . . ."

"Exactly." She punched the button for the first floor. "If I'd said I love you last night you would have thought it was just another con? Or worse, an inconvenience."

He pushed the hold button again. "Wrong again. I'm not this guy in chapter four."

"I never said you were."

"But you believed it."

She shrugged. "You're charming, attractive, smooth."

"Yeah, I am."

"I neglected to mention full of yourself."

He gave her a crooked smile, equal parts ego and self-deprecation.

"And your job comes first."

"You're right about that, too, because when I'm on an assignment my life is on the line, and I have to be all about keeping myself alive and getting the bad guy. But my job isn't who I am, it's what I do.

"This guy in chapter four, he's got a job or a hobby or a calling that keeps him from being all in when he gets involved, which means the person on the other side of the relationship has to accept those terms or move on. This guy is your father, in it for as long as the fun lasts."

"Are you going to stick around now that it's over?"

"Yeah," Trip said, still a little rattled to hear himself say that out loud, even though he'd already done all the soul-searching he needed to be right with that decision. "That day at the prison your father accused me of being a tool for the FBI."

"And you agreed with him."

"It was the truth, and there's nothing to be ashamed of in what I did."

"Was? Did?"

"It's okay to be a tool when you're being used for good, but just because I work for the FBI doesn't mean their intentions are always aboveboard. I'd have turned the loot over without a second thought. You took steps to make sure that even if you couldn't control how the FBI used the loot, people got their family heirlooms back, and those who might be concerned about incriminating papers or sensitive information they'd had locked in those safe-deposit boxes would at least be forewarned that the FBI was in possession of those things."

"You and my father kept pushing me to choose between you. Nobody was standing up for the real victims of the robbery, and the future victims of whatever the FBI had planned. I figured your employers were going to get their hands on the loot one way or another; at least this way it sort of leveled the playing field. I'm sorry I had to hurt you in the process."

He took her by the arms, drew her in until all of her was pressed against all of him. "You found a way to come closest to doing what was best for everyone, and you put yourself on the line to do it. For a con woman you have a hell of a conscience." He grinned when she frowned at him. "Jiminy Cricket with a PhD and a talent for getting people to do the right thing despite themselves."

"You're saying I'm manipulative."

"Persuasive."

She relaxed against him, winding her arms around his waist. Her frown smoothed away, and her eyes lit with hope and the love he'd seen there before but been too skittish to recognize.

"What have I persuaded you to do?" she asked, sounding unsure of herself.

"What do you want me to do?"

"Love me," she said. "As much as I love you. The rest we can figure out as we go along."

"Done. God, you're easy."

"No, I'm not, at least not anymore. I plan to be very high maintenance from now on."

"Then it's probably a good thing I'm relocating to Chicago."

Norah pulled back so she could see his face. "Really?"

"I'm thinking about becoming a private investigator. That way I can choose my own cases for a change."

"There's a lot of crime in Chicago."

"It'll probably save me some time if I can stick close to you. You seem to attract criminals."

Norah nodded. "It helps that I'm related to some of them."

Trip grinned. "What do you think Puff will say when he finds out I'm going to be around? All the time."

"I don't really care." She stretched up and kissed him, long and hard. "I'm writing another book, and I need the inspiration."

Trip made a face. "Don't tell me. Chapter four."

"Darlin'," Norah said, patting his face, "what makes you think you're only showing up in one chapter?"

Discover Romance

berkleyjoveauthors.com

See what's coming up next from your favorite romance authors and explore all the latest Berkley, Jove, and Sensation selections.

See what's new

~

Find author appearances

~

Win fantastic prizes

~

Get reading recommendations

~

Chat with authors and other fans

~

Read interviews with authors you love

M1G0610